D0680558

SHORT STORIES BY SUSAN WELCH

Crowning the Queen of Love

COFFEE HOUSE PRESS :: MINNEAPOLIS

Cover art: "Absinthe House, New Orleans" by Guy Pene du Bois, with permission of Curtis Galleries, Minneapolis, MN.
Cover design by Jinger Peissig/ Book design by Allan Kornblum
Back cover photograph by Timothy Francisco.

The author would like to thank the editors of the following publications in which some of these stories first appeared: *The Paris Review, The Pushcart Prize Anthology, Side Show: Anthology of Contemporary Fiction,* (First Prize Story for "Hatshepsut," 1997); *Colorado Review,* and *Maryland Review*. The author would also like to acknowledge a Loft-McKnight Award and generous grants from the Bush Foundation and the Minnesota State Arts Board.

Coffee House Press is supported in part by a grant provided by the Minnesota State Arts Board, through an appropriation by the Minnesota State Legislature, and by a grant from the National Endowment for the Arts. Additional support has been provided by the Lila Wallace-Reader's Digest Fund; The McKnight Foundation; Lannan Foundation; Jerome Foundation; Target Stores, Dayton's, & Mervyn's by the Dayton Hudson Foundation; General Mills Foundation; St. Paul Companies; Honeywell Foundation; Star Tribune/Cowles Media Company; the Butler Family Foundation; Beverly J. & John A. Rollwagen Fund of the Minneapolis Foundation; & The James R. Thorpe Foundation.

Coffee House Press books are available through Consortium Book Sales & Distribution, 1045 Westgate Drive, Saint Paul, MN 55114. For personal orders, catalogs, or other information, write to: Coffee House Press, 27 N. 4th Street, Suite 400, Minneapolis, MN 55401.

Library of Congress CIP Data
Welch, Susan, 1949-
Crowning the queen of love : stories / by Susan Welch
p. cm.
Contents: The time, the place, the loved one–Darcy–Broken music–Stalking Angel Dewayne–The oracle–Queen–Lagoon–Geology–Hatshepsut.
ISBN 1-56689-058-6 (alk. paper)
1. Women–Social life and customs–Fiction. 2. Love stories, American. I. Title.
PS3573.E4544C7 1997
813'.54–dc21 96-49317
CIP

10 9 8 7 6 5 4 3 2 1

Contents

Dedication:

To my mother, Lee Ruth Rickel

To my daughter, Leah Andrea Welch

And Ruth said, Entreat me not to leave thee,
or to return from following after thee:
for whither thou goest, I will go;
whither thou lodgest, I will lodge;
thy people shall be my people,
and thy God my God.

—The Book of Ruth, Chapter 1, Verse 16.

*

The author wishes to extend warm thanks to her father, Elihu H. Rickel, and sister, Alice Rickel...to Gedeon, Richard, Bernie, and, of course, Nicky...My dear friends, writers and readers, who have helped with the creation of this book: Paulette Bates Alden, Jonis Agee, Mary Brand, Nancy V. Emmons, Heid E. Erdrich, Pamela R. Fletcher, Maria Damon, Valerie Miner, Martha Roth, Fiona McCrae, Joan M. Knudsen, Mary E. Knudsen, Mary L. Knudsen, Helen Hoy, David Galligan, Leslie Adrienne Miller, Ian Graham Leask, James M. Lessley, David M. Lindahl, and Robert P. Sorensen. Thanks to The College of St. Catherine. With special appreciation to Robert Patrick, poet, composer, novelist, and playwright extraordinaire, for his work on the manuscript.

The book has profited very much from the dedicated efforts of Allan Kornblum, Chris Fischbach, Susan Wakefield, Megan Scott, Jinger Peissig, Becky Weinberg, Christine Butler, and Betsy Loushin, of the fine staff at Coffee House Press.

The Time, the Place, the Loved One

I SPEND A LOT OF TIME alone now. It doesn't bother me. The others took up too much time. I am glad that they are gone. But it is January and now and then I think of January in Minnesota, how in late afternoon a rusty stain appears along the rim of the sky and creeps across the ice. The stain seems to stay there forever, spreading beneath the banked tiers of white sky, until it fades suddenly into the snowbanks and is gone. It is bleak then, as if the sun has just slipped off the edge of the world. Then there is only the ice and the freezing wind on the ice as the sky gets blacker and blacker through the long, deep night.

I hardly ever think of Minnesota now that I am content in Florida. There is a garden with a trellis and orange trees. The branches bend to me as I pluck the fruit, then spring back. As I bite into an orange I can taste the juice of the tree still in it, all its green leaves. The thorns on the rosebushes tear my skirt. The house has pillars and a courtyard; it is not far from the sea. Mal has given me all he promised. When Mal leaves work he picks up my daughter at her school and she drinks lemonade while we drink scotch, sitting in the gazebo. By the time my head is clear again we have gotten through dinner and put the little girl to sleep and are upstairs, lying on the bed.

So I hardly ever think of Minnesota, how dark and still the winters are there. There was an apartment once, but I don't miss it, I just think about it sometimes when I consider how completely I have gotten out of the cold. From the street you could see a pale lamp shining through the window of the apartment, and the reflection of the lamp in the window; it was high up on the second floor above a store. Signs hung beneath the windows—Grimm's Hardware, Shaak Electronics—and together with the streetlights they cast a white glow into the big room all night long. Sometimes, coming home, we would see the snow falling silently in the beam of the streetlight, as if it were all a stage set.

Across the street was an all-night restaurant and sometimes people would leave there late, and yell to each other before they got into their cars. The first night I saw Matthew he was rushing down the stairs of our building to confront some boys on the sidewalk near the restaurant. If I hadn't pressed against the railing he would have collided with me in his descent. I stood watching him through the glass of the door as he told the boys to be quiet, people were trying to sleep. They hooted and snickered as he turned to leave. As he came in the door, almost in tears, the boys were screaming in a mocking, falsetto chorus.

"They laughed at me," he said, bewildered, shutting the door against them, staring out. We started up the stairs together. He was tall and very thin, stooped even, pigeon-breasted in the T-shirt he wore in spite of the cold. His hair was a mass of ringlets and golden curlicues and it seemed full of its own motion like something alive at the bottom of the sea. For a moment, standing in the hallway, he looked very beautiful and strange.

"I live here now," I told him. "In that apartment, there."

His face was haggard, lantern-jawed, but his eyes were gentle as he stared at me. "Come over and visit me tomorrow night," he said. "I'll bake you some brownies."

All day long I thought I wouldn't go. I stood for a long time in the hallway, looking from Matthew's door to mine, before I turned to knock on his. When he called "Wait a minute," I thought he was a girl, that's how light and high his voice was.

His apartment was immaculate. The wooden floor gleamed. There was a rug made of swans' heads and necks, dark and light, facing in opposite directions—the neck of a dark swan provided the relief so you could see the neck of a white swan and so on. It was impossible to hold both the white and dark swans together in your mind at the same time. There was a bed at one end of the large room, a table with two chairs, and windows that faced the street all along the wall. There were no pictures up, just plants on a shelf, purple passion, jade plant, wandering Jew, and a bulletin board studded with funny clippings, cartoons, and a picture of a bald woman in a long smock.

"I see her all the time at school," Matthew said. "She goes to all the rallies and concerts and just walks around the university."

He was wearing a T-shirt that said MINNESOTA and a pair of jeans that hung on him. I saw that he was not handsome at all. He was bony and long and his joints, his elbows and wrists and probably his knees, were huge, like a puppet's.

"How old are you?" I asked.

"Twenty-one," he said, but he looked sixteen or seventeen. "You?"

"Twenty-five."

"I couldn't imagine what your age was," he said. "People are always drawn to you, your looks, aren't they?"

"My mother was beautiful. She's dead," I said.

I looked out the window and saw how the dark was settling in. When I was eighteen I won a beauty prize, Princess Kay of the Milky Way at the Minnesota State Fair. They sculpted my face in a sixty-pound block of butter, put the bust in a refrigerated glass case, and ran it round and round on a kind of merry-go-round so people at the fair could look at it. I liked it and went every day to see it, standing on the dirt floor near the glass, wondering if anyone would recognize me, but they never did. My father told me I looked like my mother in the sculpture, but he thought it was dumb of me to stand around there all day. He made me come home.

"What in the world brought you to this place?" Matthew asked, and then I told him how I had come to be there. I must have been lonely, or starved for someone so nearly my own age. I know that's what made me pour out my feelings to him so. I told him how I had met Mal when I took a job at his publishing company, and how he had left his wife and children for me, and how he had taken me to live with him five years ago, right after my father died. I told him how Mal called me his suburban Botticelli, and how he took care of me and taught me all he knew. Now Mal had sold out his interest in the Minneapolis company and we were moving to Florida, where he had a new business. But I had never been out of Minneapolis, my parents had died here, it was all too sudden. I begged him to let me have a couple of months, work in the business as it changed hands, get used to the idea of leaving as he got our new life settled. I had found this apartment in a familiar area, near the university, where I, too, had gone to school. Matthew was looking at me so hard his jaw hung.

It was late autumn, just before Halloween, and Matthew and I watched out the window as the sky went down from copper to livery red to mother-of-pearl. The streetlights blinked on and so did the signs above the stores. The room darkened with the sky, but the signs and streetlights shed pools of incandescent light on the bed, the floor.

"What kind of person would leave his wife and children?" Matthew asked.

I sat with my head in my hands. "I don't know, he felt so awful about it. They'd been married twenty years. He told me not to think about it. He said it was my face; he loved my face." I pressed my fingers into my cheeks. The flesh gave like wax. But suddenly I was asking myself, what kind of person was Mal, to leave his wife and children. I had never thought of him in that way before.

Then slowly Matthew began to tell me about himself. It was hard for him to talk, he didn't charm me with what he said or the way he said it, no, not at all. His voice was a whisper and sometimes it cracked as it came out, no, not a man's voice at all. He had been in love with a girl and she hadn't loved him, but still he kept loving her and loving her and finally he had gone crazy.

He told me what it was like to be crazy. Everything seemed to have a secret meaning, cracks on the sidewalk, a phone that rang once but not again, the world was full of hidden messages.

"It sounds wonderful," I said. "I would love to feel that everything had a secret meaning."

He shook his head and his curls bounced. "You don't know what you're saying. No, it wasn't wonderful at all. It was horrible."

"And the girl?"

"She's gone. Gone a long time ago."

It was hard to talk to him, I had to strain to hear him, his murmurs. It was as if he were used to talking in whispers to himself. His father was a doctor, his mother wanted him to be a doctor, but he couldn't do it, his grades weren't good enough, he couldn't concentrate. So instead he was taking this degree in psychology, maybe something would come of that.

I don't know what it was, I didn't want to leave him. After awhile he got up and turned on the lamp by the window, then he put on a record.

"I like that a lot," I said. "Mal and I don't listen to any rock, just classical. Bach. Vivaldi. Telemann. A lot of baroque."

"Don't you know any people your own age?"

I looked at him. "Hardly any. There are a few girls at work, but I don't see them much."

It was late when I got up to go. I walked along the shiny dark floor to the door. The lamp shone on the green leaves of the plants and reflected white in the window. I could feel the cold on the street below seeping in around the window frames.

Matthew followed me and stood with me by the door. I thought I had never seen such a delicate-looking man. I could almost see the blood beating in his temples. He took my hands in his huge bony hands. I felt it only for an instant but my hands were throbbing where he had touched them.

A FEW days later I found a copy of the album we had been listening to wrapped and pushed under my door. When I walked over to Matthew's apartment I could hear the bass pounding in the record he was playing. I stood in the hall for a moment but the door opened.

"I heard your footsteps," he said. But how could he have heard me over the music? We stared at each other. He looked gawky and stupid. I wondered why I had come. "Listen, I've got a coupon for a pizza," he said. "Do you want to go?"

As we walked he took my hand in his. I couldn't take it back, his own hand trembled so.

"They removed a rat's memory surgically today," he said. And all through dinner we talked about how the rat experienced everything for the first time, every time.

When he himself had gone crazy, Matthew said, he thought about the same things over and over again. He had thought then that he was refining memories, getting down to their essence and their core. Now he realized that was impossible.

His way of talking was innocent and strange. He thought differently from other people, and I had to listen carefully to catch his meaning. Neither of us ate much. We pushed the pizza back and forth between us.

"Do you want to come back over?" he asked as we walked out into the bitter cold. He took my hand again. I just wanted to be with him, I don't know why. Perhaps I admired the sculpted, jutting angle of his cheekbones. He made some coffee and got out a box of fresh pastries from the bakery downstairs. He sat across the table from me, staring down at the coffee, his long legs stretched out until his feet nearly touched mine. The white light enclosed us in a long oval. He shook his head and ruffled his fingers fiercely through his curls.

"Your hair is so unusual," I said.

"I was helping my father give EEGs last summer," he said. "One lady saw me and wouldn't let them put the electrodes on. She thought that was what had happened to me."

We laughed. At that moment I looked at him and he

looked at me. I felt a dizziness, a tightness near my heart. I was snug, safe in his apartment against the cold—I'm sure that's what it was. I have thought about it since.

He put a record on and we were silent, sitting in the pool of light.

After awhile he came over and knelt beside me and wrapped his arms around my waist. I could see the top of his head, his bobbing curls.

"Matthew, I have a lover."

He ignored me and put his cheek next to mine, holding my head. I could see the fine grain of his gold skin, how tight it was on the bone.

"Do you want to go lie down with me?" he asked and I nodded, yes.

I looked into his face as he undressed me and saw that his eyes were all pupil. For a long time he stroked the place where my hip met my thigh, running his fingers over the pale blue traceries of the veins.

"I love you," I said. Yes, I remember I said it, and I said it many times; I don't know what came over me. And I thought, this is the most wonderful night of my life, nothing will ever be this sweet again. We stared at each other in the light of the streetlamps and the Grimm's Hardware sign, and we made love. All night long we looked into each other's eyes. He was so young I could see that his eyes were brand-new, just budded in their sockets.

Sometimes even now I fancy I can feel Matthew's tongue, scratchy as a cat's, and the way he wrapped me up in his long, long arms. But I scarcely think of him at all now. In fact, I have entirely forgotten him. If it weren't for the little girl, considering her as much as I do, and the way the days are so long for me here, I doubt that I would think of him at all.

Three days later I went to work again. The phone was ringing as I walked into my office and I picked it up, knowing it was Mal. There had been a short circuit in one of the stereos in the electronics store and all night music from a rock station had pounded up to us through the floorboards. Elton John, Matthew told me they were playing. "Love Song." "Come Down in Time."

"What are you telling me?" Mal asked. "You were walking along, just minding your own business, and you got hit by a freight train?"

Light from the apartment flooded into my eyes and behind them as I held the receiver, the pure light on Matthew's face as he twined me with his legs and arms.

"I never should have left you alone, I knew it was a mistake," Mal said. And when I didn't answer he said; "I'm coming up there."

He was waiting for me in the office the next morning. For a long time he wouldn't believe that I was serious, that I wasn't coming down to Florida.

"I suppose his teeth are all white, not stained like mine," Mal said. "And I suppose he has all his hair and a flat belly, that's what you're thinking when you look at me, isn't it?"

"No, it's not," I said, but now that he'd said it it became true. All I was worried about was that he would kill me, and then I wouldn't be able to be with Matthew.

I wanted to tell him how fond I was of him, how grateful I felt, how it hurt me to see his eyes glaze as he slumped against the window. But I stood speechless.

"I gave up everything for you. I can't let you go," he said.

For a moment I thought of the filthy warped floor in the hall of my apartment building, the way the brown paint on the floors bubbled and peeled. "I was a child then," I said. "That was for then."

I turned my face away as he held me.

"There's nothing I can do," he said. "I can't live without you."

For an instant I prayed, begging that Mal would not die.

Then, miraculously, he was gone. He had me fired from my job, but I found another where I just had to type. I bore no grudges. I was walking on love's good side. I had Matthew.

FROM our first night together, Matthew was always in my thoughts. I suppose you could say I lived for him. He wanted us to be twins.

"One consciousness in two bodies," he said. "That's what we are." He looked at me in a way that made me feel holy. No one had ever paid this kind of attention to me, no, never. He painted our toenails the same color, green with silver dust. When I got a pimple, he would often get one himself, in a similar spot. We wore each other's clothes, bought matching shoes. We walked alike, talked alike. It was no longer lonely being me. We could be each other.

We had been together two months when I found out I was pregnant. Matthew had told me not to take the pill, there could be no mistakes between us. Anything that happened was right.

When I told him, he smiled. "That's wonderful," he said. "I can't wait to tell my family. Now we'll get married."

We drove out to the suburbs for dinner so I could meet his parents. He had told them about me, but they had resisted meeting me, until now. We drove to a ranch house with a swimming pool behind it, big as a gulch. His father was a tall, silent man who left in the middle of dinner to go to the hospital. His mother had Matthew's jagged features but none of his softness. She hated me on sight.

After dinner she took me aside.

"Do you realize what a sick boy he is?" she asked. "You're a grown woman, you should see these things. He's been institutionalized for long periods."

"I love him," I said calmly. "He loves me. He knows exactly what he's doing. And it's medieval to think of mental illness as a permanent condition."

"What do you know about it?" She stared until I dropped my gaze. "Have you ruined your life, eating your heart out over him?"

We left before dessert.

"Cheer up, honey. We have to go out and get some sour cream cherry pie, some cheesecake," Matthew said as we sat in the car in his parents' driveway. He started kissing me, digging his fingers into my thighs. "There's a great place near here. You'll love their hot fudge cake," he said. "I can't take my honey to bed before she has her dessert."

We went to a delicatessen where cakes and pies dipped up and down on little ferris wheels. "It tastes as good as it looks, too," Matthew said. We held hands and fed each other hot fudge and cherries on heaping spoons. The rich goo dripped like wax. We nudged and stepped on each other's feet the whole time, pressing each other's soles and toes till they hurt.

"Why doesn't she like me?" I asked. "Is it because I'm older?"

"She'll get over it. Don't worry about her," Matthew said. "All she knows is her Bible. That time when I got sick—she thought it was God's rebuke to her. She's just going to have to get used to it."

I scraped some hot fudge on my plate with my spoon. It dried fast, sweet cement. "You're so old for your age, Matthew. I'm surprised she can't see it. I've always known I could depend on you."

He fed me the last bite of hot fudge cake. "How about some more?" he asked. "Come on, honey, you know you want it."

"Let's have the hazelnut torte," I said.

"Great," Matthew said. "Great. My mother would die. She believes in minimal sweets."

"Mal too," I said. "Seaweed and spinach. He made us eat seaweed and spinach every stupid day." We both grimaced, wrinkling our noses.

Matthew stared into my eyes and jammed my feet tight between his. "Hi, baby." I saw his mouth move, but no sound escaped his lips. The waitress put the torte before him. Shrugging and rolling his eyes at me he plunged his fork into the crest of hazelnut lace.

WE GOT married and I moved all my things into Matthew's apartment. Our lives went on much as before.

How did those days pass? They went by so quickly I swear I can't remember. We had everything in the world to find out about each other.

He took pictures of me with an expensive camera his parents had given him for his birthday. He gloated over the prints. "Look how you're smiling," he said. "How happy I must make you." He set the time adjustment so we could be in pictures at the same time, hugging or kissing or with our heads together, staring at the camera. "What a beautiful couple," he said.

He played his guitar as we sang duets of rock songs. He was charmed by my flat singing voice. He even admired my upper arms, which had started to get pudgy from all our desserts. He flapped the loose flesh with delight. "That's one of the things I love about you the most," he said. "Chubby arms, just like a little baby."

One freezing night as we walked home after a movie, our boots crunched into the moonlight on the snow. Our gloved hands fitted into each other like the pieces of a puzzle.

"What should we name the baby?" he asked.

"I don't know," I said.

"If it's a girl how about Phoebe, after the moon," he said. "The moon is so beautiful; look how we're walking on silver, baby. And it always seems to have so many secrets."

"But we don't like secrets, Matthew," I said. "We don't believe in secrets."

"I bet she'll look like the moon," he said. "You'll get round like the moon and then the baby will come out and look like the moon."

I woke up once during the night. He was sleeping with his arms around my neck. He slept silently, like an infant. How could he be so quiet? The lights outside flooded his bulletin board, the shiny wooden floors, the carefully arranged cabinets. The radiators hissed, then fizzled to a stop. Outside the window the full moon shared the secrets of the shadows on the dark street, his beating heart. I almost woke him up to tell him. I wanted to say, I could die now. I am so happy I could just die.

For Valentine's Day he wrote me a song. I sat on the bed while he played it for me on his guitar. He didn't need to breathe with my lungs filling his, the song said. He wanted to die from drinking my wonderful poison. I listened, filled with wonder.

As he played I watched his hands. For the first time I saw tiny scars on his wrists, fine and precise as hairs. When he finished playing I put my fingers to his pulse.

"Your wrists, Matthew," I said. "Look. Where did all those little marks come from?" He had never told me, yet he said he told me everything.

He withdrew his hands, fixing me with his long stare. "Let's stay in the here and now. Why talk about things that happened a long time ago, things you can't remember right anyway. What did my honey get for me?"

I had forgotten Valentine's Day. The next day I bought him a shirt and an expensive sweater. He thanked me but seemed disappointed. His mother could have given him the same. He had been involved in his gifts, mine were clichés.

The next day I got a valentine from Mal, forwarded from the old office. He loved me, he was thinking about me, he wanted me to come back to him. As I put it in the wastebasket, I found the valentine I had given Matthew folded at the bottom.

IN THE dead of winter, the windchill was fifty below for days at a time. We would sit on the bed and watch the smoke rise out of the chimneys in timid frozen curls. When we came home late at night, walking across the huge university campus, we would have to kiss and hold each other for twenty minutes before our noses and fingers thawed.

On Sunday mornings we would have breakfast at the restaurant across the street. We sat facing each other, our legs locked, talking about what was happening in our lives. I treasured my separate life, for it provided me with stories to tell him. Nothing was real until I told Matthew about it.

After breakfast I walked him to his part-time job at the laboratory, where he was working on a hearing experiment. Chinchillas were made deaf in one ear and then trained to jump to one side of a large revolving cage or another, on the basis of certain sounds. If the chinchillas didn't perform correctly, they got a shock. That was Matthew's job, running them through tests and shocking them if they made mistakes.

I went with him once and saw the little animals in their cages. They were furry and adorable, bunnies without ears: how could Matthew, the gentlest of people, stand to shock them?

"They have to be shocked when they're not doing their job," he said. "It's horrible, but that's the way life is."

"Since when do you believe life is that way?"

One evening he came home shaking. A chinchilla had died when its eardrum was being punctured for the experiment.

"Matthew, why don't you quit that job?" I asked, looking up at him from where I sat at the table. "Don't you see what it's doing to you?"

"It's not doing anything to me. I'm fine," he said, standing there trembling. "Do you think you're better, that you wouldn't do that job?"

I stood up and rushed to him. "Matthew, are you angry at me? Please don't be angry at me. I just want you to be happy." I hugged him tighter, tighter. "Do I give you everything you want?" I whispered into his shoulder. "What can I give you?"

"You're everything I want," he said.

"But is it enough? You're so much better at being somebody's lover than I am."

"Yes, I am good at that, aren't I," Matthew said, and I could feel him thinking about it—there was a hum in him like currents in fluorescent tubes.

Then he held my shoulders and looked deeply into my eyes. "Come here, baby. Let me tell you about this experiment I've been thinking about all day."

We sat down at the table holding hands. "When they fasten electrodes to the pleasure centers of a rat's brain the rat will do nothing but push the bar that activates the electrode. It won't eat, it won't drink, it won't sleep, it just keeps pushing the bar for the pleasure sensation until it dies of starvation and dehydration."

We sat silent. "That's interesting," I said. I watched his

hand as it moved slowly up my arm to my shoulder, then curled around my neck.

"You," he said. "You."

LATE afternoons Matthew would go to the bakery downstairs and come back with boxes of sweets. Then we would sit at the table, listening to the voices on the street, feeling how the winds lightened and the air became less bitter as spring blew in our windows. We watched the sun on the grain of the table. We cut éclairs with knives and fed them to each other. When Matthew ate chocolate he was in such ecstasy he had to close his eyes. I could see him shudder. It was like when we were in bed. Being around all those sweets made me greedier for them, it was strange. The more I ate, the more I wanted. It was like being in bed.

I got fatter and fatter from the sweets.

"If you can't get fat when you're pregnant, when can you?" he asked, feeding me another pastry. Yet Matthew never got fat.

I ate cakes, petit fours, upside-down tarts. At the soda fountain around the corner he fed me hot fudge sundaes.

"Eat, baby," he said. "I love to see your little tongue when you lick the syrup."

My breasts became huge. I swelled like an inflatable doll. All night long Matthew would lie in my arms as I lay there puffed with life and the splitting of my own cells. When we woke up he went downstairs and got doughnuts, filled and frosted pastries called honeymooners, pecan rolls.

BEFORE long it was spring verging on summer and we took long walks along the Mississippi, breathing the crisp shocking air that rose from the torrents of icy water that came with the thaw. Sometimes we took sandwiches and stayed out till two in the morning. On one walk a pale, ovoid form approached us. It was the bald woman whose picture was on Matthew's bulletin board.

She stopped Matthew, held on to his arm, mumbled to him. She had been at the zoo, she said, and had fed the elephant peanuts. It had lifted them out of her hand with its trunk, she said, holding up her palm, showing it. Its soft trunk had tickled and nudged her hand, gentle, tender. She could feel its hairs.

"Do you know her?" I asked Matthew, watching her as she disappeared. But Matthew wouldn't answer.

One afternoon after a rock concert we followed a path along a cliff near the river; below us the Mississippi glimmered like diamonds. We walked hand in hand but I was waddling fast to keep up with Matthew's long strides.

"Let me catch up," I said, and he stared at me, his eyes hard.

"You know, I've been thinking," he said, walking faster. "We're really not that much alike."

I couldn't catch my breath. The air was freezing my fingertips even where Matthew held them.

"Like how so?"

"Like makeup," he said. "Like you wear makeup and I don't."

My eyes watered from the wind. "But I've always worn makeup," I said. "I'll stop wearing it if you don't like it."

"That won't do any good," he said. "And you take up a lot of the bed. It's hard for you to keep up with me when I walk."

"But I'm pregnant, I've got fat," I said, nearly in tears. "If I weren't pregnant and if you didn't force all that food on me, this wouldn't happen."

Tears were streaming down my face, but Matthew was walking fast, not seeming to notice.

"I don't make enough to support a baby," Matthew

said. "It's all going to be different. It seems cruel. Sometimes I think I can't do the job."

"You know I've got savings. And your parents will help." Now I couldn't stop crying. I halted in my tracks, jerking my hand out of his. The Mississippi roared below us. I waited for long moments by a tree, waiting for him to come back. And suddenly I knew that we would never again be as happy as we once were.

Finally he came back, retracing his steps, and looked at me.

"I'm sorry," he said. "I never want to hurt you."

I looked into his eyes and saw how young and frightened he was. I will never leave you, I said to myself. You need me and I will always take care of you.

That night in our room, rainy air billowed the curtain inward on our long embrace. There was the smell of skin, warm salt flesh, clean.

"Please, baby, whatever you say, never say you stopped loving me," Matthew said.

"Oh, never. I would never say that."

"You would never start hating me, would you? You would stop long before that."

Stop? He had never said anything about stop. "No. I would stop before that."

"We would stop while we still loved each other. And now . . . are you going to hug me all night long?"

THE next day, on impulse, I called up Mal from work.

I couldn't even wait for him to get over his shock. I rushed into it. "You won't believe this, but I've just got to talk to someone. About Matthew. It's just interesting, you won't mind? He's absolutely terrified of getting fat. He's the skinniest man you've ever seen, yet he's worried about fat. Once he went on a fishing trip with his father and he ate a whole pound bag of M & Ms and he was so appalled he didn't eat anything else the whole trip. And by summer he had got so thin he could see the sun shining through his rib cage. Can you imagine anything so stupid?

"He loves sweets, you know. We live near a bakery, and sometimes he'll get so many good things and eat them, then do you know what he does? He sticks his finger down his throat and throws them up. Really, I've seen him do it."

Mal listened, silent, until I was done. "Why don't you leave him?" he said.

"Because I'm happy, that's why," I said, suddenly desperate to be off the phone. "Besides, I'm very fat. Do you think you could like me fat?" He didn't answer. "I was just kidding about him throwing up. Do you believe me?" Mal was silent. "Well, maybe he did it once or twice when he was drunk.

"Do you know why I'm fat?" My voice grew shriller in the silence. "Because I'm pregnant. I'm going to have a baby in two months."

I pressed down the button, hoping he would think we'd been disconnected.

I CAME home from work that afternoon and found Matthew lying naked on the bed, his stereo earphones on, one leg propped straight up against the wall. He was so absorbed in the music he didn't see me coming up to him, see how I was staring at the long red marks on the inside of his thigh. As I sat down beside him he took his leg down quickly and removed the headset, smiling.

"It's spring," I said. "It's gorgeous out, Matthew."

"It's pretty," he said. "Have a good day?"

"Did you?" He said he hadn't been out and, leaning back again, he pulled me down with him. I moved away.

"Matthew, let me see your thigh." He watched me docilely as I lifted his leg. It was as if it were a specimen we were both going to examine.

"What are those red marks from?" I asked.

"Me."

"How did you do it?"

"With my own little fingernails," he said.

They weren't scratches, they were deeper than that. The gold hairs on his thigh spoked innocently around.

"Matthew, why did you do it?" He brought his leg down.

"Don't worry about it. It's nothing. It's something I do sometimes. I put iodine on it, it won't get infected."

"But why did you do it?"

"Because I was having evil thoughts."

"About what?"

He shook his head. "Don't worry about it." He eased me back down. "Don't worry your little head," he said. "Baby. Double baby." He started moving his hands up and down my body.

I pulled away. "Wait."

"What's the matter, baby?" he asked, touching me all over. I felt his tongue in my mouth and I closed my eyes.

ONE night he came in late, very agitated.

"There was this guy following me down the street just now for about a mile. He was this juiced-up black guy even skinnier than I am. He was muttering, calling me sweet cakes, doodle bug, bony maroney. Can they tell about me?" he asked, looking into my face. "Can they tell I've been crazy? Do I give out special vibes?"

I thought of the tense air he always had, the speed of his walk on those long legs.

"He followed me all that way. He kept saying, 'Think you're pretty hot stuff, you creep, you creep.'"

And the bald lady, had he seen her? Matthew wouldn't answer.

"People can't tell," I said finally, but he wouldn't stop looking at me.

"Why are you staring?"

"Because you're so nice and fat," he said, still staring.

Behind that gaze there was an intensity that had nothing to do with me. I felt something ungiving in him, the tightness of his skin on the bone. "Stop making me eat," I said. "You're turning me into a monster."

"But honey," he said, smiling. "I likes you fat." Then his expression changed. It was a dark look he gave me. "You're eating with your own mouth," he said.

I CALLED up Mal again. "Can you imagine?" I said. "He washes his hair every morning and every evening because he doesn't want dirt to accumulate too close to his brain. He's afraid it will penetrate and sink in. And he scratches himself with his fingernails when we have a fight. When I told him to stop buying me so many sweets he thought I hated him and you know what he did? He put a long cut down the top of his arm with a knife."

"He's crazy," Mal said. "Don't you know you've got a mental case on your hands? Why don't you get out before he does something to you?"

"He won't do anything to me," I said, but it was a long time before I could hang up the phone.

WHEN I came home that night Matthew was sitting at the table with a stack of pictures. I sat down beside him.

"What are they of?" I asked.

He looked annoyed but said nothing. I slid the pictures over and started going through them. They were all of him. He had taken twenty-four pictures of his own face: laughing, smiling, stern, pensive, in profile, in three-quarter view, from the back.

"These are really good," I said. "When did you take them?"

"I've really changed a lot," he said. "I suspected it, but I can tell from the pictures how drastic it is."

"How have you changed?"

"In ways." He put his hand over his mouth, staring at me and then staring at nothing.

"Why are you so indifferent to me?" I said.

"I'm not indifferent." He took the stack of pictures and began looking through them again, humming to himself.

"Why don't you take my picture?"

He continued to sort through the pictures, humming.

"Why don't you take my picture, Matthew?"

There was a long silence. "Sure, I'll take your picture sometime," he said, and I saw how his hair flared out in the photographs, like a sea fan.

I REMEMBER every detail of the next few days. It was the hottest part of the summer in Minnesota. Night after night I went sleepless in the still air, hanging over the side of the bed so Matthew would have more room. I was so huge and moist my nightgown clung to me like a membrane. I had to take it off and lie naked on top of the sheet. Whenever I tried to meet Matthew's eyes, he looked away.

"It will all be different after the baby comes," I whispered to him, but he pretended to be asleep.

One evening I could hardly walk when I got off the bus after work. With every step my fat thighs rubbed against each other. They had become so sore and chapped they had begun to bleed. As I walked past the bakery the heat rose in waves; behind the window, a sheet of sunlight, I saw wedding cakes, gingerbread men, cookies with faces, shimmering.

I heard music coming from our apartment. I twisted my key again and again in the lock. Surely Matthew could hear me? I punched my knuckles against the door. I tried the key again and the lock suddenly gave.

The room was filled with smoke. Matthew was sitting on the bed with the bald woman and a short black man who was even skinnier than he was.

"We used it all up," Matthew said. "There's nothing left for you."

"Who is that?" said the bald woman.

"She lives down the hall."

"I do not live down the hall and you know it, Matthew," I said. "I live here and I'm his wife." I stood there awhile and nobody looked at me. I put down my purse and sat down next to it on the floor.

"These are my friends. They're like me," Matthew said. He looked at me with the eyes of a little animal, eyes that were all pupil, all black, absorbing everything and giving nothing back.

"He's a cabdriver," Matthew said. "You wouldn't think of having a cabdriver for a friend, would you? Or a bus driver? I like cabdrivers."

"I would so have a cabdriver for a friend," I said, but I couldn't think of a single friend I did have. Matthew was my only friend.

"You wear makeup and you're fat and you only want to be friends with editors," Matthew said. "Oh, yes, and friends with Uncle Mal." The bald woman edged closer to Matthew on the bed. Her hand brushed my pillow, the pillow I had brought to Matthew from my old bed. She whispered in his ear, moving her hand to his hip, to the front of his pants.

"We're going now," Matthew said, standing up.

"Wait a second, I'll come too," I said.

"Do you want her to come?"

"No way," said the bald woman.

"See? They don't want you to come," Matthew said. "They're my friends and they're like me and they don't want you to come."

I stood still as they passed, stupefied by my pain.

"Matthew, please don't go!" I said. "It's just a tough time now, baby. Isn't it?"

He stopped in the doorway, staring down at me. A vein like a root throbbed in his temple. His face blurred in my gaze and I saw his eyes staring wide at me as we made love on that bed, silver ghosts in the wash of pale neon. I saw the snow falling silently as we hurried home in the cold, looking high up for the glow of the lamp in our apartment.

He put his hands on my shoulders. His palms and fingers cut into me like brackets. "Stay here," he said.

I watched him from the window but he did not turn to look back up at me.

I lay on the bed watching the ceiling get darker and darker. I don't know how long I lay there or when the pains in my back and stomach started, they blended so imperceptibly with the other things I was feeling, staring at the ceiling, lying on the bed. Then I lay down on the floor, on the rug of swans' heads and necks, hurting so much I imagined I felt them moving under me, nudging me with their bills. I waited and waited there for Matthew to come back, but he didn't come back. It must have been a couple of days later that I called a cab to take me to the hospital. The baby was tiny. She was born feet first, the wrong way. They gave me a drug that put me in a twilight sleep, that turned everything pink until I saw her after she was born. She came out curled like a snail and stayed calm in her crib sleeping all the time. She fit over my shoulder like a chrysalis, a tight little cocoon.

It was Matthew's father and mother who came to see me at the hospital and who took me home. I wanted to go back to our apartment, but they wouldn't let me; they said Matthew wasn't there and I needed somebody to take care of me. They took me to the house in the suburbs, but Matthew wasn't there, either. He had taken too many drugs and hurt himself, and they had to send him away somewhere, they wouldn't say where. His mother gave me the Bible to read.

He came to see me once. I was still lying down most of the time. He came and sat down beside me near the big swimming pool. He had seen the baby. "She wasn't like the moon," he whispered, or did I dream that? He sat down on a chair next to me in the sun for a little while and he cried.

He got up and started walking toward the house, muttering something.

"Matthew, I know you didn't mean to hurt me," I said, but he kept walking, shaking his head.

"He didn't even recognize you," his mother told me later, glaring at my face in the sunlight.

"Then why did he cry?" I asked. "If he didn't recognize me then why did he cry?" Words from her Bible swam in my head—he whom my soul loveth. We could do anything, be anything, with what we had. Hadn't he always told me that?

I rushed into the house, hoping I could still find Matthew, but he was gone. I took the keys to his mother's car off the kitchen table and ran to the garage before she had a chance to stop me.

Then I went out to look for Matthew. I looked everywhere nearby, up and down the streets, and when I couldn't find him I drove back to our old neighborhood. I parked in front of the old apartment and went upstairs and knocked and knocked on the door but no one answered. I tried my key but it wouldn't fit into the lock. I pushed at the lock until the key had scratched my fingers and made them bleed. Then I sat down by the door on the floor in the hallway and remembered how there had been heaven in that apartment, time had stood still. No matter what he did, Matthew knew. We had made love all night, in the light of the streetlight and the Grimm's Hardware sign. If I put my cheek to the wood I could feel the vibrations of those nights, still singing in the floorboards of the apartment.

MAL came to the house in the suburbs after I called him. He cried when he saw me, and I saw how his cheeks were now crosshatched with tiny red veins. Matthew's mother wanted to keep the baby for herself, but Mal wouldn't let her. He took me, and the baby, and brought us to this beautiful house, where we have been so happy. It is not far from the ocean and we go sailing a couple of times a month if the wind is not blowing too hard. I am thin again and Mal has bought me wonderful new clothes. The little girl calls him Daddy and has never known another father.

I thought Mal would ask me to explain a lot of things, but mostly he hasn't.

"I know you've never loved anybody but me," he said. "I knew you'd come back. That's why I waited." That was four years ago. And more and more I think Mal was right.

Once we were sitting under the trellis and Mal asked me what I was thinking about when I looked so preoccupied and far away. I told him an apparition gripped my mind sometimes.

"It's a picture of a man who looked like a boy and a girl

at the same time, a man with hair like a sheaf of golden wires, with eyes as black and shiny as lava chips. You remember, it was a man who confused me, a man who studied the memory and even tried to look into his own head. I must be making it up, don't you think? For no real person could be anything like that."

Mal was annoyed, he said it was certainly something I had made up. I'd made a mistake and had altered the memory to turn it into something more compelling, so I didn't seem like quite such a fool. It was basic psychological theory, he said.

That was a long time ago. I am content with my life and light of heart. I know how evening rises up in the blue noon, and I know every moment by the angle and quality of the sunlight spreading on my lawn and my courtyard. I stand in the courtyard and watch the days and walk through my garden and wait for my daughter and Mal. For surely, as Mal tells me, I am the happiest of women. But it is always summer here and sometimes I remember how the winter was in Minnesota, how dark and drear. And it is just occasionally, as I watch Phoebe's copper hair growing into tighter and tighter curls with each passing year, that my mind strays back to that dead and gloomy time.

Darcy

Darcy's chair folded up the way a rain bonnet does, compact and flat, and was put under the bus with the luggage. She scanned the bus as the driver carried her on, her eyes feverish and alert, her crushed body stuffed scarecrowlike into awkwardly hanging cowboy clothes, gleaming with spangles and sequins. When she saw Nora try to look away, it was decided. "Put me by the babe," she said in a throaty, narcotized voice, and the driver set her down.

Nora's nostrils flared as she moved her bag for Darcy, who smelled musky, like a slightly soiled child. Darcy rested her feet in cracking lavender plastic cowboy boots, on top of the seat ahead at impossible angles.

She inclined her head coyly at Nora's dressy outfit, velvet skirt and silk blouse, silly for a bus trip, really.

"Say, what's your name," Darcy said to a small boy who stood in the aisle sucking on his finger with lips the color of plum skin. "I'll bet I can guess your name. It's Zippy the Pinhead, isn't it?" Darcy laughed. The kid gaped at her. His mother, across the aisle, looked benignly on, leafing through the book in her lap. "Do you know what my name is? I'll bet you can't guess, can you? It's Darcy. See, I could guess your name but you couldn't guess mine. Aren't you Zippy?"

The little boy gave her an enraptured look. "Is that your car, Zippy?" Darcy asked. "I think it's *my* car." She made a feint for his toy and he squealed. "Say, how old are you?" The child drew closer. "Come on, Zippy, tell me how old you are."

"Talk to the nice lady, tell her how old you are," prodded his mother, her gnawed lips compressed into a thin little grin.

Just behind Nora sat an old man whose left eye never stopped crying. She heard him murmur approvingly. Darcy surveyed the passengers on both sides, who watched the scene between her and the boy with doting smiles.

"I won't say how old I am until you say how old you are," she said. The bus was rumbling out of the station. Lights erupted overhead, crackling along tired old circuits.

The child held up his fist and blurted out, "Two yis old," which Darcy apparently misheard.

"Too old?" She turned to Nora to verify his words, and when she got no response she said, to everyone in general, "Too old. He thinks he's too old. Well, Zippo, if you're too old then you're older than me because I'm not too old. Can you get over that kid?" she exclaimed to Nora. "He thinks he's too old." She leaned over and tried to catch the child in her frail outstretched arms, but he ran down the aisle. "That's all right, go ahead, try to escape, I'm still going to get you."

She relaxed in the seat, passing on a conspirator's smirk—wasn't the child adorable? "My name's Darcy, what's yours?"

"Nora."

Darcy pressed her upper arms and spine against the seat, thrust her head back, a stretching exercise. "Well, at least you talk. I thought I was going to get the silent treatment. Some people think they're too cool for Darcy."

After humming awhile she turned to Nora again and said, "Where are you going?"

"Cleveland."

"You from there?"

"No." Nora's reply hung blunt in the silence.

"That's all right, you don't have to be specific," Darcy said, laughing deep in her throat, hundreds of tiny pieces of glass tinkling—her eyes never leaving Nora. Darcy groomed herself, stroking her blouse—it was yoked, it had deep ruffles, there were red roses embroidered on the snap pockets, outlined by sequins. "Where are you from?"

"Minneapolis."

"No kidding. Minneapolis." She let out a long, deep breath. "I stayed there once, in an apartment with my mother. I had three brain operations in five months. Ha, ha, ha. Now I live in Black Duck Falls—dumpy town, dead little town—but I go back to Minneapolis all the time. Say, you don't mind if I take off my boots, do you? My feet are killing me."

Darcy removed her gaudy doll boots with the smooth, unmarked soles that had never been walked on. Her naked feet curled coquettishly on the top of the seat before her, the toes crossed like fingers, chicken feet boiling in a pot.

"Let me tell you about my boyfriend," Darcy said. "He's twenty years older, a Vietnam vet. We met in a rehab center. He can walk now, but his ears got messed up real bad over there. He was attacked by sea snakes, these weird snakes that are only poisonous part of the year. Ever hear of them? He's hearing impaired, not totally deaf, though." Darcy squinted at her. "He has a job. He's getting along. There're all kinds of programs these days for the differently abled." Darcy moved closer, peering harder. "You don't know what I'm talking about, do you?" she said with satisfaction. "Formerly 'Deaf and Dumb.' Formerly 'Hire the Handicapped.' Nobody uses those old rubber stamps anymore. I bet you'd call me a cripple, wouldn't you."

Nora winced. "I wouldn't call you anything," she said, but she sounded sorry. Her long white fingers wiggled in Darcy's direction. "That's a beautiful necklace," Nora said. "What kind of stone is it?"

Darcy's eyes crackled into focus. "A sandstone agate," she said. "It's very rare. Want to buy it?" She eagerly turned.

"No, that's all right."

Darcy bent nearer. "Look, what this really is is a bolo tie," she said, swiveling to give Nora a better look. "You fit the strings around your collar, see? They're genuine leatherette." Darcy tightened the cords till it looked as if she might choke herself. "Adjustable, see? Check out the scene on the agate. It's a dune."

"I really wouldn't have anyplace to wear it," Nora said miserably.

"Well, think about it," Darcy said, the turndown sliding right off her, and she massaged her pockets. She was leaning over so far that Nora was pressed up against the window. As Nora squirmed, something fell out of her purse. "What's that?" Darcy asked, instantly alert.

"Vitamins," Nora muttered, scrambling to pick the bottle up.

"Ha, ha, ha, that's funny. Darcy needs more than vitamins to make her feel good. Are you a health nut?"

Nora shifted in her seat. "I don't think so."

"Not me, either, are you kidding? Look at me, I'm a disease nut. Ha, ha, ha." Darcy grabbed Nora's bottle, inspected it, looked at her shrewdly. "Prenatal . . . aw."

Nora couldn't stop her own pleased smile. "Yes," she whispered.

"I was pregnant once," Darcy said. "Didn't think I could get pregnant, did you? Thought I was a roller skate. But I was, sure as can be. They said it was in the tubes, never would have been born. But it was in there." She looked at Nora through blank brown eyes. "The guy ran out on me anyway, the slime." She pushed Nora with a tiny elbow like a chicken wishbone. "Not like my boyfriend now. He's so crazy about me. It's about time I got one who really wanted me. I've told the guy to get lost lots of times, but he just keeps crawling back." Darcy stroked back her lank mousy hair. She turned to Nora as if something had just occurred to her and demanded, "Are you married?"

"No," Nora said. "Well, almost."

"Does he know about this?" Nora shook her head. "Boyfriend doesn't know?" Darcy started to laugh.

"He'll be happy," Nora said, and the words swarmed around them like gnats. "He'll be happy," she said again. "That's why I'm going to Cleveland. You see, my fiancé works in a K-Mart in Parma. Pretty soon he'll be promoted to assistant manager. And then I'm going to be married." Nora fumbled to find her wallet. She handed Darcy a picture of a very white young man in a very white shirt and black tie.

Darcy handed the picture back. "Lots of luck," she said. "You'll need it."

"We've been planning this for a long time," Nora began again, but it seemed that Darcy had already forgotten her and was looking for the little boy. Outside the window were lilacs, everywhere lilacs, blossoming on a hill in the countryside; they passed a ramshackle red building in some little town, what town? The bus driver didn't even call it out. They saw a decaying, shambling barn with the paint peeling off, rotten boards, and, all around, lilacs, just hanging, shivering there.

"Zippy the Pinhead, I've got you," Darcy squealed, voice piercing and oblivious. She pulled the boy to her and sank her fingers into his shiny, taffy-colored hair, covering him with kisses. Oh, the ardor of those kisses, and the heated, fervent look she flashed back at Nora when she felt her stare.

"Say, do you know what sign I am?" Darcy bent her head inward, nodding for Nora to do the same. Then, looking wickedly around, she unsnapped her blouse at the chest, pushing toward Nora a round milky breast with a pink nipple being attacked by a purple and magenta crab tattoo. "Oh, Nora," said Darcy, "isn't that pretty? Isn't that pretty, honey? Hey, you like me, don't you?" she said with a cackle, and Nora, desperately, nervously, started to laugh. "Oh, I'm funny, am I?" said Darcy, starting to button herself up. "So just how do I amuse you?"

"No, no, it's nothing," Nora said, and when Darcy kept looking at her, she said she was sorry, she was just so tired, she'd been on the bus for hours.

While Nora pretended to sleep, Darcy drummed her fingers on the armrest, looked out the window, took out a pack of cards. Then she roused Nora, tapping her on the shoulder. "Look, we're coming to our dinner stop," she said. "It's about time." The smitten little boy bobbed into view. "Hey, Zippy, look, it's Booger King. Don't you want a booger from Booger King?" The boy's mother smiled a pained smile. As the bus stopped, Darcy stirred. She gripped the tops of the seats and hoisted herself up, then, as adept as any trapeze artist, traveled crabwise along the headrests to the front of the bus.

"Will you get my chair?" she asked the driver, then looked back to Nora. "You can take me around Booger King, all right?" she said.

In her tasteful, implausible outfit, Nora wheeled Darcy into the restaurant. "Excuse me, excuse me," Nora said, trying to get in line, but she was blocked by several young men from the back of the bus. A black one was handsome, with a glorious head of succulent-looking, sausage-like dreadlocks. He took off his sunglasses and turned to look at Nora, staring as if to ignite her.

"Don't rush so, baby," he said. Nora tried to push past. "You are so fearful," he said. "Why won't you speak to me?"

Nora stared back. "Because I don't know you," she said, standing there lovely and proud.

"I think you're prejudiced."

Nora's mouth trembled. "That's ridiculous. I'm not."

"I think you should talk to me a little about this ugly prejudice you have," he said insistently.

"You're really wrong," Nora said. "You have no right to say that."

"Then why are you running so fast to get away?" He peered at her intently.

"We've got stuff to do," said Nora.

"Look, she's your friend, isn't she?" he said, nodding at Darcy. "Well, how did she get to be your friend? You didn't always know her, right? You stopped and talked to her, that's how you got to be friends with her, right?"

"I'll be friends with you, honey," said Darcy, and a white guy started to laugh.

"Looks like you got a live one, Wilson," he said. "Way to go, Killer Joe."

With elaborate politeness, Wilson leaned over and took Darcy's hand. "Pleased to meet you, Ms. . . ."

"Anything you want to call me, you hot thing," said Darcy. She wouldn't let go of his hand. "Just keep talking, sweetheart."

"We'd better get our burgers, or it'll be too late," squeaked Nora, plowing Darcy past the men. Darcy looked back, licking her lips. They got into line and waited for whoppers and chocolate shakes.

"You should be more friendly," said Darcy as they sat down. "In my profession, you learn to be open. You learn to connect with other people, find out what they're all about. You learn about your place in the world."

"What is your profession?"

Darcy wiped her mouth with a piece of ketchup-smeared waxed paper. "Switchboard operator," she said. "I lost my job, took a tough bounce, but I always hit the ground running . . . ha, ha, ha."

At the Burger King door, the driver barked, "We leave in five minutes."

"You've hardly eaten a bite," Darcy said, sucking her fingers and gulping down the last of her shake. When Nora didn't answer, Darcy began to primp in the napkin holder, gazing approvingly at herself, combing her hair with a tortoise shell comb right there at the table.

"Hey, Nora." She snapped her fingers. "Say, Nora, would you get me some cigarettes?"

Nora bit her lip. "Sure."

"Some Marlboros," Darcy said. "Make it the hard pack."

Nora wheeled her back to the bus. The driver hadn't reappeared, so she held out her arms to Nora, sweetly. Gravely, Nora lifted Darcy up.

The bus pulled onto the road. Nestled next to Nora in their seat, Darcy once again took off her boots with their elaborate stitchery . . . leaves, arrows, ran up the sides of each, surrounding a plumed bird. The toes were capped with imitation lizard tips, Darcy informed Nora.

Then, rubbing her hands, she said, "I need a cigarette bad. Want one?"

"You can't smoke here."

"Ah, chill out. The driver don't care. Anyway, they're smoking in back." Both of them turned to look at the area around the chemical toilet. No females were anywhere near, but Darcy saw Wilson and waved. "I guess I'm gone for awhile then." Darcy shrugged apologetically. "I got an awful habit." She hoisted herself up and, using the head-rests, began traveling to the back of the bus.

"Mind if I sit here?" she asked in her sleepy voice.

"Sure, go ahead," said Wilson's friend, a freckle-faced redhead wearing a leather vest over his bare chest.

"Got to have a cigarette," she said, and she laughed her merry laugh. "Sure you can have one," she said to her new seatmate; he took the pack and pulled out two, three. "What the fuck are you doing?" she said. "Give me back my smokes."

"Watcha gonna give me for 'em?" he asked.

"No fuckin' way," she said. "I got more to sell than you think. Come on, give 'em to me."

The front of the bus was silent, with Nora, Zippy's mother, and the other, older passengers seeming to listen intently to what was going on behind them. The back of the bus was a clubhouse, smoke-filled by the sprawled young men and Darcy, who now sat on the edge of a seat like a child-sized puppet, her useless legs folded to the side like wings discarded after the Christmas play.

"Thanks, Wilson. Thanks for getting my cigs back from that creep. What's his name? A.K.? That's a weird name. Hey, Wilson." She blew smoke at him. "How old are you, eighteen?" She inhaled deeply. "I'm twenty-three. You're practically jailbait, the way I see it. What sign are you, Taurus? Oh, Libra. Libras are off the wall. Want to see something? Oh, forget it. You're too immature. Why are you looking at me like that?"

Wilson teased her. "Why are you so suspicious?"

"Because I hate men, that's why, what do you think?" Darcy said, not missing a beat. "Look at that Casanova, that A.K. I give him my cigarettes and what does he do? Just blows me off. I've never been so insulted." No one said anything. Darcy, inevitably, filled the silence. She focused on a chair several rows behind Nora. "Hey, you moron in the orange shirt and stupid-looking hat."

Across the aisle from Nora, the little boy's mother slammed her book with a sound like a pistol shot. The noise was so loud they could hear it in the back. Darcy looked forward. Amazing how ominous and overloaded the atmosphere had suddenly become. People were nervous, glancing around. The boy's mother sat with a look of stunned fury, back straight up.

"Why don't you go back to your seat?" said the guy in the orange shirt. His cap had a preserved sunfish on the front of it.

"You're supposed to be asleep," Darcy chirped, but something caught in her voice.

"I was, but it's kind of difficult," he said. "You're sitting across the aisle, not across the bus."

"What's your problem, hard up?" She wouldn't take no for an answer. "Give your hand a break. I bet I know somebody who'd get you off. For free, too. Hey, Wilson, go over and do that guy. You need the experience."

"If you weren't a woman, or whatever you are, I'd smash your face in," he said.

"Just try it, dirtball. I've got upper body strength."

Wilson said, "Hey, baby, I think you should leave. Go on, git."

"Who pissed on your Wheaties this morning? What's the matter, Wilson? I give you a rush, don't I? Oh, no, I can tell. You don't want tuna with good taste, you want tuna that tastes good."

"Oh, so that's what the smell was—tuna," said A.K. The young men's laughter echoed from the back of the bus as from a dark cave, dangerous and private. They were whistling, stomping their feet. The filthier Darcy's language got, the louder they whooped.

Voices drifted to the back: "They ought to kick her off the bus."

"The Lord hates people like her," croaked the man with the weeping eye. "He'll shut her down early, may his will be done."

The young men in the back uproariously laughed. "Thanks, preacher man." Zippy's mother stared straight ahead. And Darcy sat there with a small smile, as if she knew they wanted to pull her apart—the job was started, after all. In the haze of smoke she wiggled the toes of her snow-white feet.

Nora looked startled when she saw Darcy peering tentatively around the side of their seat.

"Hi, it's me. I'm back," Darcy said with an inquiring look, as if she weren't quite sure that Nora would welcome her. She continued brightly, in a stage whisper, "They've got rum and pot back there," and she slid in. Nora gave her wide berth.

The little boy scooted forward and tossed his car into Darcy's lap.

"Hey, lady, isn't this your kid's toy?" Darcy leaned to pass the car across to the boy's mother, who turned to look at her and pointedly did not say anything. Darcy tried again. "Look, I don't want him to forget it."

"He hardly needs that toy anymore, things being what they are. In fact, I wouldn't let him touch it," the woman said. Darcy received the slight with all the antagonism intended. Her face seemed to swell as if she'd been slapped on that side, her arms crossed in front of her like objects she had just found, they had nothing to do with her. Her bravado was flagging. The whole bus sat silent.

"Hey, Darcy!" The young men in back were calling her now. "Come on back here. I've got something for you to do since you're out of cigs." They pounded their feet. They had put their mark on her. "You don't need no cigs," A.K. chided. "I've got something that will keep your mouth full."

"Why don't you just shut up?" Darcy squeaked over her shoulder, but she was smiling. "They're getting fresh," she said to Nora, who gave her a terrified gaze. "It gets old fast, don't it?" But anyone could see that deep satisfaction stained Darcy's flushed face as they stamped their feet in unison. She was preening. "Do you think I should go? Just to shut them up?"

"Wanna give me a try, Darcy? Once black, never back."

Darcy elbowed Nora in the ribs. She called loudly to the back of the bus, "I been there and I came back. Eat your heart out, Wilson."

"Hey, Darcy, watcha gonna give me to eat?"

In an instant she had scuttled back and was sitting next to Wilson. "Start on these," Darcy said, waving her bare toes in front of his face.

"Shut your mouth, there's a little kid," someone said.

"Well, pardon me, I'm sorry, I didn't see him." Darcy spoke in a gentler tone. "Hey, Zippy, want your car?" The boy walked toward her. Darcy tossed the toy. He was too little to catch, so the car hit his chest, ricocheted, then landed under a seat. "Whatsamatter, why didn't you get it?" The boy began to whimper.

"Billy, don't touch that. Come back here." The mother craned her neck, looking at her son, but he was already running to her.

"I didn't mean to hit him," Darcy said half heartedly. The boy's mother was shaking with rage. She seemed barely able to contain herself.

"We're getting near my stop, Wilson," Darcy said. "If you're ever in Black Duck Falls,. give me a call."

"What do you mean, if I'm ever in Black Duck Falls. I'm in Black Duck Falls right now."

"You want to get out with me?"

"I sure do. The place is named after me, I might as well get out here. What do you say, everybody?" Wilson and his friends laughed.

The bus pulled onto a cloverleaf, past a sign that said "Black Duck Falls, Home of WCOW Radio: Five Miles."

"Come on, Wilson, get me a smoke from A.K. Thatta-boy, thanks. I'm leaving soon. You gonna miss me?"

"I don't know whether I'll miss you, but I'll miss your mouth."

Darcy made kissing noises. "Yum, yum, yum."

"Hey, what did I tell you, there's a little kid."

The child was back beside Darcy, gazing at her out of the corner of his eye. "Hey, Zippy the Pinhead, do you forgive me? Come on, get on my lap, give me a kiss." It was awkward for her; she had to lean far over as the bus bounced on the badly paved road, and she nearly toppled, pulling him up to her. "Come on, little sweetheart," she said, "talk to Darcy," and she began to hug the boy and kiss his cheeks passionately.

The boy's mother jerked to her feet, all gangly arms and legs, and rushed down the aisle. She grabbed her son by the arm, yanking so hard that he started screaming. Darcy wouldn't let go. "He'd rather be with me and you know it."

The mother flushed a horrible prickly red. "If I was you I'd jump out of the bus right now and let it run me over."

"I'm sure you would, as stupid as you are."

The woman lunged with all her might, pulling her son away and sending Darcy sprawling in the aisle.

For a moment she lay there, unable to right herself. She thrashed and squirmed, shuddering as the bus shuddered, but no one made a move. And then, all at once, Nora, who had been craning her neck to watch, got up and ran, hurtling herself toward the boy's mother, stopping just short. "Can't you see she hasn't got anybody in the world?"

The mother looked at Nora in astonishment—Nora in her silk blouse, keeping her balance by holding on to the headrests. The bus bumped down the interminable night-time roads. From somewhere came the smell of sweat curdling, sweetish, sticky. Finally Wilson lifted Darcy up, and together he and Nora took her back to her seat.

Nora kept her arm around Darcy's small jellyfish frame. "You know what you are? You're just like a little baby," Nora whispered haltingly.

"I'm no baby, you stupid sap, and don't you forget it," Darcy hissed, twisting away from the arm, and then she sat there limply. It wasn't hard to crumple her, she was crumpled anyway, after all, wadded up on the seat. How aggressively she came on, how easily she gave in. The bus's brakes wheezed. They were nearing the station.

For awhile Darcy and Nora sat in silence. Then Darcy began crooning in a peculiar singsong: "Under the bus, is that right? Shut down? If you weren't a woman or whatever you are . . . what could that possibly mean? What do you think I am?" She was in a trance, muttering, shaking her head, as if she were used to murmuring like this, always.

All at once she looked over at Nora and said, "Thanks for getting that fucking bitch off my back." Then, with a sly look, she said, "Now how about the bolo tie. Are you ready to make a deal?"

"Well, I really hadn't thought . . ." began Nora.

"You're showing good taste," Darcy said cheerfully. "This puppy is my pride and joy." She began unhooking it from around her neck. "That'll be twenty dollars. Don't look so surprised. You've got to pay for quality, Nora." Nora hesitated. "Well, if you don't want it, I can always put it back on." Sadly, she began refastening it.

"Oh, no. That's all right. I'll take it." Nora dug into her bag, found a bill.

"There. Now you'll always have something to remember Darcy by." Darcy smiled tenderly at her, putting the cash into a lavender leatherette pouch that matched her boots, swirling with arrows, cactus designs, fancy stitchery.

After that she snapped to, jabbering at Nora as before. "Well, it looks like this is goodbye. You're a nice person. Maybe I'll see you in Minneapolis sometime." She leaned past Nora, getting a view of the station. "Say, I don't see my boyfriend. I wonder where he is, the shithead." She swung herself into the aisle.

"My bags are all under the bus. You think the driver will still get them?"

"Of course he will, he has to," Nora said, and, sure enough, the driver was already coming down the aisle for her, his face scornful.

"You can name it after me if you want," Darcy said to Nora with a wink, looking over the driver's shoulder, and that was the last Nora heard from her.

Darcy looked sunken and very small, plastered to her chair when the driver got it out, as if she had been soaked and stuck on it, her body as insubstantial as a spider web.

Nora tapped the glass and waved her hand. Darcy peered at the bus but couldn't seem to make out where the noise was coming from; she scanned the length of it, gaping. Then she rolled alone into the terminal and began trailing back and forth.

"It's lucky she left when she did," said Zippy's mother to everyone in general. "If she hadn't, I'd have thrown her out with my bare hands."

"She's gone, the Lord be praised," said the teary-eyed man. "Satan's got ahold of her. She won't be around long."

Nora took her vitamins out of her purse, tried to remember if she'd taken any. Why had Darcy said she needed luck? It seemed an obvious question, but she hadn't dreamed of bringing it up with Darcy at her side. She wished Darcy would come back, so she could ask her now.

Nora watched Darcy wheel from one end of the storefront terminal to the other, scanning all horizons, her bags in her lap. Her glitter reflected brilliantly on the sheet of plate glass; soon her speed set the spangles in motion till they seemed to leap and fade like fireworks.

Broken Music

Since yesterday, Victoria and Pavel, the required Polish guide, had been eyeing each other. When she left her mother alone in a circle of deferential fellow tourists at the gate of the Warsaw Jewish Cemetery and threw herself into her designated front bus seat, a place of honor for her mother, she wasn't surprised that Pavel ambled aboard to chat her up.

Victoria had never been away from America before. The richly overgrown cemetery had stunned her with the old-world charm of its ancient, sometimes Byzantine grave markers, the horror-movie morbidity of the single sunken mass grave where thousands of unnamed Jews—"probably all our Rudman and Taub relations," her mother had muttered—lay tangled. Covering thirty-three hectares, whatever that was, the cemetery had sprawled as far as she could see in the mist of the spring morning, a seething landscape choked by weeds, shrubs, and young trees that had burst all efforts to contain their unruliness. Victoria was astonished. And now here was adorable, foreign Pavel, shimmering blue eyes, ice-blond bangs, standing lazily in the aisle flirting with her.

"Are you a Jew?" he said, although he must know that a Jewish organization had rented these buses, hired these guides. Perhaps he took blue-blonde Victoria for one of the German nationals from Dusseldorf who had joined the tour as a penance.

"Are you a Jew?" he said again. A Jew, a Jew, a Jew.

No, not a Jew, not exactly. An American, a half Jew, couldn't he tell, looking at her generic pink-cheeked face. No, not a Jew, not like the picture on the Elders of Zion kosher vodka in the duty free shop of the airport she had seen at 1:00 A.M., 6:00 A.M. Warsaw time, the day before. . . No, not like that, the line drawing of the rabbi in tallis and yarmulke and dippy, flouncy sidecurls with a huge hooked crooked nose, beady eyes, thick lips twisted in a greedy smile . . . No, not a Jew like that, but a part Jew, nevertheless, an American . . . impossible, wasn't it, to convey that to him, with his thin bright shell of English?

She thought to explain to him the story of her Jewishness, but he literally took her breath away. She wanted not to look anything she was. She wanted not to look thirty-two. She wanted not to look like a tax lawyer. Instinctively she groomed herself, smoothing her hair, running a finger over her lips. She knew the shiny royal blue "official tour jacket" flattered her coloring.

"Well, sort of," she managed to whisper. "Well, more or less."

"Ah, not a Jew. Not really," Pavel whispered to her, squatting to be nearer to her. "But some of the Jewish women, they are the most superb of all."

Her mother stomped up the bus steps, stopping short behind Pavel. "Hi, Mom!" Victoria said, sending Pavel into a smart rise-and-retreat and sliding to the window so her mother could have the aisle seat. Her mother made a "shu-shu" sound with pursed thin lips and gestured Victoria to keep the aisle seat and let her hide by the window.

Still, everyone reboarding the bus gave a special bright-eyed smile in her direction and said, "So! Fania!"

As a girl, Fania had been an inmate of Auschwitz. She had been tracked down for the tour by Joyce, the relentless tour leader from New York, who passed now, beaming at them both. Pavel tucked his shirt in, sat in his little chair beside the driver, and lifted his microphone. With a wee wink at Victoria, he announced, "Please to take your seats; we have four hours to Auschwitz to make."

"I don't need to see more of Poland," Fania growled to Victoria.

The panoramic front window was like a solar panel, with Pavel as the sun. Victoria seemed to be the only one attending his almost-English commentary about the country they passed through, although cynical Jimmy, the lawyer across the aisle, occasionally parodied it: "This is a tree. This is a bird." Pavel aimed his speech at her. His short-sleeved shirt showed off his velvety, supple arms. A couple of times he even pursed his lips as if to blow her a little kiss. Fania's head fell heavily onto Victoria's shoulder.

When the bus made a stop in Krakow, Fania jerked awake. She shook her shiny head of hair, a sheet of mahogany. She had a bold, red-cheeked face with a stolid gaze and squint marks that trailed to the middle of her cheekbones. "Don't wrinkle your eyes," Victoria used to say, not wanting to see the lines carved in ever more deeply, but she'd given up that plea years ago. In the broad noon light, her mother's face looked creased as a walnut.

Like nearly everyone else, Fania got off the bus. Victoria asked Pavel to close the door against the fetid, corrupted Krakow air—an ecological disaster area, the guidebook said of the place. This air was a threat to historic structures and was making the residents sick. She showed the page to Pavel.

He sat next to her, flattened his spine against the seat

and swelled his chest, pressing expansively back against her arm, her shoulder. "Hah—exaggerated! Exaggerated!" he said. Feeling she had to, she shifted away from the pressure of his body and scrunched up next to the window. He was young, yes, hardly more than a boy. He pointed at a trolley car. "Look over there—not so dirty, hah? Or that church over there?"

A faint film of wild green frothed over the parks, the avenues: the Krakow spring, a patina on a long-buried shipwreck. Before the war, there had been almost sixty thousand Jews in Krakow, in an ancient community dating from the fourteenth century. Now there were how many? Six hundred? Six? She flipped a page in the guidebook: "The citizens of the new Poland are wild with excitement, on a wildly erratic roller coaster ride from communism to capitalism."

Fania returned, again ahead of her fans, and took the aisle seat Pavel grudgingly vacated. Fania was insulated now by an absurd pair of sunglasses—*Terminator* sunglasses!—she'd surely bought at the Krakow gift shop. Jimmy now sported a bizarre hat, a round tan rain hat like Paddington the Bear's from the children's story.

Victoria had felt a fleeting attracton for Jimmy in the bar of their hotel the night before. He was funny. Sitting in the bar, they'd watched Polish "Wheel of Fortune" on TV.

"It's all consonants," Victoria said.

"Yeah, can't you just see them . . . uh, Pat, I'd like to buy a vowel . . . wait a second, we haven't got any." They were fatigued from their long trip and getting drunk. "I'd like to see a contestant hit bankrupt and blame it on the Jews."

Uneasy, Victoria said, "A little thin-skinned, aren't you?" and he had replied, "Just you wait."

Later, in the hotel lobby, one of their fellow tourists had asked, "Why are we doing this trip by bus? Poland has good trains." Jimmy had guffawed and said, "Please, you can't take a bunch of Jews to Auschwitz by train!"

Now Victoria sat on the bus, studying her guidebook. This area had been inhabited since prehistoric times. The legendary Krak was supposed to have founded the city, subduing a ravenous dragon by feeding it animal skins stuffed with tar and sulphur, which it fatally devoured . . . as the modern-day inhabitants sucked in their pestilential air.

Jimmy took a flag of Israel out of his knapsack and spread it over his window. "I don't want to see this Polish city," he said in a loud voice.

Pavel spoke on, not seeming to notice. "Centuries of Polish kings lived on Wawel Hill: Prince Boleslaw the Shy, King Wladislaw the Short . . ."

As they halted at a stoplight, a passerby, seeing the Jewish flag, walked the length of the bus, giving all of them, the Jews on the bus, the finger.

"Look, Mom," Victoria said, oddly focused on the vacant-faced, dirty-looking man moving in the spirit of an age-old ceremony. He held an arrogant finger in the air as he trolled them, his whole arm stiff, jabbing again and again.

"Ignore it," said her mother, just as the man bent, right by her window, to spit at them. Jimmy moved the flag to give the finger back . . . but the man seemed to notice nothing, see nothing, his face drugged, impervious. When the bus started up, the man hurled himself in front of it, forcing it to brake with a loud screech.

Victoria fell back against her mother.

"And stupid, too," Jimmy said. "Who spits and throws himself in front of a bus that could run him over?"

"Don't react. Don't give him the satisfaction," her mother said through tight lips.

Fania had never talked about being in a concentration camp. Victoria had always known that it was not to be spoken about. Once when she was a little girl, sitting on a stool by the cash register in the gift shop, she had heard a customer ask her mother what the numbers were on her arm—her phone number? It must have been a very hot summer day because always, in her memory, her mother wore long sleeves. Ha, ha, ha, her mother had laughed, and it was as if Victoria, at seven, were seeing for the first time, on the softest inner part of her arm, the blue numbers with the crossed sevens and the dash with A on the end—or was it L, for Luck, the small Polish city from which her mother's family, incomprehensibly, had come.

Fania moved closer, and Victoria felt her soft and pliant side. "Have you noticed what Hoffmann and his wife are doing?" An Israeli colonel was along on the march, one of the organizers, and since yesterday her mother had singled him out, him and his wife, a poised and elegant woman who always seemed to be flirting with him. "You can tell when people have a good sex life, can't you," her mother said. "In the bathroom, I mentioned to Mrs. Hoffman the speech he made this morning—so forceful, so powerful. She said, 'That's not the only thing he's forceful and powerful about.'" Her mother laughed.

Victoria shook her head. "Honestly," she said, but this was the mother Victoria had always known, inclined to ask even her own daughter how her sex life was. Fania stopped her constant broad winking at Victoria and her husband only when Victoria told her that Jason was moving out. After he had gone, she had felt very little, nor could she say that she was surprised. Although she thought of herself as a pleasant person, the marriage had revealed her as bland, unable to connect; she didn't see herself as someone who knew how to keep a relationship going.

"How are you doing, Fania," said Joyce, the tour leader from New York. Cherished creature, said the smile. Treasured one. "We were wondering if you had any names."

When Fania didn't answer Joyce, Victoria squeezed her mother's hand and put an arm around her. Then she shrank back. She always did this, and it irked her: she would fawn over her mother, then catch herself doing it, and recoil into numbness, distance. Fania was perfectly capable of dealing with Joyce herself.

"We're writing down names of people who died in the camps," Joyce said. "We're writing them on these little wooden plaques, then we'll plant them in the earth when we have our ceremony at Birkenau with the other groups. Are there any you want to remember? You can write their names right here."

"Are there any people you want to remember, Mother?" Victoria said hesitantly. She wanted to push away the effrontery of Joyce's insistent bright face.

"Maybe later," Fania said. Joyce lingered a moment before moving off.

Victoria drummed her fingers on the armrest, looking out the windows at the rolling hills, the birch forests of Upper Silesia, through lines of flickering trees, a rich and lustrous green. Her mother, too, gazed through her dark blublockers into the silvery shivering of those leaves.

I am Victoria, daughter of Fania . . . "What was your mother's name, Mother?"

"Esther."

"And her mother's name?"

"Sarah."

"And her mother's name?"

"Rachel. Before that I don't know." I am Victoria, daughter of Fania. I am Fania, daughter of Esther. I am Esther, daughter of Sarah. I am Sarah, daughter of Rachel.

Her mother was poking around in her backpack, the blue backpack emblazoned with the Star of David that had been handed out to everyone on the tour. Fania took out a curling sepia snapshot of people squinting in the sun against the backdrop of a wooden house—her mother was a freckle-faced little girl, standing in front. She tried to hold the picture steady in front of Victoria's face, but it would not stay still. "My mother," she said. "My father. My sister, Devora Rudman," she said, pointing to each face in turn, as if Victoria were supposed to see something beyond strangers trapped in an offhand group more than a half a century away. "My mother, Esther Rudman."

"Shall I write your sister's name, Devora?" Victoria said cautiously.

"My mother, gone," Fania said. "Don't know what happened. Devora: Came in, never came out." She had to push the pencil hard, strain against the splintering wood, to inscribe.

"You write: My cousin, Resa Rudman."

Victoria started writing. In her mother were enough names to populate a block, a village, a city of the dead. Her mouth open, stabbing the pencil into the wood, Fania wiped her brow with the back of her hand. "Came in, didn't come out . . . Jonah Meisel, Rachel Blum, Rebeka Korvic." Fania filled her plaque, and after that she had more than enough for Victoria's paddle, on both sides.

Victoria sat sullen, jealous and shocked by all the names. "God saved me so that I could have you and that you would be happy," her mother had said to her more than once, and Victoria had never questioned these calming words that bestowed such dignity, such continuity. But this muttering woman with the craning neck was not the one who had reassured her.

Every time she saw an image of a swastika symbol, or of that con man with his absurd mustache, saluted by his followers, Victoria's fingers had skidded fast to get her past the page. It must ruin a person to know this. If you thought about it, if you spoke about it too much, how could you live? When shows about the Holocaust appeared on television, Victoria turned them off. She flipped through quickly when she saw the gruesome pictures in books and magazines. She didn't want to hate people.

All her mother's behavior implied that this was the right course. Only once that she could remember, or twice, had her father said bitterly to her, "You have no idea of what went on over there. You have no idea of what your mother went through."

Now Fania gave names for Jimmy's plaque, and for the plaque of the woman behind her, a woman with a gleaming-gray page boy and smooth skin but with long pruny lines wrinkling the skin above and below her lips . . . Eleanor.

"Where did you get the wonderful vest?" Victoria had asked Eleanor earlier that day as they were leaving the hotel. The vest was a magnificent tapestry of jewels and gold and scarlet thread, intricately wrought, obviously hand done. . . . No connoisseur of clothes, even Victoria knew that a year of someone's life had gone into making it.

"Oh, I have no idea. We travel all over the world," Eleanor had said, shrugging off the question with a smile. But now, as Fania dictated, Eleanor wrote down names: Jakob Bedzin, Lila Kalisch. She wrote reverentially, taking dictation. "They came in, but they didn't come out."

It was the twenty-seventh of Nissan, a Jewish month Victoria had never heard of before, and a solemn day of mourning: Holocaust commemoration day for the Warsaw Ghetto Uprising. In the state of Israel flags were at half mast, entertainment businesses were closed . . . and Jews from all over the world were descending on Poland to walk the three kilometers from Auschwitz to Birkenau.

"The Nazis hid this camp away in the country to keep it from the Polish people," Pavel began again through his microphone. "That way they kept secret what was happening to the Jews."

Victoria saw her mother shake her head.

"There he goes again," Jimmy said under his breath, and then he said loudly, "That's not true. The Polish people knew exactly what was happening."

Victoria could hear some of the charms on Eleanor's vest tinkling.

"The Poles didn't know," Pavel repeated rancorously, his gaze blazing down the aisle. "It should not be forgotten that Auschwitz is a tragedy for the Poles, too, and that many Poles died there. It's our memorial, too."

Hisses and boos broke out on both sides of the aisle. "That's bullshit," Jimmy said. "The scale was incomparable. The Nazis took the Jews away and your people heard the screams."

Joyce took the microphone from Pavel for just a moment to remind them once again of the righteous gentiles, Germans and Poles, who had risked their lives to save the Jews. That very morning in their hotel she'd met a Polish farmer who had built a shelter for Jewish friends during the war, hiding them under his barn.

"Here we turn the corner into Auschwitz," Pavel said. The bus turned off the main road and into a crowded parking lot. It was so anticlimactic and dull that Victoria didn't want to admit they had really arrived.

She looked at the milling tourists with a sodden feeling of panic, then put her arm around her mother's sturdy back.

Pavel tipped his cap to them but her mother did not bother to reply with word or gesture. As they disembarked, some people gawked at them, coldly staring.

"Look at them—the Poles. See how they act?" her mother said under her breath. They tried to navigate politely through but the onlookers stood unmoving in their path. They had to jostle their way across the parking lot and were soon walking toward a grove of fragrant springtime trees.

"Over there," her mother said, "on the night I came, it wasn't dark. We were blind from the floodlights, and off in the distance—" she turned so she could point in a certain direction, but all they could see were budding trees—"were pillars of fire." Fania gawked at signs that pointed the way to a snack bar, a hotel.

Walking beside them for a moment, Jimmy said, "Look what I found—an Auschwitz postcard." He showed Victoria a shot of a long prison building, a pile of hair. "I ought to send one of these to my ex, don't you think?" Jimmy said. "Wish you were here . . . wish you had been here."

They fought their way through the crowd, passed through the black arched sign above a wrought iron gate: "Arbeit Macht Frei," work makes free; the black spindly letters were coy and curling, the sign forming a sheltering arch for them to walk beneath.

How was Victoria to know that Auschwitz, at first, would look like a college campus . . . a charming campus in the spring with its orderly brick buildings, its cobbled walks, its lovely supple green trees springing out of the earth like fountains. They trampled the damp streets, past bright lawns, with Eleanor, the prune-lipped woman from the bus, and then with Jimmy. "Mansard roofs, neat brick buildings all in a row," Victoria murmured to her mother.

Fania marched on her sturdy strong legs, a seventy-two-year-old woman keeping up easily with much younger people. Victoria reached out to lay an arm across her tough square shoulders, then hugged her.

"You poor sweetheart," Victoria said impulsively, voice hushed with tenderness. "Even then it was this that kept you going, wasn't it. This," she said again, squeezing her mother's upper arms and back even harder, warmth flooding out of her.

Her mother stiffened. Her shoulders rippled, but she made no sound, though her mouth was set. She shook her head. "To go on and on when you know what the world is like," she said. Intimidated, awkward, Victoria lagged back a few steps.

Yes, it could have been a spring campus in New England until you walked, on shuffling feet, into one of the orderly brick buildings, descended dark stone stairs into hell. Damp cement and glossy, tempered alloys of steel, bare bulbs stuck fast to iron pipes, thick metal doors, everything battened down, cemented, inescapable.

Victoria stuck her head in a door. "This is the washroom where women stripped before execution," said a sign. She saw a crude concrete basin, exposed rivets and struts.

Another door, shellacked and locked shut, had a peephole: "In September 1941, the first experimental mass killing of people with Zyklon B took place in this basement."

Block 11 was cavernous, with echoing corridors, its ceilings spattering a uriney light, for the air itself seemed saturated by the substances a trapped, terrified animal would extrude, and by the inexpressibly evil smell that knew everything, that would always remember . . . the superbly silent musty smell.

She saw blood still sprayed on a stone wall after fifty years.

She saw pictures of smiling Nazi officers pulling a prisoner in a striped uniform out of these very doors.

Victoria suddenly thought of Pavel, but he was nowhere to be seen. Her muttering mother, weighed down as a pack horse, walked impassively past the pounds of hair, gray with age and chemicals. She stopped only once to stare at a pretty white sandal that had fallen away from the pile of shoes, a jaunty thin-strapped sandal that a young woman might have picked out on a happy day . . . a carefree delicate sandal, torn loose from the others, at the edge of a dusty pile.

Just as they left, Victoria pulled Fania to a stop in front of an imperfect picture, enlarged until it was grainy and indistinct . . . a furtive picture, taken at a slant—a blurry black and white photograph of women running naked through a forest clearing in the early morning or evening: the sun was overexposed, blazing low in the birches. Birkenau, 1944, read the sign: Jewesses driven to a gas chamber.

They paused in the courtyard of the Auschwitz theme park, the crowd milling while pollen, blossoms, and feathery seeds floated in the April air, the air of Nissan. Victoria was cold.

People were watching them, a woman with her family, a woman in a green polyester blouse, her arms hanging out of the sleeves like great loaves of white bread dough, a woman who gaped arrogantly and stared, entitled to stare, like the man who had given them the finger.

Victoria stared back. The woman shook her head, rolled her eyes, glaring at her, at Fania, with malice: What are you doing here?

The effrontery . . . it was unbelievable. Victoria glanced behind herself, then to the side, for a backup, for reinforcement against this unfairness, but there was no backup.

"Even after the war they tried to kill us," her mother said all at once. "They were afraid we'd tell the world what they did." Coarse and pitiless looks came at them, unblinking, from the woman, her family, other Polish tourists, taking in the long lines of people pouring through the streets of Auschwitz with Stars of David on their jackets.

Victoria put her arm around her mother. Why should she feel wounded by the looks, and afraid?

"You Jews," said a boy standing with the woman.

"Keep going, keep going," said her mother, nudging

her to walk past, but Victoria hesitated before him, her face aflame.

"You must have done something very terrible for the Lord to punish you this way."

Speechless, Victoria ran after her mother. "What did I tell you?" her mother said.

Hoffman, the Israeli colonel, was bounding over to where they stood in the center of the cobbled walk.

"Come on over here," he said. "We're meeting by the gate to begin the march. You're holding everyone else up."

His curt, brusque tone broke the spell, and Victoria trembled with relief to have a task, something specific to do. Her mother hated to hear, always, that she was holding anybody up, and she prodded Victoria: Hurry, hurry. Deconditioned, defamiliarized, she could hear Jimmy now; we are mimicking them, our ancestors, even in that. They followed the colonel to where the group was milling under the Arbeit Mach Frei sign.

Ashamed of herself, Victoria kept her arm around her mother, who whispered the rest into her ear. "I was taught to be honest and kind and to think well of others . . . if I had not unlearned that fast I would be dead. Everyone I met lied to me."

"Did you take this walk, Mother? Did you walk from Auschwitz to Birkenau?"

"I'm sure I did. I worked in the crematoria."

"What?"

"You knew it, of course. I was a Sonderkommando. I took the bodies from the gas chambers to the ovens."

The information settled and sifted over Victoria gently like a feathery coating of ash.

On their way out of Auschwitz they passed the snack bar where Poles stood eating what—Polish sausage?—looking at them as if they were the ones who were preposterous.

Walking, her mother began talking to her in a low monotone, breathing hard, licking her lips. "Back in Luck, too, before I ran away to the woods, I worked for the SS. I cleaned the school they took over for their headquarters. One afternoon, a boy I went to high school with came by and told me: 'They killed all the Jews in Jaslo today. They piled them into trucks, drove out to the country, and had them dig their own graves.' One day I came back to the ghetto and they were all gone—my poor old father, my mother, my cousins. My sister and I who had been cleaning, we were the only ones left, and we ran away. We did not flee for our lives. We fled to avoid the humiliation of having to dance naked before our own graves, to be shot to death by the Nazis and boys we went to high school with . . . "

It was a cool damp afternoon, but her mother moistened her lips as if her throat were parched. "We hid for months in the woods. Then some farmers told the Nazis where we were hiding. They put us on a transport." Her tongue lolled out again.

A lovely walk in the misty rain on a spring day, that's what it would have been in Minneapolis . . . they passed Polish people going about their daily business, school, work, with barely a glance at them. Small groupings coalesced and fell apart, so it was not unusual when a young man, who turned out to be a Polish Jew, fell into step with them.

"Ask him how he can stand to be a Jew here," Victoria said.

It was good to see her mother in her usual mode, lively, interested in others. Victoria plodded along. In the crowd around them were young people, old people, speaking Spanish, French, English.

"He says he's quiet about being Jewish," her mother said. "He says the younger generation is different. They're ashamed of what their parents did."

"Tell him Poland doesn't deserve the Jews," Victoria said, a rainy wind blowing in her face. "Where is their medicine, their technology, their science? We saw a medical school that looked like a stable yesterday, Mother—tell him that Poland is a slum."

"I speak a little English, you know," Shlomo said, so faintly Victoria could barely hear him. When she sought to shake his hand he sprang away as if to avoid the strike of a snake. "I'm sorry, I don't shake hands," he said, loping off so fast that a smile actually passed between her and her mother.

"Orthodox," her mother said. "They never touch a woman. They'll go to the opposite side of the street."

"He's crazy to want to be in Poland," Victoria said, "don't you think?" Her mother, staring into the middle distance, did not respond. She plodded along dully. "Mother," Victoria said, "Mother? How do you feel?"

"I feel like someone who isn't supposed to be alive."

They passed the paved part of the road and began to walk in dirt. With every step, Victoria was aware of the pungent aroma of the soil.

"This is where the tracks came—to Birkenau," her mother said. They had arrived at the famous profile of the watchtower, and Victoria looked past.

"It goes on forever," she said. While other tourists used the bathrooms in the watchtower building, Fania and Victoria looked at Birkenau's vast fields, consumed by what they saw. They walked out onto the mud, for it was raining gently now, a fine mist, and their feet began to slosh in the thick black mud.

"The sky used to be black with smoke," her mother said. "It stunk for miles."

They walked to the place where Fania had undergone selection; she and her sister had walked to the right, while others from the transport were sent to the left.

Soon smoke from their corpses blackened the skies. Where her mother's barracks had been, only a chimney remained.

They marched in the mud to the wreckage of the crematoria. Polish security men were everywhere, talking into their radios. After all those years, the reek of smoke and blood still inhabited the crumbling towers of burnt bricks.

Kneeling at the makeshift shrine of an exploded crematorium, Fania lit a candle, but the mist was growing thicker and it would not stay lit. Off to the side, Victoria stood, hands in the pockets of her blue jacket.

She let her gaze settle on the forest in the near distance. The scene reminded her of something that wouldn't quite take shape. Fania cupped her hands around her candle, then lit it again. Victoria inhaled the old smoke, then the pungent sulphury tang of her mother's matches, till gradually it came to her that the trees before her looked like the background of the black and white picture she had seen of the women running. The blurred picture of the frantic women being driven had been taken very close to this spot, on a spring evening, the setting sun overexposed, blazing through the trees, printing desperate slanting shadows across the grass.

"Devora," her mother said. "Devora. I always thought the two of us would get out together. We made it through the whole war . . ."

"And that was what kept you going?" Victoria said encouragingly.

"Yes, that was one of the things that kept me going. And then," Fania said, "right in that barracks there"—she pointed a finger to an area far in the distance—"right before we marched away from here, she was lying sick on her bunk and an SS came and injected her with air."

"With air?"

"Yes, it goes right to the heart, it kills." Fania scanned her face. "He wanted to murder as many as he could before he ran away."

"Oh, Mother," Victoria said. "You must have felt horrible."

Her mother looked at her, unblinking. "I only knew that I was starving."

"But you smiled, Mother—you loved your sister." Squeezing her eyes shut, she hugged Fania tight. "Deep down you were always the good person you are now."

Fania seethed beneath her embrace till Victoria let her hands drop. The swollen tongue poked out again. "No one knows better than I what people are really like."

Her mother knelt to plant her sister Devora's silver ring beside the plaque. "Poor Devora," she said.

It was all Victoria could do not to pull harshly on her mother's arm. She could scarcely stand it. "Mother, I'm here," was all she could say. And when her mother didn't look her way, she said, "The ceremony is starting."

Under threatening skies, the crowds quieted in front of a platform erected beside a blown-up crematorium. A man spoke to them: These Jews who died were good, gentle people; they were learned people. But they had no power. They cried out and the world would not listen. Now, because of the state of Israel, Jews all over the world have power, and their cries will never again go unheeded.

"We are here, and we have not forgotten," he said to the mass graves, the lonely fields stretching empty and far away. "We are here."

The rain began pounding down in earnest and some of their crowd began to flee back toward the main watchtower of Birkenau. Beneath heavy black umbrellas at the periphery of the group, the cluster of Polish security men began to snicker. Fania and Victoria exchanged looks. They had no umbrella.

The icy rain drenched her neck, soaked beneath her collar. "Should we go?" Victoria asked.

"Stay right where you are," Fania said. "Don't you move. Never let them say that a little rain came and the Jews ran away."

Victoria glanced over her shoulder, wondering if the cadre of Polish guards would think such a thing. But when she really looked, and looked hard, the expression on each face was different.

They knelt in the mud and planted their other wooden plaque scored with names. They murmured along as a magnificent voice pealed out the Kaddish. Then they took the long walk back, with the rest of the procession, through the muddy fields, past the barracks, past the disabled fences, barbed wire still hanging.

Victoria strained to remember the romance of the cemetery that she had visited a few brief hours before. She tried to bring into her mind the joy she had felt at the green pathways, the soaring stone, the reckless and sacred jumbled together . . . but the descendants, the great-great grandchildren of the people so grandly entombed in the Warsaw Cemetery, she now dug up with her every footfall.

Near the tracks of Birkenau, the buses were waiting. Climbing up the steps, Victoria noticed that the river of black mud had lapped up to near the very tops of her tennis shoes.

Pavel sat in his official spot, gazing thoughtfully at her. His eyes seemed to glimmer with sympathy. As her mother walked by, Pavel came up to Victoria. "Was hard, I know," he said.

Eleanor, entering the bus, stopped to glower at Pavel's grasp on Victoria's wrist. She stood there until Pavel let go, then went past them.

"Vicki," Pavel said. "Vicki. Do you have a telephone?"

"What?"

Her hand flew to her face, sticky with grime and tears. He hadn't caught up with the speed of what was happening to her; his message was forever too late.

Eleanor was calling out to her mother. Fania went docilely halfway to the back of the bus.

"Why do you speak only to her?" Pavel said.

"Because she's my mother," she said.

"Beautiful girl," he said, "you don't need to talk to your mother. You need to talk to a man." He drew closer. "Vicki," he said. "Are you a doctor?"

"No, I am a lawyer," she said, smoothing her Israeli flag. "I collect taxes. I go after people who don't pay their taxes. Do you understand?"

"Ah ha," he said, a huge smile growing on his face. "Ah ha," Pavel said. "A tax collector. Then you must beat me." He showed her his scrawny, whippet-like little butt.

Eleanor was speaking loudly, urgently, to Fania. Victoria cocked her head backward.

"How did you survive?" Eleanor was asking. Victoria saw her mother shrug. All over the crowding-up bus, people were silent, listening to the woman question her mother.

"Eleanor, leave her alone," said her husband.

"It's just an honest question. I want to know," Eleanor said. "When so many others died, how did you survive?"

"I don't know," her mother said, but she did not try to get away.

Across the aisle, Jimmy shot her a look. "You better go get her," he said, and when Victoria glanced at him askance, he said, "She's being attacked."

"What?"

"It's that old Darwinian thing—that the people who survived were . . ." He bent across the aisle, whispering to her. "You know about the Sonderkommandos. They cut off the hair, pulled the teeth. At Nuremberg there had to be a special finding . . ." His voice trailed off. Victoria looked at him incredulously. "Haven't you heard that?"

Victoria shot out of her seat and with loping strides she intruded herself between her mother and Eleanor.

"Come on, Mom." Her mother seemed stuck to the spot, limp, hanging her head in a way Victoria had never seen before. "Come on, Mom."

"I don't know why," Fania was saying dully.

Victoria tugged on her. "Come on." It was not until she jolted her arm, pulling it sharply, that Victoria was able to shepherd her mother back to their front seats.

"They keep asking me how I survived," her mother said. Victoria was speechless at her look. "How do I know how I survived?"

At last, the buses began to pull away. It must have been twenty minutes, half an hour later when Fania began to massage Victoria on the arm. "The Polish guy is hot for you," she said with a wry glance. "I noticed he kept looking over at you the whole time. He's a handsome man, too."

Flushing, Victoria watched her own reflection in Fania's glasses.

"These people just pretend to like us," Victoria said. "They don't really like us."

"Vicki, do you have a telephone? Vicki, are you staying with your mother?" he had asked.

Incomprehensible that she had answered, "No, I have a room by myself."

Watching the sun set in a little village that she could now swing by fearlessly, with no thought of being killed, Victoria saw a castle on top of a hill with a steep rock face, not a striated rock face but pebbly, stony. She saw two brown chickens pecking in a yard. And then, in a grove of flowering fruit trees, she saw a calf standing on one side of a gulch, separated from its mother, while a boy and a woman tried to get the balking creature to step across the ravine. Completely absorbed in what they were doing, the boy and his mother cajoled the calf, whose stiff front legs were firmly planted. The boy tried to push the tiny bony hindquarters then moved up to kiss the calf's nose, hugging its neck, pulling gently on the rope. The whole scene was impossibly illuminated by caramel-colored sunset light.

They would be woken before dawn to go to the airport and back to the States, so she and Fania decided to skip the ceremony that night and go straight to their rooms to rest. Victoria rushed off the bus, avoiding any further words with Pavel.

Somehow, though, she knew she would not get so easily away. She was barely asleep when the phone woke her. When she picked up the receiver, no one was there. Lying there, she stroked her thighs, unable to sleep, numb to what she had seen that day and thinking only of the blue sear of Pavel's eyes. The phone rang again and she spoke to the silence on the other end: "Pavel? Pavel?"

He was so crazy about her she almost took pity on him. She had tears in her eyes thinking about it all. Life goes on. This has always been the way of the world. The new generation doesn't have the scars of the last. This is how we overcome hatred, with love, with love.

As she lapsed in and out of fitful sleep, she dreamed that Pavel came to her, put his hand on her breast, and that she welcomed him warmly. She hugged him, they pressed closer, then hugged again, a little kiss on one cheek, then the other, a soft nuzzling of curls. Somehow they were alone together in one of the buildings of Auschwitz but it was a sanitized room, perhaps a room at the Auschwitz Hotel—the white Polish plungers all over the place, plunger light switches, plunger sinks and plunger bathtubs and toilets. A Polish Disney World of Auschwitz. . . . She lapsed into a trance from Pavel's dream-inducing, sleep-inducing, death-inducing eyes. She was so ready for him, it was embarrassing, her body yielding up its substance, flowing ever up and spilling over and over again like a fountain. His golden hair was lifted in currents of air, he swirled around her, blazing through her with the light of his bleached-out eyes.

Waking with a start she saw, waiting near the door to her room, her Rockport walking shoes with the mud of Auschwitz drying on them.

But what had awoken her was a knock on the door. She rose to greet it. In the doorway, for a moment, she let him caress her. "You're a sexy American girl," he murmured into the soft hair at her earlobe.

"Do you think so?" she hummed back.

He pecked at her with passive, tentative, sticky little kisses.

"You Jewish girls," he said. "You hot Jewish girls, you're all witches, aren't you," he said, his tongue lacing the curve of her ear. Then he kissed her so hard it made her lips numb, and she felt her whole body convulse. "What do you want, Vicki?" he whispered to her. "Tell me what you want."

The next morning, sitting in the plane next to her mother, Victoria started to cry.

"And why now?" her mother said.

"Pavel, the Polish guide? He came to me last night," Victoria said.

"Did you let him in?"

"Just for a minute," she said. "I let him kiss me . . . and then I closed the door. But I let him kiss me right there in the entrance to my room, even though I knew he was against the Jews."

He had been all over himself with enthusiasm, awkward, ill-timed, like the character on Saturday Night Live . . . the wild and crazy guy. For an hour after she shut him out, he scratched on the door like a cat.

"Then you won," her mother said. "Forget about it."

"But I feel so bad, Mother." He'd felt her clinging to him, hungry against his breast. "What do you want, Vicki?" He'd pressed her tightly, he'd slid his hand down fast, crumpling her slick gown, all disarrayed. When she slammed the door on him, his fingers had been wet with her.

"Let me tell you something . . ."

Victoria stared out the plane window, flying at seven hundred miles an hour away from the sunrise.

"Before we ever left Luck, when I was still living with my family, I was working for the SS, cleaning the schoolhouse where they had their headquarters. Every day as I washed and scrubbed, one guy came in to watch me."

Victoria tried to imagine her mother with a patina of youthful innocence. "He was so handsome. But of course, they were all handsome—so tall, so strong, so clean. This one was blond, and his eyes, a heavenly blue." Her mother sighed, inclining her head. Of course, she, too, would have noticed Pavel's charm—his eyes blue as air. "How can I tell you what it felt like to look at him?"

"Did you love him, Mother?" Fania said nothing. "Was he your lover? Did he help you escape?"

Her mother laughed harshly. "Love a Jewish girl? They would never admit to such a thing. It was a capital crime. No, when I scrubbed the toilets he peed on my hands."

Victoria breathed in her mother's fire, her fierce look. "Never to allow self-pity, or to give in, or to let them hypnotize you into believing you were a lower being . . . that was the only victory . . . Victoria."

The morning sun shone so blindingly into the windows that people all along one side had pulled down their shades, inducing a kind of artificial twilight. Her mother's face looked creased as old parchment.

"Too much history," Fania said. "Nobody needs it." She looked lonesome, sad. Craning her wrinkled tan neck, she looked around, dressed in the expensively tacky gift shop stock that always grated Victoria: over tight pants, she wore a black knit top with gold-reinforced peek-a-boo holes that stretched in a pattern of sun rays from her bosom to her throat like the breastplate of ancient queen.

Where was the voice for Victoria to counter this story, this story that led to the blurry frantic picture of Jewish women driven to their death? It was the voice of Shiva, destroyer of worlds. It was the voice of Lilith, who brought death by night. Seeping into her and through her, against her will, was all that she had fought against for these long years, all that she hadn't wanted, this hate.

She put Fania's hands to her lips and kissed them, freckled, rough-skinned hands that sunk with their own gravity. Victoria's young hands folded into them and stayed, enclosed.

"Oh, Mother," she said desolately. "We're so easy to kill, aren't we?"

"Oh, no, we're not." Her mother's grip tightened, drier than dust. "We're so very hard to kill."

Stalking Angel Dewayne

GLENNA HAD TAKEN to visiting the gourmet twenty-four-hour grocery store every Wednesday after her summer class, walking the aisles and asking prices until she could hear once again her own voice and not the headlong unstoppable voice that had started coming out of her now that she was teaching so much. As soon as the store's door hissed closed behind her, there was only music and murmuring and soothing, mechanical sounds. Northerly's was full of cheap thrills. The live lobsters were gone, so she couldn't commiserate with them, but it *was* possible to wring her hands in front of the trout. They clustered together near the bubbling aerator in their tank, against a scenic painted-paper backdrop of deep green ferns. On this fateful Wednesday she was peering at one browner and more speckled than the others, that swam in the small space with sweeps of its long tail. She was contemplating its impending death, that probably would be, in its enactment, little different from her own: some jolting shock to consciousness, and then a darkening, the swift gurgling away of a drain emptying.

The trout yawned.

Glenna pushed herself past, standing guiltily in front of the meat counter, sick of the trout. It would never anticipate death. Even her friend at the college who had worked with chimpanzees said she didn't figure they thought about death much. Still, it vexed Glenna that she grew weak if she didn't eat meat occasionally and thereby impose annihilation on fellow creatures in order to live herself. In the wild, she would probably be bringing down small game. As it was, she stood looking at steak behind glass, fighting visions of stockyard carnage, innocent furred cattle heads in a pile, and her own evolution from a race of predatory apes, when she spotted Spence Angel Dewayne in the produce aisle, fondling a pear.

She gagged on her words to the butcher. It was indeed Angel whom she saw. He was inordinately fond of monograms, and even from twenty feet she could see the SAD imprinted on the pocket of his shirt.

A couple of dazed late-night shoppers glanced his way as he moved toward the plums, parting the waters. He didn't seem to notice the stares but continued at his own pace, careful, wary, whistling a tune. He was singular, of course, a dark-skinned person among pale caucasoids.

He looked up just as she was approaching, and turned swiftly, trying to hide behind the tiers of bunched bananas, but it was too late. He held out some bananas as if to propitiate her.

"Angel. Angel. It's all right. I understand."

He pretended to smile. She had forgotten his eyes, a bewitching honey color. Even though she had been coming here expressly to run into him, she was shocked, somehow, to find him actually walking through the aisles in his summer suit, examining bananas and carrying in his cart cream of tartar and white figs.

"You really don't need to run away from me like that, Angel," she said.

"I wish you wouldn't call me that."

"I'm sorry," she said, moving closer as he, tossing his head significantly, indicated the nearby aisle: "Isis is here."

"Isis?"

"She's getting some stuff for baking cookies." He took this moment to feign being casual, show her the macadamia nuts in his cart. "Some off-the-wall recipe she came up with. So naturally we have to come to Northerly's at ten o'clock."

"You're still with Isis?"

His sufferings with his estranged wife and his pangs about their impending, or maybe not so impending, divorce, had been the substance of what he wrote about in the extension poetry class she had taught by default the previous winter, replacing a fired colleague at the junior college.

Glenna had been so curious about Isis for so long that she had to take a look. She searched the adjacent aisle till she spotted her near the Bisquick, a small woman with tea-gold skin and huge long eyes. She admired Angel's offbeat taste in selecting such an eccentric-looking yet luminous creature.

Glenna said, in an undertone, "She's gorgeous. She looks like Vanity—or Lena Horne."

Angel scowled. "Lena Horne," he said sourly. "Never did like her much. Too white."

Glenna ignored this comment. She tried to keep her voice down. "That address you gave me last winter," she said. "That was a phony fake address. That wasn't your house at all."

"Maybe you'd have found it better if I'd planted a row of watermelons in front of it."

Her face felt as if it had been slapped. Surely she should have passed initiation by now. "Very funny," she said, then hurried on. "Whenever I called your office they said they'd leave you a message. I must have called twenty times."

"I never got any messages," he said, looking at his cart. For a moment she almost believed him. She still hoped that much.

"We really need to talk," she said, but just then Isis turned the corner and came toward them, smiling inquiringly.

Angel pulled on his ear. It was obvious that he didn't want to introduce them but Glenna was frozen where she stood, gulping in what she saw. Isis's face had a wackiness to it, a crazy delicacy, with its curving, important-looking nose and small chin. Glenna smiled at her.

"Isis, meet Glenna Swenson," Angel said at last. "The person who taught the poetry class last year that I told you about."

All at once the warmth ebbed from Isis's face. She settled into herself, her gaze growing sidelong, indistinct. "So this is the midlife crisis groupie." She laughed behind her hand. "Barbie on steroids, isn't that what you said, honey?"

For a moment after Angel grabbed Isis's hand and led her down an aisle, Glenna looked after them, stupefied and furious. Something had told her not to approach him. After all this time of searching in vain, finding him had somehow boded ill. And then, after what seemed like a long while, she, the queen of late-night extension classes, unpinned herself from where she stood stuck in the grocery aisle, and walked dazedly away.

The rows of frozen dead things no longer caught her attention. She swept past. She had always known that she was bigger, brighter, more beautiful than most people, with her dark brown eyes and golden hair, and if that made her a target, well, at six feet, with strong arms, and long legs, she could take it. Still, it had been a disaster for her to veer from teaching "Grammar Refresher," her usual course, and it had been disastrous in a shocking and unexpected way.

She went to the place near the cookie aisle where you could drink complimentary coffee while sitting in a plastic chair. She did not want to go in humiliating aloneness to her car until she was absolutely sure Angel and Isis were gone.

Glenna had always disdained the easy marks, the people who took the easy way. All her life, simply because she was white and blonde, and had an irresistibly faithful and vulnerable look, or so she fancied—like a particularly nice collie—the world had come to call. It grated her. Such interest was not personal, it was toward a familiar image that was duplicated every time anyone picked up a magazine, turned on the television, or looked at a billboard. How was she supposed to get any satisfaction out of this kind of adulation?

Still, in the crunch with Angel, it had been this edge she'd used, and she'd pitched with everything she had.

As she waited in line beneath a sign that said "Ten Items or Less," which she enjoyed ridiculing in grammar class, she saw that Angel was coming back into the store, heading toward her.

"I'm sorry," he said. He led her out of line. She saw only the glossy threads of his impeccable suit. "I told you she was crazy. I never know what she'll say."

"Did you really mock me like that?"

"Of course not," he said indignantly, blinking hard.

She let it pass. "So are you back together?"

He nodded. "Everything's still the same."

"Still not divorced?"

"Nope."

He looked down at the linoleum, perhaps oppressed, as she was, by the pounding glare of the fluorescent panels. She could smell smoke on his clothes. So he hadn't quit yet. After the evenings she'd spent with him last winter, her clothes had also reeked of smoke. She could still see him lighting up, shaking his head as he sat on her couch, saying, "Women make you smoke. My granddaddy told me that."

"I tried to call you. You were never home," he said now. When she did not respond to this ridiculous assertion, he said, "How about tomorrow night. Are you free?" He actually seemed contrite. "I'll be up at the lake. Feel like taking a drive?" She shrugged. "This time I'll make you a map."

He pulled out a small pad and started to draw. She watched his deft hands. "You're not going to be on call?" she asked. He shook his head. "Your pager won't go off?"

"Not when I'm that far away. Six o'clock. It's a nice drive," he said. He ripped off the sheet and offered it to her. "I'd better get going."

A few minutes later, Glenna was out in the parking lot, leading a bedraggled bag boy. The day had been miserably humid, and the soles of her shoes stuck to the hot tar; a thick aroma came up to her in sweet, suffocating waves.

Some experiences blazed through you, leaving a charred core at your center and changing you forever. How could you let them go? She put her head on the dashboard, thinking about it.

HER deceased husband had been an entomologist, a collector of insects who also hunted big game. Her marriage to that much-older man had not been a happy one, and she disliked thinking that her identification with animals, living and dead, was in reaction to him, but as she walked into her home that summer night, and thought of Angel's visit six months before, she breathed in the mustiness and remembered Angel's comment: "You live in a mausoleum."

It was going to be a long night.

She thought of grilling her little steak outside on the hibachi, but came in when she felt the close, urgent press of the mosquitoes. Half an hour later, sitting in the living room, she was washing down the last bite of meat with vodka. The taste of the animal's fear was in its flesh, a residue of chemicals released in the beast's awful panic at its moment of death. She knew it was true, no matter how people scoffed when she told them. She put her greasy plate next to the deer-leg lamp. Four polished hooves rested on the end table, descending from thin, graceful legs cut off right above the delicate little knee bones.

She had always thought she would throw this out, along with the other trophies, at her first opportunity, but somehow she hadn't. Though her husband had been gone these long months, something still stayed her hand.

"What in the hell is that?" Angel had said last winter, visiting her for the first and only time.

"My husband's work. His hobby was taxidermy."

He had chuckled. "Ah. The origin of cosmic roadkill."

She always hated it when he called her poems that, yet knew, even then, that she had taken a risk, writing poetry with her students. She sat back in her chair. Of course she could remember that night, that first night last September when it had all started. Rushing through the darkening streets to get to the class on time, she had run over a squirrel.

Half an hour later, standing in front of her students, she had been barely able to speak. She could hear each of her words echoing in the vast marble anteroom of the St. Paul post office where the college had located this community outreach class. From three sides of a huge square table, the students had sat looking at her.

"Are you Biagini?" an Asian woman, not a native speaker of English, had hammered out in explosive syllables.

"No. I'm Swenson."

With a little cry, the woman got up and ran out, shoes clattering on the polished floor. Glenna had tried to shrug it off, but no one else smiled.

Right in front of her, a woman's mouth had gaped in an endless, luxurious yawn; Glenna couldn't stop looking into that bottomless pink mouth, wide as a hippo's. The post office overlooked the Mississippi and she allowed herself a fitful glance out the window at its gun-metal surface, cold lava. She felt surrounded by a barren and hopeless silence. Had she really seen another squirrel come back down out of a tree and, chattering, try to rouse its dead friend?

The students stared dully. Now several were yawning. Could they tell that she knew nothing about poetry? Picking up her clipboard, she had started checking off names. Twenty-five people were on the list, and more than half were no-shows.

Angel had been late for class, she remembered that. The rest were already at work when he came in. "Free write," Biagini had tersely told her when she had called him for advice. He'd been terminated a few days earlier for getting a student pregnant and spoke resentfully, for he thought Glenna, as head of the composition department, should have intervened on his behalf. "They don't know anything anyway. You don't have to know anything yourself. Just have them free write."

"We'll save the introductions for later," Glenna had said. "Right now I want you to get in touch with your poetry-writing self." She read a sheet from Biagini's office files: "We don't start jogging or dancing without loosening up our muscles. By the same token, we limber up our mental muscles to start writing. So put down anything that comes into your head." If she'd known this was the junk Biagini was serving up, she would have fired him herself. "No worthless thoughts. No wrong ideas. If you say something and you know it isn't exactly right, then continue, try again, and say, no, it wasn't like that, it was more like this."

Some of the students had actually listened to her. They bent their heads to their desks and began writing furiously.

It must have been then that Angel came in, hands in his pockets, affecting nonchalance, whistling lightly under his breath, as if he didn't know they had already started. Glenna remembered feeling amazed and gratified to have the rarity of a distinguished, older black man walking into her class. How confident he had seemed with his measured strides. Small and wiry and compact in his dapper suit, bringing his own mood with him, breezy, completely incongruous, as if on his way to a social engagement.

"Name?" Glenna had asked and he had given her an arch look, his lower jaw outthrust. But it lasted only for a moment.

"Spencer Angel Dewayne. Dr. Dewayne." He sat down. She perched next to him and started speaking in a low voice, trying to explain the assignment. The absurdities of Biagini's instructions were even more mortifying as she recited them for this man.

He took a pair of glasses from his pocket and put them on. "Just write a stream-of-consciousness?" he asked, looking up.

"Why, yes."

His glasses fit into a raw dent in the bridge of his nose. The lenses had a rind of greasy fingerprints as if they had been smeared by a sticky-pawed child.

Pretending to be friendly, but isn't. Pretending to be scholarly with that dignified air, those rounded glasses perched on the edge of his nose, but he isn't.

She gave him a smile of fanatical encouragement, then walked back to where she had been sitting at the front of the class. He was trying to be casual but it was a lie. Resentment ran through the center of him like a wick.

No bad thoughts. No wrong ideas.

Most students were laboring doggedly over their notebooks. As her eye roamed the room, she noticed the monogram on the new arrival's briefcase: SAD. She remembered thinking that this was odd. And then she, herself, started writing. After an hour she had finished five sloppy pages. She had them still: "The clouds were shiny and twisted all along the horizon as dark fell/Membranous, a slick pink/musculature gleaming live beneath skin."

She winced now, but at the time she hadn't. She had been proud. She sometimes viewed the clouds through her husband's telescope, and they did look like living tissue. Her pen idle, she had turned to ponder her students, one by one: the snoring woman in a shiny jumpsuit, the handsome blond with a reddish mustache, the doctor, ever more dour.

"Why don't we go through what we've done and see if there's a poem in there," she had said. "Volunteers?" The students sat staring. "Come on, folks, this class is for you. You won't learn anything if you just clam up." No one, not even the self-assured doctor, had met her gaze.

Teachers were supposed to have the poise to endure silences, and Glenna usually could use them to her advantage. When students accused her in their evaluations of being dull, she wasn't crushed. They always said they'd learned. Tonight's snores, however, were obnoxiously obtrusive. They were duplicated maddeningly in this echoing room.

"I tried something myself," she said, clearing her throat loudly. "Here's one of the lines: 'When you came out of nowhere, squirrel, I veered but heard a bump.

Could I have saved you or myself after I heard the thump?'"

Her offering did not have the inspiring affect she had anticipated. In fact, the doctor seemed to be chuckling to himself, a soft guffawing.

"Mr. Angel," she said through clenched teeth. "If you have a comment . . . be specific."

"Dr. Dewayne," he said. "Go by Spence." And then he tried to catch his breath. The students began to murmur among themselves. Even the woman who had been sleeping sat up, rubbing her eyes, craning her neck to look at the doctor. "The same thing has happened to me," he said finally. "You feel terrible, don't you. You just want to turn around and go home."

Glenna had grasped her clipboard. "It came out of nowhere. I absolutely never saw it," she said. "I thought they were all up in their trees this late."

"They get slow, don't they, like the flies and bees in late summer. It's as if a sign has come to them." He slapped his notebook on the table, calling everyone to order. "Dust to dust. Who teacheth us more than the beasts of the earth, and maketh us wiser than the fowls of heaven?" His bass voice filled the room, its tones resonant as the strains of a church organ.

Then, gradually, miraculously, other students rushed in to help. A pasty-faced young woman with bright scarlet lips read a poem about her abortion. A middle-aged shoe store clerk read about her husband's ambush of her in the ladies' rest room at work. No longer yawning, the woman in the zip-up jumpsuit spoke about her date rape. Knud, a handsome blond car salesman, was having incest flashbacks.

Finally, she called for the break. Angel headed for the lobby, taking out a cigarette. The woman in the spandex jumpsuit followed close at his heels, and when Glenna passed them to use the rest room she heard her chattering to him, all agog.

GLENNA stretched her legs onto the footrest with its smooth blond hair, rams' horns portruding from all four sides. She poured herself something green from the crystal decanter near the deer-leg lamp, wondering why such self-disclosure had taken place in the class. Maybe people were relieved to have permission to talk in public about these intimate, personal matters. They were obviously desensitized to confession, sophisticated about the language of recovery from watching "Oprah," "Jenny," and "Donahue." In any event, the group quickly seemed to lose all embarrassment and self-consciousness.

As for Angel, he hadn't started in on the divorce and Isis right away. No, he wrote during that first class about the recent death of his mother in rural Alabama, some courtly prose about Lily Belle, a tiny lady, not one hundred pounds . . . and the day she died all who had known her brought silk scarves to the church to show the bright colors she had woven into their lives.

Why was it that she still remembered that? Perhaps because every day for the past six months she had been trying to recall all the details she had heard about Angel's life.

His devotion to his mother seemed to touch every heart. One by one students had told him how much they supported him. They dispensed with written autobiographies and chatted informally about themselves, that diverse group: a security guard and two unemployed single mothers, a food-service worker at the nearby hospital. Spence Angel Dewayne also worked at the hospital occasionally and had an office close by, which made the class convenient for him. Lately separated from his wife, he needed something to do in the evenings.

A postal worker suggested they tell their zip codes. The clerk said it would be fun if they knew each other's shoe sizes. Glenna and Angel had the biggest feet. Angel asked for blood types, which most people didn't know. Glenna invited everyone to bring snacks and drinks from now on. After that first night, the class never lost its bizarre mood.

It hadn't been till a later meeting that Angel wrote a poem about his estrangement from his wife, an inconsolable lament. Glenna had kept a copy. She lifted up the top cushion of the rams' horn ottoman and dug it out.

If you don't understand my love, I don't care.
Though some people may agonize over the definition, I don't.
You know it when you feel it.
You want to spend every waking minute with her, near her.
Nothing you give do you view as a sacrifice or too much.
Her moves are designed for you . . .
Everything is welcomed by you.
And now she is gone, lost forever to me.
I have nowhere to go.
The foxes have their holes, and the birds of the air have their nests,
But the son of man has nowhere to lay his head.

She remembered how his dirgeful voice had reverberated in the quiet of the post office. The longer she had listened, the lonelier she had beome. A woman with dead-white skin and vampire lips started crying.

Finally Glenna had said lamely, "You sound like some kind of Old Testament prophet."

When he looked at her his eyes had glowed like little red coals. "Well, I no longer believe in a redeemed world, if that's what you mean."

That was the third or fourth class. Despite his occasional confessions, Dr. Spence Angel Dewayne had remained unapproachable. She was often aware of his belligerent pug face, his furtive eyes darting as if he were judging her, judging them all. Sometimes he smiled good-naturedly, but she could hardly read the language of his changing countenance that was playful, brooding, forbidding, by turns.

It wasn't simply that he was more educated and articulate than the other students; it was that he seemed not to make much of it. His deep, thundering voice and polysyllabic, biblical locutions were his by birthright: the class soon knew his grandfather had been a Baptist minister. He easily could have dominated the young single mothers, the struggling salespeople, but he didn't. Most of the time he was respectfully reticent—at least Glenna had presumed he was respectful until just before Thanksgiving, when the two of them had met, quite by chance, in the post office lunchroom.

He had sat scowling through the whole class that night. When he caught her eye as he came down the cafeteria line and she saw him heading for her table, she recoiled. She had to put on an act with students, never let herself relax, but it was even more of a strain with someone as intimidating, as judging, as Dr. Dewayne.

Yes, the post office lunchroom. Glenna put her head back on the couch, dreaming in the darkest part of the summer night, drinking the strange green liqueur poured into the decanter by her husband, god knows when, letting her big toe scratch at a ram's horn. She sat in the sunken living room of her spacious house and tried to think back to that evening so many months before when she had lingered late, after class, chatting with one of her students—not an unusual thing to do, not at all.

"Your heart beats a hundred thousand times a day," Angel had told her, but when? "And if you cut out the heart of an animal, the pieces of its heart keep on beating."

He had sat down with her that night, and gradually, so gradually, had yielded up his charms. He had asked about her at first, quickly setting up a camaraderie, professionals at their ease. She had told him about her long drive, out to Lake Minnetonka, where she lived alone, a widow, yes, her husband having died the previous year. He had died suddenly in a hunting accident. She was still stunned by it. Her husband had been older than she, and once had been her teacher—it was a familiar story, and probably one he, too, had heard before. As she spoke, there was one word she thought but did not say: *lonely.* She would be lonely over the holiday. Even Siri, her only true friend, would be out of town. Well, as for Dr. Dewayne, he had to work on Thanksgiving Day—it was no big deal to him, but he had a date first thing in the morning to take his family to the airport. He and his wife both came from the same little Alabama town; they'd come here to seek their fortunes twenty years before. Yes, it had been strange. They were still called "Negroes" then, as Glenna might recall.

She noticed for the first time the tawny gold of his eyes, in such contrast to his dark skin.

Night-shift postal workers straggled in to look at flat bowls of pudding and yogurt, stale sandwiches. The two of them lingered over the terrible coffee. She gnawed on a cookie, getting ready to go. But he wasn't done talking yet. He examined the flatware, sighed, and all at once it struck her that his deep voice was too big for this lunchroom, for the starved existence he was leading.

He was fifty, had she known that? At thirty-five she felt far away from fifty, yet he wasn't old. The only real signs of age were the little daisies of white in his hair. Yes, he'd had a tour in Vietnam as a twenty-six-year-old doctor unable to get out of the draft, serving in a platoon of rednecks, as he said. "To tell you the truth, I was in more danger from my own battalion than from the enemy."

"Unbelievable." She could barely swallow her bites of stale cookie.

"I was finished with my residency. All my friends were out in the world, right, starting to make money, and old Spence got drafted." He lit a cigarette, jerking his head away from her as he expelled the smoke. "So where do they send me? To an all-white battalion. Southerners, mostly." He laughed.

"Even before I got there I heard about the bitching. A lot of the communications guys were black, you know, and they told me about all the shit that was flying, word for word. 'Hey, they don't want you over there, man. They're doing everything they can think of to get your orders changed.'

"Once I was there I slept with a gun beside me every night—not for protection from the enemy but from the other soldiers."

"God, it's horrible that you had to undergo that," Glenna stammered.

He fixed her with his golden eyes. "You think it's only there? Why just today a woman refused to let me perform surgery on her—in a public hospital. 'Give me a real American doctor'—that's what she said."

That's when it had happened. It was on that night that she had come down with him, breathed him in and caught him. Surely he must have known. Surely she wasn't the first to fall. He must have been aware of how susceptible some might be, the awe in which they might hold him.

He'd thrown his stories out to her as ground bait. At his leisure, he would decide what he wanted with her. Yes, she had been taken over. For that long Thanksgiving weekend she had sat correcting papers in front of the large-screen TV and thought of him and little else.

They'd had coffee a couple of times afterward. Once he had told her of his difficulties when he and his wife first came to Minneapolis. He'd had to ask one of the orderlies in his own hospital where he could get a haircut. "You know, my hair can't get any longer than this," he said, turning around to show her, explaining himself to her like a congenial anthropological subject.

Then there had been the time when he'd read aloud one of his poems and she complimented him after class on the way he spoke. He had leaped on her words. "Not like a nigger, hah?" he had said, his words lashing.

Quickly he had apologized, in his own way. "I've told you about my mother's father, Reverend Angel. Well, my daddy was a principal in an all-black high school. He spoke the most beautiful Oxonian English. I'm sure, between him and my granddad, I picked up a few things." He had restored comfort again and was flawlessly agreeable. "But it wasn't just my dad and my granddad. My history teachers, my English teachers? Outstanding. Those all-black segregated high schools in the South were great places to learn. The brilliant black scholars and teachers who couldn't rise any higher in that society ended up in the public schools. Kids like me got a windfall."

He was nothing if not an entertainer.

She tried to recall more of the experience of teaching poetry writing: she remembered most the frozen ice fields on her drive into town, the swath of daylight that shrank and grew briefer and briefer with every class. It was one of the classes close to the end when, after turning in nothing all quarter, the woman with the vampire-white face and crimson lips submitted "Stopping by Woods on a Snowy Evening" as original work. She had handed the poem over with a fixed, glazed expression, then turned and disappeared, as if in a trance. It had been a classic moment for Glenna. Righteousness brought a fierce tingling to every nerve ending in her body, a sensation which, as a grammar teacher, she experienced often. She had been prepared at the next class, waiting to pounce. But the woman never returned.

Other than that, the class was uneventful and surprisingly pleasant. During the free writing that they did for at least an hour every time they met, Glenna continued to transcribe the profoundly symbolic small murders she saw every day on the roads. By semester's end she had pages of notes that had led to a series of poems on scraps of paper that she leafed through now, by the light of the deer-leg lamp: "Porcupine in the Grass," "Blackbird on the Aerial," "Hedgehog on the Shoulder," and "Bug on the Windshield: He Won't Have the Guts to Do That Again," suggested by Angel as comic relief. The problem of species massacre was not confined just to trophy hunters with blood lust. Delved into, the subject matter became even more disturbing: deer, foxes, turtles, frogs, raccoons, muskrat, skunks, opossum were slaughtered at roadside by the revolting encroachment of humans into their habitat, humans crowding everything else off the planet.

The poems weren't holding up very well to the reading she was giving them tonight, as she sat listening to untold hordes of crickets and frogs singing in the background, but during the period that the class was going on, she had felt genuinely inspired.

GLENNA's friend Siri from the biology department had been unimpressed by her tale of what was going on with Dr. Dewayne. She thought human females were self-sufficient, needing only sperm donors, and only occasionally finding men who were worth all the trouble, which this indecisive man certainly wasn't. "I can't believe you're really this hung up."

They were eating rain forest crunch popcorn and watching TV. A Burger King ad came on and Glenna muted the set.

"Whenever I see him . . . I'm just filled with joy," Glenna said. "I haven't felt like this since the early days with Magnus."

Siri frowned and they sat in uneasy silence. The show they were watching returned, a special on the devastation of the Northwest salmon runs.

"You ought to move out of here," Siri said. "All Magnus's stuff is driving you crazy." As the salmon swam upstream, they encountered a dam. They kept trying to leap up over it, their whole shiny bodies involved in the convulsive effort, unable to express anything else. She felt it herself, pushing forward, mindlessly hopeful, beating her tail.

"Lighten up," Siri said. "Can you spell H-O-R-N-Y? But I didn't know you were *this* horny."

For a long time Glenna lay in the huge bed she had shared for ten years with her husband and for one night with Angel, but sleep would not come. Between her legs, she rubbed a deft elliptical design, again and again, but nothing seemed to work. If she didn't get some rest, she would look bedraggled for her meeting with him in fifteen hours. She would not be able to trust herself and might say weird and regrettable things. Despite the vodka and liqueur she had drunk earlier, she was still too excited to sleep. She drew a hot bath for herself and put in green mineral salts and looked at the tops of her knees.

They hadn't even bothered to have a final class meeting. Instead they had gone to the warehouse district of

Minneapolis, where Angel knew a restaurant with a sumptuous, cheap buffet. By this time, he was the class leader. Everyone trusted him. If he recommended the food, they were all in for a treat. But the building Glenna drove up to on one of the darkest evenings in December was skinny, faltering, and old. Inside she saw Angel at the far end of a long hall, dapper in one of his exquisitely tailored suits, waving.

"Am I in the right place?" she asked.

He smiled, full of fun. He liked a party. "You made a wrong turn." Turning her around, he brushed her wrist for a moment, and she felt her skin quiver. She followed him, her feet shuffling on the dusty floor, cheeks flushed from the cold seeping into this long hallway. "Listen to me. You'll be glad you came."

The warmth of the setting, the golden lamps, prevailed easily over the darkness and icy chill. At first she was bewildered by the music, the lively holiday chatter, the people flying about on all sides; only gradually did the sights around her assume an order. A lone guitarist held the stage, a bearded man with a bent head, intent on the voluptuous strains of his music: "I Wonder as I Wander." He played mournfully, passionately, segueing into a rendition of "Stardust" that somehow wasn't incompatible. He hummed and sang as he strummed, gradually starting in on a new melody, one she had never heard before. Glenna sat trembling in her seat. This song whispered mysteriously to her, waylaid and enticed her. Or perhaps she was stirred because Angel had seated himself at her side.

As she tried to talk to her students, she saw that their faces had taken on a milky shine; they looked translucent and enigmatic. These people, whom she had seen once a week for three months, whose poetry she had read, whose stories she knew, now felt like her friends. Rochelle, wearing, as always, her zip-up jumpsuit, hugged her as they walked together to the buffet. Glenna felt lucky she had been able to know Rochelle and the rest of them.

In line, she turned away from the delectable smells of the meat and piled her plate high with chips and guacamole dip, macaroni and fettucine, salad. A chocolate cake at the end of the buffet looked particularly good, with thick luscious swirls of ivory frosting, chocolate and caramel festoons.

She was just helping herself when all at once she felt a little tap. Rochelle had gone. Angel had nudged her and all along her side she felt flickers of excitement. "My goodness, you're a greedy girl."

She looked guiltily at her plate, then back at his face. "Don't worry," he said, "I like greedy girls. They're the only kind I like."

He was smiling amiably. "Why don't you try some of the tenderloin tips? They do awfully well with steak."

It was bad enough that from time to time she ate meat. It was even worse when someone saw her doing it.

"I try to keep away from that stuff—you know, meat."

He nodded. "Of course. I should have known. Greenpeace."

"Let me ask you something—as a doctor," she said.

"Sure," he said.

"I've heard that a cow's or a pig's adrenal glands give off toxic chemicals when they're being killed . . . when they try to flee and they can't," she said. "Doesn't that make sense? Scientifically, I mean."

He nodded his head agreeably. "I'll tell you something. If you were in the wild, the other animals would sense your fear. Your empathy would make you vulnerable. You wouldn't last that long. Yep." He smiled congenially.

He picked up a cracker, slathered it with dip. Then he bit it in two and held the second half out to her, as if proffering crumbs to a sparrow.

Back at the table, Glenna found she couldn't hold on to her fork. She was messy and insatiable. The table in front of her was splattered with crumbs and pieces of avocado. Occasionally a student would ask her a question, still expecting her to be the teacher, but with Angel at her side she had grown demure.

When Avis, the shoe store clerk, asked Angel if he were still separated from his wife, he shrugged sadly and nodded. Glenna watched. She wiped her sticky face with her sticky fingers, tacky with guacamole.

Delicate, sweating glasses were handed around: more champagne. He had ordered it for everyone. She drank till she could feel her eyes swimming, everything melting and shining, but he was drinking, too, drinking all the while. She hummed softly to the music, which was affecting her so secretly, so viscerally.

They sat talking long after the others had left. His wife had gone to Alabama with the boys. He had to stay here to work, all Christmas season. Oh, of course there were places he could go, he had several invitations, but—well, she knew how it was. She nodded her head, his friend, his confidant.

All those things just came over Glenna—his beseeching eyes, his dejected, forlorn expression, his powerful, stooping shoulders. She noted well his brown skin against his shirt, the color of white narcissus. She prayed that she could be as seductive as the music and that Angel, at her side, would never be able to turn away.

"Tell me how you decided to practice medicine. Did you always want to be a doctor?" she said at last.

"I wanted to help humanity—if you can believe that." She watched the strong square hands clutch the glass. "Yeah, everybody was behind me. My father died when I was young, I told you that, and I became the man of the house. My sisters, my mother, they helped put me through medical school." He took a drink. "Everybody pitched in. I couldn't let them down."

He was still the honorable, industrious son he had probably always been. "So everyone counted on you."

"I welcomed the burden. I was going to help people," he went on. His look grew impassioned. "You remember when Martin Luther King died?"

She blinked. "Yes, somewhat."

"Well, after that, everything changed for me. I just stopped being as hopeful. Before that happened, I always wanted to do something for humanity, regardless of race—something more than patch up a body, fix a bone. And then they killed him. All these years later, and they're still trying to tear him down. These kids out there today, do you think they have hope? It died with Martin."

"I thought a lot of people didn't like Dr. King," she said, but her voice trailed off lamely. The racist jokes she had heard from her husband and his friends over many years, Glenna couldn't begin to enumerate. Martin Luther King had been a favorite target. She was filled with shame. It had seemed so abstract. Certainly she had railed at Magnus, insulted him, for the remarks had cut at something in her, but he had turned it into a game, gibing her as Angel gibed now about Greenpeace.

"Some people thought he should have changed his stance when he went up North, been more confrontational, but I believed in the idealistic course. Hah."

Smoking, drinking, sorrow.

"The kind of medicine I'm practicing isn't what I went to school for," Angel said. "Sometimes it's all I can do to get out of the house and go to work. Today we had an old guy whose insurance wouldn't pay for his treatment. He really needed it. We all knew it, but we took the guy off, then wrote up a report on how he benefited." He sipped more champagne. "This isn't what I took up medicine for."

All at once the guitarist left the stage, and the room seemed robbed of its friendly atmosphere. They barely spoke as they finished their drinks. No longer was she irresistible. He asked for the bill, waved aside her protests. Finally, he got up abruptly and she followed him out into the parking lot. Lightly falling snow had dusted the cars, leaving the roads glazed.

He turned to leave. Leaning on his arm to keep her balance, she said, "You'll keep in touch."

"Keep in touch? Sure. If you want to see my name you can always look for it on the obituary page."

She reached out to hold him back, but he had already started away. "Spence . . . Angel," she said, and before she knew what had happened she had lost her footing on the ice. She heard him rushing back.

"Well," he said. It was awfully cold out. Her fingers were already beginning to freeze.

"Something seems to be wrong." With his help, she staggered to her feet.

"I guess I'd better see you home and check out that ankle," he said with measured words.

She turned away to hide her delight. "OK."

As she drove, the guitarist's melody found her again, twined itself into the rhythms of her body. So the music had not scornfully cast her off. She smiled to see Angel in her rearview, fast upon her, following her along the freeway to the moonswept landscapes that surrounded her home.

In the circular driveway, he pulled up behind her, looking up at the house, showing no sign of being impressed by the imposing colonial facade. As they walked in, however, he came to a frightened stop. Throngs of insects were swarming the walls in choreographed schools, crawling out from behind the hall mirror, swirling around the ceiling. Walking closer, you could see that the insects were old and shabby, shellacked wings decomposing, with sightless, pickled, petrified eyes.

"You actually live here?"

"You like scientific classification, don't you? You'll enjoy this." Next to free-flying insects were cases of specimens—butterflies, moths, and beetles, with little white cards under them, identifying names and dates—hundreds of tiny eyes, with frozen, fixed gazes. Each insect was specially placed with thoughtfulness and wit. They were arrayed like knickknacks. "These were Magnus's pets," she said. "I know I should get rid of them, but every time I try I start thinking about what a monumental effort it was to do all this, to assemble it. . . ."

He had stopped and laughed when he came to the ledge over the fireplace. Three stuffed frogs were dressed in doublets and waistcoats, playing musical instruments in a glade, the whole scene grotesquely perfect down to the last detail, the frogs' long flipper feet twisted like stiffened seaweed.

The frogs seemed to smile. What else could those huge mouths do?

"Magnus made that himself at a workshop," she said. They'd passed the heads of the cape buffalo and grizzly bear, the footrests covered with smooth blond fur, the box propped up on real snakes' bodies and heads.

As she built a fire, he had inspected the bin of antlers next to the couch, then picked up an animal skin that lay on a chair. She sat there now with the same soft pelt to her cheek. It was all hard on one side, like cardboard, but soft on the other. How insubstantial the pelt felt, how silky and personal the fur, how fragile the anchorage. She could pick it off with her fingers.

He had made, without her, a quick tour of all the rooms that lined the main hall.

"Just getting an idea of the place," he had called out to

her. He's paranoid, she thought. He thinks I'm setting up some kind of a trap.

"Did you see the birds in the back bedroom?"

"What have you got in there? An aviary?"

She tried to hold it back. How amused he would be if she explained her role as rescue person for the Minneapolis Companion Bird Society.

"Fifteen parakeets." She peered up at him in the dim glow of the logs.

"Jeez, Glenna, you're a nut. A nice nut, but still." It was obvious that he was nervous. She couldn't even get him to sit down. What could she do to put him at his ease? She brought him his drink, scotch and water, without his having to ask. She knelt at the grate of the fireplace, poking at logs, hoping he would help her, a vain hope. He walked around with his drink, shaking his head as he inspected Magnus's petrified wasps and termites.

"Want to look through the telescope?" She walked across the sunken living room and opened the drapes to the scene of moonlight on the lake. Perhaps that would lure him closer. She took the lens cap off of her husband's telescope and spent a few moments trying to focus it.

"We've got a lake place, too, in Wisconsin. Minong," he said. "Or, I should say, I do. Isis and the boys never go there."

He joined her at the window, picked up the edge of one of the silky mint green drapes. "My house in Arden Hills, where Isis is living . . . now that's big, like this. Did I tell you that when I first moved out there the police stopped me as I was trying to get into my own house?" He chuckled. "And I can't tell you how many times, when Isis answered the door, she'd be asked, 'Is the lady of the house in?'"

As Glenna had moved closer to him, she had felt a sweet shudder go down her back. The melody hadn't left her. She hummed it silently to herself as they looked together at the view of Lake Minnetonka, its banks sluiced with moonlight.

"The ankle's hurting," she said with a grimace. "I guess I'd better sit down." She lured him to the couch by offering him another glass of scotch, patting the place next to her. Then she had poured a drink for herself from the crystal decanter, the green she sipped now, the ancient draught her husband had drunk for years but that she would never be able to replace. She had no idea what it was.

He had put his hand to her ankle and she had put her hand on top of his. Though he was trying to appear indifferent, his skin was scalding to the touch, like a lightbulb that has been burning for a long, long time.

The cape buffalo head loomed over them. More than once she saw him glancing up.

"My husband had polio when he was a kid," she said. "He walked with a limp." She leaned over and threw open the lid of the rams' horn footrest. Staying close to him, she slid down to her knees, rummaging through the hollow cache beneath the cover. She pulled out a picture, which Angel looked at cursorily. It didn't do Magnus justice, of course. How could the heft and size of the man be conveyed in a picture, the northern lights in those insane violet-tinged eyes. "He just didn't want to be a victim."

"But it's not all one way, is it?" Angel said tersely. "Aren't the eater and the eaten in collusion? The eyes of predator and prey always meet at the fatal moment."

Across the footrest, she looked into his face. She saw beads of sweat appearing on his forehead, emerging from his widow's peak. She couldn't break his resistance. Rising to touch those drops, she leaned toward him, still on her knees. He took her face between his hands as if to stop her, running his tongue over the line of her lips and then, with the greatest restraint, he kissed her. His fingers rested gently on her spine.

"This position isn't good for your back."

Next to him on the couch, she could still feel all around them the hush, the tension of their silence. She pressed herself into him until his lips grew softer and more pliable, his kiss tender, sending waves of sensation deep into Glenna. She moved his hands to her body, pulling up her blouse so he could kiss her breasts. He licked them and the sweat that bathed his forehead dripped onto her chest. She felt his hair, a fragrant, malleable mound. She smelled the starched fragrance of his white shirt, his body's clean musk.

"Wait a minute," he said. "Wait a minute." And he pushed her away.

"What's wrong?" she said.

"I shouldn't be doing this." Why, why, why? The skin was so tight along his cheekbones—as tight as the tendons in wings.

He sat up, reaching for his cigarettes, giving her a chummy, confidential look: "Women make you smoke. My granddaddy told me that."

As the smoke surrounded her, she sat there with her blouse open, waiting for him to notice the moonlight on her lovely breasts, and looked into his eyes. "Will you come with me?" She was putting herself at his mercy. He had to be kind.

His hand was trembling as she led him down the hall. She thought of the fire she had made, of wood that doesn't seem to be burning until you prod it with a poker and it collapses in a shower of sparks. There had been smoldering inside him all the time—he was hot and thick with it.

In the bedroom, she took off her clothes, huddled beneath the covers. As he undressed, she saw with a shock his smooth naked body, and how it came to get her . . . how that nakedness knew how to use her.

As she watched him come to her she had a vision of that first night with her husband in this very bed. How enamored she had been of his impassioned voice, his crest of white blond hair, his pearly, ice-filled arctic eyes. She had seen him before wearing only suits and crisp shirts. But seeing him naked, she had known, as she knew now with Angel, how much it was a lie, everything that had come before.

Angel peeled the sheets down off of her body and she shivered. The music was suddenly so loud in her head that it seemed to clang, and take her over; it was all she could hear. Gently he had moved down between her legs. She felt she had always known it, how vulnerable and tender he was. But in love his body was hard and slow and exquisitely sensitive. In the dark he had been smooth and sleek, a free thing and wild. He had covered her with his cloak.

And as with her husband she had felt afraid . . . of the willingness that had been aroused in her, the blind giving, that made her want to be dominated and led, made her want to please, above all else, so that she would be offered such pleasures again.

When she woke in the morning, he had gone. Outside, the little winter birds were ecstatic, waiting on the branches for her to fill the feeders, trilling away to each other as they swooped from tree to tree. Her body had felt heavy with Angel, inhabited by him in the morning's pristine quiet.

But that was to be her only peace for a long time. It was two weeks before he had called her again. Trying to get in touch with him, she had gone through an awful moratorium, waiting for him to answer the increasingly imploring messages she left at his office, the only number where she got an answer.

Never had she felt it before, such an absolute and terrible loneliness. She had not felt it when her husband was alive, even though they were for many years estranged. She had not felt it during this year that her husband had been dead, because the mystery of his departure had made him more present to her than ever, and given her feelings for him gravity and depth. She rambled about in confusion, spending hours at the college, in search of her lost assurance and competence, living for the moment when she would go home and see the red light blinking on her answering machine. But the only one who called was her friend, Siri, whom she met over coffee in the afternoon, for she would not risk spending an evening out on the off chance that he might call.

"You've got to get out of that awful place," Siri said. "That's half the problem."

"But I like it. It's my house now."

Siri shook her head. "The only good thing Magnus ever did was get himself shot in the head, mistaken for a deer." It was Siri's favorite joke. "Magnus was a bastard, too," she went on. "You have to stop looking for the alpha male."

Through endless days Glenna waited, paralyzed, humiliated.

Then one noon between Christmas and New Year's, as she walked the house in her unlifting gloom, the phone had rung.

"Tonight?" she had asked.

"Well, if it's inconvenient, we can—"

"Oh, no," she had halted him, breathlessly. "It's fine, I can do it."

For the long silence he gave no explanation, except to say, incongruously, "You know, I always like to think of myself as a good person."

Later that night, as she walked into the lobby of a Japanese restaurant in Minneapolis, she was not angry when she saw him. She drank in his presence greedily, in long draughts.

Had she deliberately tried to dim him in her imagination? Indeed she was unprepared for how handsome he was in all the intensity of his bearing, a dark candle burning from the inside.

As they walked in and sat down opposite each other on the floor, she had twitched in her silver mini-dress; he was his usual composed self.

In her exuberance, in her joy, Glenna had stretched her legs in all their glossy sheen across the mat and rubbed her feet against his gold-toe socks. A single instrument played in the background, shivery, important-sounding notes. They were overlooking the Mississippi, sitting side by side with other patrons on reed mats before low tables, so her teasing jabs were probably evident to the couples on either side, but Glenna didn't care. She had actually thought that he was dropping her! So grateful was she to be with him now that her heart, her feet, did a little dance. She kept pummeling him and soon her toes tapped against his thigh to the rhythm of her fluttering heart, thank you, thank you, thank you.

Always that would be a bit of bliss for her, always she would remember—how proud she was to be there with him.

They murmured things to each other—like lovers. She was not afraid to nudge at his feet with hers, and not afraid to gloat—for he had called her back, finally—she was not ridiculous.

"Tell me what's good," she whispered. She felt the strains of music like the gentle stroking of a sympathetic hand.

As frying steak sizzled before them, she decided not to make an issue of the curling meat slices. She would accept being a bloodthirsty carnivore if she could be one with him.

"Spring is on the way," he said congenially.

Was this small talk? She glanced, mystified, at the ghostly brine of the half-frozen river, flowing sluggishly just outside the restaurant window.

"No, honestly, it won't be long now. I got proof of it today. My Burpee's seed catalogue arrived. I think I'm going to plant a rose garden this year up at the lake."

The waitress brought chopsticks, small bowls of soup. "I didn't know you were a gardener."

He brought his hands down forcefully on both sides of his luhala mat. "I'll have to order the rose bushes, of course." He continued his exposition as the waitress stirred the meat. He told her about his favorite roses, and how he intended to plant them down to where his retaining wall abutted the lake. He would create paths full of roses, winding trellises of roses. He wanted the Abraham Lincoln rose, big, dark, and red. He wanted a Pascal, the purest white.

They were served and left alone, but he continued this discussion in his familiar mode, a raconteur. He was just describing the delicate lavender gray of the Sterling Silver when an unfamiliar voice boomed and a man's hand appeared. "Dr. Dewayne!" She had looked up, face all sunshine. The intruder had swooped down low, putting his curious mug right between them.

"That's a nice plate of sukiyaki you've got there," he had said.

Angel smiled slyly back. "Yeah, and I'm going to eat the whole thing, too," he said. They laughed.

Glenna had bent her head as they conversed. When they were alone again, Angel told her that the man had been a colleague, a plastic surgeon. Perhaps they had seemed comical to a plastic surgeon: he so short, dark, and compact; she so large and white-skinned, spread out in her retro mini, her whole body listing toward him.

Then he had looked down at his chopstick, turning it every which way, and said, "What do you want with me?"

"Want with you?" she repeated.

"You must have guys all over you."

She shrugged. There was no way to convey it to him. It was his whole life that filled her with desire.

"But why?" He was looking at her with a fixed, dazed smile. "What is it that you're after?"

"Isn't it obvious?" she said. "I just want to know everything about you."

"But isn't it obvious to you?" he said. "Don't you know that I'm emotionally bankrupt? You've read my stuff. Anybody who'd want to be involved with me—considering what I have to give now—would have to have something wrong with them."

She looked down at the spilled broth on the table, suddenly aware that she was chewing meat, that she had slices of dead animal flesh in her mouth and was trying to liquify stringy tissue with her grinding teeth. It was all she could do to gulp the mouthful down.

"Oh, come on," she said, blinking her eyes, straining to seem an ordinary person methodically eating a meal. "You can't generalize just from that. You've got to give yourself another chance." She had grown tone-deaf, to blare out at him such platitudes, but she could not stop, and her voice was shrill. "Don't say you're not willing to try again." The people beside them had turned to stare. Immediately sensitive to the prying looks, he grew silent.

All at once his pager beeped.

"What's that?" she asked, nonplussed.

"I've got to call the hospital."

And as she had sat there alone on her mat in the buzz and hum of sociability in the Japanese restaurant, in her pretty dress, with her long pretty legs stretched out, she thought of the lonely house, the vacuum of her own life—oh, please, don't make me go back to that. How presumptuous she had been to think she could earn his trust so fast.

She stared out at the ice-clogged waters of the Mississippi and hoped she would not be delivered once again to that mausoleum to sit in isolation and wait.

When he returned from using the phone and sat down opposite her, he was silent for a few moments.

"What's going on?" she asked.

He shook his head regretfully. "I've got to go to the hospital. It's an emergency." As the waitress knelt next to them in her obi, holding out a tray, he signed the bill. He had given her his credit card to expedite matters while making the phone call. It was all happening so fast that Glenna felt jerked along like a dog on a leash. When he stood and walked out, she followed.

"I'm sorry about this," he had said in the parking lot. She had moved over closer, to grasp at him, feel his skin. "Look, I don't want to hurt your feelings."

"When can we get together again?" she asked.

He cleared his throat, did not meet her eyes. "We'll make plans for you to come over." He had furrowed his brow. "I'll give you my St. Paul address. It'll be sometime in the next few days."

She sighed, relieved. "Yes." Now she was understanding his perspective. What he was putting her through was a brutal but ritualized hazing, as medical students are hazed when they first come to a hospital. She had to get beyond it to earn his trust.

Reluctantly, she turned away. Patience was an art she had never sufficiently studied. Now, for him, she would master it.

She had felt full of self-belief and confidence. She had been longing for just such an avalanche that would leave her no choice about what to do next. Feelings like this were always reciprocal. She knew it in her deepest core. No one ever had such emotions all by herself.

In the next few days, she had blown every rule she

knew. She had sent him orchids, a box of Godiva candy, a book of poetry by Langston Hughes.

They all came back. There was no such address. When he didn't return the calls she made to his office, she had parked near the hospital and stayed there for hours, hoping for a glimpse of him, but was never so bold as to get out of the car. Once, late at night, she even thought she saw him leaving with the vampire nurse who had dropped the class, but she didn't even work at that hospital, did she?

She finally accepted that there had been no emergency—he had activated the pager himself and was trying to ditch her. It seemed hard to believe. She had been a fool. If she hadn't gone to Northerly's that night she most likely would never have seen him again.

IN A few hours Glenna would go up to the lake cabin to see Angel. Now she lay in her tub. The fragrant papaya scum swirled, thick as cream. She sat there, rubbing the insides of her forearms. That was the way she wanted to be on the inside, silky smooth and warm and dry as a mole—no gushy, seepy make-your-own-sundae kind of girl.

She hadn't meant to fall in love with him. She hadn't even liked him. And yet it had happened. It was his escape that had taken her by surprise. She'd never dreamed he would ignore her so utterly. Only Magnus had been, in his own way, so cruel.

With him, too, she had undergone at the beginning an overwhelming and transforming experience. She had felt close to him, and singled out. Certainly it hadn't turned into what she had anticipated, but it had changed the course of both their lives.

Magnus had wooed her in the classroom and pursued her on summer vacations. He had separated her from her family by deeply insulting her parents. At the time she had been thrilled at his fervency, the way he stopped at nothing, but once they were married she couldn't hold his attention. "You were only interesting when I didn't have you, Glenna." What then was the good of being thought beautiful? Aggressive nurturer, he had called her. Not that she had sat waiting around for him. She'd had numerous flirtations, and even once a brief affair. She and Siri volunteered together at the bird society and at the zoo. But much of the time her empty marriage gave her she had spent building up her demesne at the junior college, creating a career, and planning her departure. Who would have dreamed that the death of the man she thought meant nothing to her would have stopped her in her tracks?

When she got out of her bath she walked into the living room to take a final sip of the green liquid. It seemed appropriate that she should finish it off. But as she lifted up the decanter to drink, it slid out of her hands and broke against the tiles in front of the fireplace, where its shards sparkled amidst what was left of the emerald liqueur.

The loud noise of the decanter shattering had caused panic in the roost. She spoke to Astrid soothingly, and to Hero, missing an eye, and Demeter, whose beak needed trimming again. She fed them and filled their water dishes, she vacuumed and wiped down the shower curtain spread over their floor. She tried to calm them down, the iridescent green and yellow ones, the tiny blue and white ones, in such wild disarray.

As she worked, she dreamed, and thought of Angel Dewayne at Northerly's. She was sure that she had detected in him a welcoming, a certain suppressed joy. It was indeed possible that all along he had simply been fighting his attraction to her.

Naturally Siri would misunderstand him. How could she know the trouble Angel had gone through in his life, the difficult experiences he had endured. He had to make sure that Glenna was strong enough to take it. And now she was being given another shot. Who knew how long he would want her to stay up there? As she was packing some clothes a few hours later, she threw in outfits for two days, three.

She was on the road by early afternoon, in heat so oppressive that reluctantly she turned on the air conditioning, letting the freon encapsulate her in crisp soundlessness. At the bottom of one hill she nearly hit a doe that looked back at her, its lovely fluted ears quivering. She slowed her pace and continued on with the windows open, her legs sticking to the seat.

She passed the little towns of Sprocket and Bracket, listened to the flat, yodeling voices coming from the radio. The winds were growing so strong that soon they were whistling scarily all around her, as if she were being blown up to Minong whether she wanted to go or not. The harsh sounds of the winds were frightening. It was midway into her trip that she pulled into a clearing near a roadside market and bought herself a cool drink, which turned out to be sticky syrup. She was in a strange place drinking a nauseating beverage in a car that shook with every gust of wind. She got out of her car and walked into an open field, finding a place to sit under a tree where she could compose herself.

And then she saw it.

It must have been a blue jay. The torn-off head was lying sedately beneath the bush. It was an old woman's head, eyes closed; she saw it wrapped in a shawl . . . so tight lipped, so alone.

She saw the curved bill, the mass of ecstatic feathers, the white down scattered, and the brilliant blue wing, lavishly lacquered and outspread, like a fan.

A fox must have gotten it, or a hawk.

And all at once it came over her that if she went through with this, continued on her way to see him, she would be dead. She knew what he thought of her. She knew what he had said to Isis about her. She was a joke to him, a mockery; she should turn right back.

Getting up on her knees, she knelt beside the bird. She couldn't just leave it there: a little grave for the remains. She dug it with a branch, pushed over the head and wing and most of the down, heaped it with dirt, covered it with a stone. But it wasn't gone, really, it was more vivid than ever—the bent crone head, tight-lipped, sealed.

The interior of her car was steaming in the humid heat. The bare backs of her legs seared as she got back in, fully expecting to go home, but at the road she couldn't bring herself to make the decisive turn. She tried to recall what she had known so distinctly moments before when she saw the blue bird, but she couldn't bring it back. Looking back at the field she saw only two dusty wheel ruts disappearing into a scrubby wood. Swerving her chin and frowning, she checked the map and continued heading north.

What was she doing, throwing herself at him in this way? She was still asking herself this question sometime later as she looked through her smeared windshield and saw the hicktown errors on the burnished wood signs in the driveways near Angel's place: "The Johnson's," "The Young's."

No sign was in front of his property, however, just a number. More than an hour early, she parked far down the cleared dirt driveway, and walked back toward a public access road to the lake she had just passed. Certainly he couldn't mind if she approached his house from his rose garden.

As she trudged through some acreage adjacent to his, she passed through woods that showed evidence of a recent fire. Many of the trees were like pompons, long scorched trunks where the fire had raged along the ground, jiggling tassels of leaves at the top ends. New growth was head high around the stumps and tree carcasses, green and buzzing. She saw deer tracks, a transparent dragonfly as big as her hand.

Hot and sticky, she made the turn onto the access road. She walked along the periphery of the sparsely populated little lake, which was just beginning to be rippled by the strong breeze. The stolid scene was deadening to her, so overcast, with sky and water uniformly gray. From somewhere out on the lake came the whine of an outboard motor. She felt a sharp bite and saw a glossy black deerfly stuck like a scarab onto her bare arm. She had to slap at it two or three times before it disappeared into the close air.

She looked up the hill, wondering if this were his cabin—it was hard to tell, though she thought she had gauged it right. And then she saw that indeed she was standing in a rose garden, but one she had waited too long to visit. She walked through a wasted, scrubby field, the flowers blown, the bushes trampled, some dry vines clinging to a trellis.

Kneeling down by a bush, examining its wilted grayish blossoms, she wondered if this were the Sterling Silver he had told her about. She inhaled as deeply as she could, trying to find its sweetness, unable to tell the difference between the scent she had sprayed on herself and the perfume of the dying flowers. Nearby she heard the crack of a twig. An animal, maybe a rabbit or a fox. She scanned a looming thicket, looked farther to the scorched forest, but no sign. The landscape absorbed sights as quickly as it threw them out, filtering all back into itself without a trace. She could just accept it, that this whole world was always a pace or two ahead of her. She could just stay here and not go up to the cabin, after all. But this resolution, too, failed her.

A few minutes later she started up the long hill toward

the cabin. She could see Angel's Buick parked in the front driveway. There was a chimney, a hummingbird feeder; a pigeon fluttered to a stop in a tree. It was all so silent that she hesitated for a long time before finally walking up and peering into a window. The first thing she saw was a rowing machine leaning in a corner and a set of weights, perfect for a vain peacock of a man.

Her eye wandered the room, almost missing him, he was so still, on a couch near the far windows, reading. Then all at once she froze. He looked up from his book, staring straight at her, as if he already had sensed her presence, his eyes piercing, fiercely red.

She waved stiffly, then moved away from the window, going quickly to the front of the cabin and down the path—a window peeper, a stalker. For a long time she stood waiting near a neat border of flowers. Then the screen door screeched as he pushed it open to let her in.

"I didn't expect you this early."

"I wasn't sure I could find the place. I'm afraid I overcorrected a bit." She kept muttering as he showed her inside. They walked through the kitchen, still littered with the remains of his lunch. He hadn't had a chance to clean it up yet.

"What can I get you?" His tone was curt. He didn't even look at her, opening the cabinets in the kitchen one by one, as if letting their noisiness express his irritation at her early arrival; catches plucked, then snapped into place. "I've got scotch, bourbon, vodka—or some Chablis and Coke."

"Whatever you're drinking."

He handed her scotch while he poured himself lemonade. They walked out into a cozy living room. He seated himself at the far end of a plaid couch.

She smoothed her tight shorts, then sat down next to him, feeling him edge over toward the armrest. She crossed and uncrossed her legs, doubtful and unsure, inspecting the room with its woven rugs, its wooden ducks on the polished tables, all the usual paraphernalia of a Wisconsin vacation cabin.

"It's so typical," she said.

"What did you expect? Tribal relics? Shrunken heads?"

Of course he would say that. Of course. She had been wrong to come here, as she had known all along. Hearing the wail of the wind, she looked out the window. Gusts were whipping the surface of the lake now, blowing stiff through the pine trees. "It was just small talk," she murmured.

"I'm sorry." He wiped beads of sweat from his widow's peak, from his crinkled forehead. "I just get so sick of being a cultural emissary. Everywhere I go in this goddam white wasteland I feel like it's my job to be educating people."

She looked at him sharply. "I can imagine what a drag it must be to . . ."

Abruptly, he changed the subject, refusing to meet her gaze, gesturing at the living room. "I guess the place looks OK. I'd like to do more, but I can't right now. I made a quarter of a million dollars last year, but between the IRS and my wife, I'm poor."

On a coffee table in front of the couch was a seashore display: a piece of driftwood, a net, and some cowrie shells. She picked up a starfish, sand-colored, with tiny pearls embroidered on its back.

"It's pretty," she said, examining the porous feet. "Tell me, do you know, are they dead when the divers bring them up?" Her words were lame, but somehow she couldn't hold them back.

He laughed in spite of himself. "You never quit, do you?" He pressed his hand to his forehead. "Well, to tell you the truth, as soon as they're dead, they start to decay. So they kill them as soon as they bring them up and put them immediately into preservative."

Depressing. She had known it would be. She poked at the little cilia, so brittle that they crumbled at her touch. "Can't they totally replicate themselves from just one arm?"

Angel laughed again. The cigarettes came out. She liked it when he smoked. He seemed authoritative. She wished he would drink, too, so she could stop worrying about entertaining him. "I'll tell you something about the starfish. It doesn't have a brain." He leaned over a bit and took the starfish from her. One of its star points was twisted, angled demurely to one side. "Sure they can regenerate from a single limb, but the applications for that adaptation are really limited. A complex creature would never have such a capacity for regeneration."

"No brain," she said.

"Quite a price to pay for being able to grow back your whole body, wouldn't you say?" he asked her, his eyebrows lifted. "Although sometimes a complex creature might wish it could start from scratch." He smiled with his lips together.

"Why won't you ever tell me what it is that you mean?" She sunk her fingers into the hot skin on his arm. He looked at her sidelong, grabbing her hand, smiling with grim satisfaction. "You just got caught by the Tar Baby," he said. "You poked at him and now you can't get away." Then he clasped her to him, and roughly they began to kiss each other. She had expected to have to seduce him, to wait for him again, but he was more than ready. For a long time they sat there stroking each other. Then he eased her to her feet.

He walked her a few steps down the hallway to a bedroom with two narrow beds, one against each wall. They lay down on the nearest, making love in a room so white it hurt Glenna's eyes. A breeze blew the white billowing curtains. She heard thunder, a fusillade of aftershocks.

"It's going to rain," she said, stroking his hot face where it lay against her breast. And then: "I'm so glad you invited me up." When he didn't reply, she moved her foot up and down his leg, sticky with heat. "My Isaiah," she said tenderly. "My Angel . . . my sweet Old Testament prophet."

He rolled away from her. Without his glasses, in the glaring light, his eyes looked raw and sore. "It's Spence. And please forget that prophet bit. I don't need you putting me into any dumb old preacher bag."

Glenna lay back, still too overcome by waves of ravishment and relief to remember the point she had come so far to make. Her belly was as white as if it had been hidden under a rock. She pulled the covers over herself in an agony of modesty.

For the first time she noticed that looking down at her, above the bed, was a large picture of Isis as a young woman, aloof and smiling serenely, her skin tinted café au lait, her sweater baby pink.

"What is this, the boys' room?" There must be a larger bedroom somewhere else. "Do the two of you sleep in another room?"

Quickly he hoisted himself over her, moving across her body to stand on the floor in the center of the room. "Didn't I tell you she's hardly ever up here?"

"But that must be why you brought me here, to the boys' room. Because you didn't want to be with me in her bed." She couldn't make herself shut up.

He began struggling into his clothes, clothes that resisted him, shorts bunching at the ankles, his white shirt buttoned up one notch off. "Did you really come up here to discuss my situation with my wife?"

Glenna studied Isis's composed face, her necklace of elegant pearls. No matter what she did, she remained ensconced in the place of honor, his trophy.

"So tell me, why did she kick you out? Was it other women?"

"Well, sure, what do you think. A big black stud like me, what else would I be up to?"

He left the room. She stared listlessly at the picture of Isis's impenetrable face. The rain rattled the windows with such force that she looked over and saw a branch of rhododendron blossoms squeaking on the rainy glass, their violet color pale and sad.

"So what do we do now?" he said. She had washed her face and was sitting under a loon picture in the living room. He came in from the kitchen with her drink and one for himself, real scotch now, which he drank facing her in a rattan chair. "Since it's raining we can't go fishing or sailing. We can't go for a walk."

She felt thrashed and roughed up. She threw out her hand at the cigarette smoke that blew her way. "I shouldn't have done that," she said.

"No one forced you," he said.

She wiped her eyes. "That's true."

"Well, I'm attracted to you," he said. "I won't deny it." She licked her lips, rough and swollen from Angel's kisses. "I've never understood what you want from me," he went on, his voice as maddeningly neat and composed as he now looked, sitting across from her, assured and far away. Safe from her.

"That *night,*" she said, wretchedly self-conscious, but hearing herself push doggedly on. "Something *happened* between the two of us." Would he deny her even this?

"Well." He spoke slowly. "Well, Glenna," he began again. "It's just that we're very different people."

What could that possibly mean? It was an absurdity. All people were different from one another, and what did that prove? She plopped her glass loudly down on the coffee table, miming him. "I was crazy about you," she said. "Couldn't you accept my affection? Are you really so angry?"

"Angry?" He raised his eyebrows. "You read all the poetry I wrote in that class, all my freewriting, and it surprises you that I'm angry?"

He slugged down a couple of swallows of scotch, and she held out her glass for more. They didn't bother with ice. They poured scotch right out of the bottle and drank it warm.

She leaned toward him, straining to reach out to him, far away, across the room. "I could help you. Why don't you give me a chance to help?" The words clattered out, droning and senseless, from a fairy tale she was telling herself.

She shouldn't be surprised by his archness, his condescending smile. She thought of what he had been to his family, the perfect son, brilliant in his career, making his mother and sisters proud. He carried himself with a solemnity born of the radiance of all their blessings.

Angel sighed. "I shouldn't have let you drive all the way up here, should I?" He chewed his lip, reflective, then turned to her.

"In some relationships there are so many givens and common ground that they grow stronger almost without effort," he said.

"But not this one," she said.

"You can't just separate people from their natural environment," he said. "You can't just view them without a context. People are embedded in a whole system of relationships."

"But what are your relationships?" she asked, leaning toward him, and when he did not reply she peered at his face, unstoppable, intent. "We had such a beautiful night." She twisted her hands. "When you taste that kind of sweetness, it's all you ever want, ever," she said. "You do everything to hang on to it."

"But you can't hang on."

"You can try."

"You can't hang on," he said again. "Don't you understand? You have to let go. Everything will be taken. We enter this world with our fists clenched tight, to grasp all we can, but we leave with our palms open. We have given all."

She rushed over to him, bent to drape her arms around his neck, but he turned away, thrusting his head against the back of the chair. "Glenna, booze and horniness can make H_2O seem like the theory of relativity."

She closed her eyes, standing by his chair, feeling herself as old and dead as the bent crone head. And then she forced herself to move.

"You going?" he said, as if surprised. "Wait a minute." She didn't turn. "I'll walk you," he said as she started out, coming up to join her. "Wait a second, button your blouse." He turned to her in that mocking way he had, attempting to adjust her clothes as he would a child's.

"Are you sure you're in shape to drive?" He nudged her. "Friends don't let friends drive naked."

"You're a funny guy . . . Spence," she said, trying to lift her chin.

"Glenna," he said, "rescue something else."

That was the last she saw of him. How singular he had looked near the border of flowers, and odd, and self-contained, as if he had just thrust up from the rich loamy soil like a dark tulip.

She left the house and trudged down toward the main road, her breasts exposed to the wet damp air. For the moment, she couldn't feel any rain though her feet slogged through puddles. The humid evening was closing in on her like the petals of a wet dark plant.

In the car, Glenna sweated against the seat, the plastic adhering to her skin. The wind blew so hard the little car shook. Every so often raindrops would splatter the windshield like paint whooshed from a soggy brush.

Could it really have been nothing, this whole thing between her and Angel? Could she have made it all up in her own mind? Dense, she said to herself. Clueless. Her very important ego was hurt. Her very important self-regard was being challenged.

Well, she had tried.

To hell with Angel. She'd had rapture with her husband, too, when they first started. The feelings had been reciprocal. In no way had she been alone. She had wanted to give herself over to him, let her life dissolve in the ecstasy of all that sweetness. And then it had changed.

I'm not shallow, she had said to Angel. Don't assume things about me. Give me a chance.

I'm not like that, she had said. But more than anything she did not want to be one of the weak ones that was hunted down by the others.

It was sad. Life was always tragic. If you tried to create some grand scheme for yourself, you were doomed. She was no good with poetry and should stick to grammar.

Seeing a small animal, a varmint of some type, dart onto the road ahead, she gunned the engine—just to scare it. It was better if they were trained.

FOR all of that long summer night, Glenna dreamed that he would surprise her by coming after her. She thought she heard the melody of his whistling, blowing across the front lawn, and more than once she had gotten up to look for him, but she saw only the thrust heads of the leaves, wobbly on their spindly throats, beating tirelessly against the fence.

Much later, coming inside, she threw open all the windows of the house, inhaling the crackling electricity of the ozone, the humid green sweetness of the summer air. She was actually laughing to herself, a forced, unsatisfying laugh at that, but something was good about it nonetheless—it was so raucous, so wild. Later she lay in bed, listening to the sighing and rustling of the darkness, and felt, in spite of herself, part of this richness, this summer fecundity, that was never used up but always being replenished.

As she tried to stay with this soothing thought, she became maddeningly aware of a whining at her ear that came again and again and would not go away no matter how many times she hit. A mosquito, of course, she thought, turning on the awful glaring bulb, only to see that her bedroom was full of them, a blurred gray swarm, everywhere alight, too many to count, the air thick with their fast, whirring bodies. She began flailing heedlessly, slapping them against the creamy velveteen-ridged paper, running them down furiously for twenty minutes, half an hour, always finding more on her face, on her legs, splattering herself and the wall with stars of her own blood.

When Glenna woke up the next morning, she had been scratching in her sleep, scratching at her sore, bitten arms and legs. The deerfly bite swelled, painful and bulbous.

She thought furiously of him doing that to her, standing in his doorway, a hacked-off, burnt-off stub of a man. How had she ever thought he was handsome? Walking through her house, she picked up the display of frogs on the mantelpiece and studied Magnus's calligraphy: "A frog went a courtin'." She looked at the wide smiles of the frogs, their long flipper feet, that Angel had found so funny.

Her breath rustling in her hollow chest, she knelt down at the fireplace, and though the day was already sticky and humid, she started a fire. Some of the wood was damp, and she needed to put in pieces of paper and blow on them before the kindling ignited and she got a strong flame going. When she put the frogs on top of the fire, plumes of flame shot out and an acrid, biting smell filled the house.

With cleaners and solvents she found in the garage, she prepared two large pails of soapy liquid and started scrubbing the pasted-on, encrusted insects from the walls in the entryway. She worked for hours, till her fingers and arms and face were filthy with shredded bodies and wings. The pine scent of the cleaners was suffocatingly strong, mixing with the caustic fumes of the fire, on which she heaped now the cape buffalo head, now the deer-leg lamp—a pyre of hairy dead things. Finally her eyes were streaming so profusely she had to stop.

She took a shower, then went back to her bedroom to rest. She picked up the phone to call Siri, tell her what she'd done. "I'm remodeling," she said to Siri's answering machine. "I think I'll start from scratch." The smell of charring flesh pervaded the house. It would take days to clear it out. She sat scratching beneath the tiny clumps of mosquito skeletons as they dried on the walls in the afternoon sunlight, a galaxy of them, with their own little blood rings. Her artwork.

The Oracle

IT WAS ALWAYS DIFFERENT in the morning. In the morning, he was reserved, apologetic even. They would walk around the little house in the pure blue summer air and it was hard to remember what had gone on the night before . . . though smoke always lingered, and sometimes broken glass.

But the cat remembered. It slunk beneath the couch and hissed at him, and then, as soon as the door opened, it ran out into the bare scrubby field that adjoined their house in the small California mountain town.

Sometimes her husband seemed almost ready to weep, distraught at what he had done. It was as if the blue morning reproached him, too. He would fix his eyes on her sadly, try to nibble her hand, beg her not to leave him. And the groveling created a queen.

She lay in her bed after one of those nights, listening secretly as he moved about, preparing to leave for work. They both taught grade school and had just finished for the year, but he had taken a summer job as a clerk in an adjoining town. Due to deliver in August, she got to be a lady in waiting.

Yesterday had been an all-day party. Wearing his clown costume for the kids' last class, Donny had stayed dressed for the staff event that evening. When they came home he had throttled her on this very bed, his ruffle vibrating, his teeth dingy against the greasepaint, his eyes popping out at her behind their spokes. He kept her pinned until she said that she had been wrong to contradict him in front of the principal. When he called her an ugly mole rat from hell, she'd wanted to laugh, but you didn't laugh at Donny at a time like that.

Before they were married, his clown routine delighted the kids at the college nursery school where they'd met. Golden-eyed and graceful as he was, he wasn't ashamed to paint his face and roll around on the floor with a bunch of four-year-olds. Tracy had been enthralled by the lazy lefty lean of him as he swooped up a child in his arms. She'd followed him around as the children had, longing to be held in those hairy blond arms, and he had seemed unable to turn away. To her, this morning, he was as conciliatory as he'd been in those days, standing in the doorway and smoking a cigarette, casting her scorching, loverlike looks—with such looks he had gotten far. She pretended not to see, but did get out of bed. Sipping on her tea, she could almost doubt this silly, humiliating, ridiculous situation she'd gotten herself into. He was handsome Donny, her winsome swain. She loved it when he put on his clown makeup—bovine fringes of false eyelashes, his smile a greasy watermelon slice.

But her contempt for him now had hardened. She was sensitive to every little movement. She shuddered each time he turned a page of the paper, never meeting his eyes. She could feel him shifting toward her, shoulders, knees; he needed her to anoint him with a forgiving look. But not until he stood at the door, ready to go, did she say, all at once, "Bye, Donny."

He breathed hoarsely; she heard a rattle in his chest. "Bye, Trace."

And just as he was about to say something more, she heard the backfiring of a pickup as it lurched down the treeless gray street. His ride. Donny waved awkwardly and was gone. Standing next to the rusty, dried-out hydrangeas, she watched him out of sight. The heat of the day was already rising.

Tracy left her cup of tea where it sat. First she went to the shower, where she felt the sweet wash of suds slide down her body; she ran her fingers over the slick skin again and again. She was ripe and luxuriant, energized by pregnancy when left alone to bloom. She dressed quickly then rushed to the chest, where she had hidden her secret treasure folded up in her grandmother's silk scarf—a thousand dollars worth of chips from the casino. They seemed to have taken on the smell of the chiffonier, ancient, secretive, relaxed. She stood there for a moment, absorbing the pungent, musty smell, then walked out to the living room.

She took one last look around the stark rented house, at the worn, mustard-colored carpet, the sparse furniture, the bare walls. There was not a personal touch in the place.

"Why don't you decorate?" Donny had asked early on.

"Decorate? Like for a party? Some party." *Crash!* He pushed her head into the refrigerator. *Bam!* He slung the cat against the stove.

And in her ears pounded the song he sang to his second-graders: "When you're mad and you know it, stomp your feet." *Stomp. Stomp.*

She threw some clothes into her suitcase, let her house keys clank onto the kitchen table, and sat down for a few hushed moments, scrawling with a flourish her five-word note: "Sorry it didn't work out." How gleaming her hand, how bold and translucent, as bright and without memory as the new morning.

Her only regret was the cat. It hated riding in the car and was, in any event, still out in the field behind the house. "Kitty," she called softly. "Kitty." But her voice stayed low. If she called too loudly, who knew what she might summon up.

Before leaving town she went to the bank and cleaned out the accounts. The teller, a woman with the cracked, parched skin so typical of people in these parts, peered at her through glinting glasses when she made her request. She knew both of them, after all. The town had only one bank, and their arrival the previous fall had been an event. "Baby stuff," she muttered as she collected nearly ten thousand dollars in stacks of hundreds and stuffed them into her large, peacock-hued straw bag.

In the car, heading out at last, she could hardly contain her exhilaration. The rusted-out old Escort had no air-conditioning, so she opened the windows wide, singing out to the vast, windswept fields, "When you're happy and you know it, clap your hands!" The sky was not so bright as before—already the heat was raising the dust. She wondered how she had lasted so long in this arid wasteland. She surveyed its vastness disdainfully. It was nothing she couldn't master. She adjusted her swelled belly in the safety belt, turned on the radar detector and floored the pedal, swerving past the sign: "Reno 180." She hadn't been down this mountain since they'd ascended last fall, newlyweds with jobs at the same little town school.

Sunlight caught her wristwatch, her ring, in a glaring flash. She had the idea that she and the baby, whom she hoped would be a girl, were going to be rich. And gradually she let a long-simmering idea take hold: since she would be going to Reno anyway to cash in her chips, perhaps she would stop by and see Octave, the blackjack dealer.

As they'd passed through Reno ten months before on their way to Shasta, Donny had wanted to gamble but asked her not to come to the tables with him: "Women change your luck." So Tracy had wandered. It was almost as if Octave had drawn her to him with his insolent slate-gray eyes. He was small, gnomish, compact. He wore a funny shoe, scruffy and outsized, that didn't match the other one.

He had swerved his chin at her, reeling her in. No one else was sitting at his fifty-dollar minimum table.

"I'm afraid," she was not at all afraid to say to him, sitting down. How she must have looked then—her round pink face with its ruddy cheeks, her shiny brown hair pulled back with a ribbon. A week later a student' s mother would say she seemed like one of the kids.

"On your honeymoon?"

But how had he known that? Already she was aware that something was wrong with her and Donny. The fights had started the evening they left Nebraska.

"That's a beautiful sunset," she had said to Donny.

"You call that a good sunset?" he replied contemptuosly. "It's a stupid sunset. You haven't seen the kind of sunsets I have."

"Why am I suddenly deserving of your scorn, oh master?" she'd asked, joking as they always did.

"Because you let me do it," he replied, and he backhanded her right then and there, hitting her arm. If only she'd left at that moment, jumped out of the car. But she was a newlywed. She'd just had a triumphant send-off—as triumphant as her poor little grandma could afford. Her life was riding on this guy. Perhaps she'd merely misunderstood.

Octave hadn't. For awhile she had just sat there at his table, sipping on a drink and staring at his long fingers as he shuffled cards like a fortune teller. His skin was deep tan; his hair was straight and soft-looking, with a taupe hue. He wore a glittery white sequined jacket like Elvis and had a diamond encrusted in the nail of both of his forefingers. All at once, he said, "You gotta move if you don't place a bet, baby."

"Fifty dollars?"

He shrugged. "You look lucky to me." His gray eyes held her fast. She took out two one hundred-dollar bills, her grandmother's wedding present. On to the table they went, disappearing soundlessly into a slot on the table. He gave her four fifty-dollar chips.

She'd slid the first one over the green felt, and he dealt her a jack and a seven. She held and lost. The next time he dealt her a nine of clubs and a king. He got a twenty. The next time she got a twenty and he got blackjack. Stunned, she'd taken up her final chip.

"I'd better not," she said, cut to the quick.

"Do it," he said, and dealt her another jack and seven.

She sat gaping. To her amazement, Octave busted.

"Double your next bet," he'd said, and she had. She doubled again. And when she'd won a thousand dollars, he had tossed his ponytail a couple of times and leaned toward her, his face so close she could smell the odd juniper tang of his breath. "That was pure, sheer luck," he said. "You are chosen. You'll be lucky all your life." She had felt herself cresting toward him over the blackjack table, the exalted coming together that she'd dreamed of with Donny.

"How much can I make today?" she asked him.

He'd arched his eyebrows, raised his hands. "Ten thousand. Fifty thousand."

But just then she'd seen Donny coming her way, and quickly hidden her chips.

How carefully and lovingly she'd sequestered her little trove, guarding it in its sleep, till she'd taken it out on this day to live for her again.

By the time she got to Reno, she was cooking inside the glass and searing-hot metal of the Escort. She'd get a new car with her winnings. A Lexus or at least a Legacy. At high noon she pulled into a parking place on a side-street near Octave's casino, jostling for a place with a large tour bus from a retirement home. As she got out, miserable and scalded, the bus occupants flocked around her cheerfully, as pretty in their pastels as a cluster of parakeets. Farther down the block, a goofy, grinning cowboy, fifty times larger than life, took off and put on his hat at her approach, then did it again. She could almost hear him talk to her, in Donny's voice: *You are so stupid.*

The only customer in the hotel lobby, she loitered in relief, breathing the crisp, refrigerated air. The whirring sounds of the machines tinkled in her windblown ears like the soothing bubbling of a waterfall. How well she remembered this embracing dark. It imposed no expectations. It knew you did not like the daylight, it knew you did not like the bright lights, or to be looked at; it knew your favorite thing was to be in the gloom and to be left alone with the soft cheerful jingling all around you of the piping, trilling machines.

She got herself a room on the twentieth floor and looked far out over the scrubby desert, back up into the blue mountains from whence she had come, and where Donny, about now, was probably calling her.

She sponged off her face and arms, then lay down on the bed, trying to breathe deeply, clear her mind, but now the only thought that came to her was that her baby was due, her time was coming fast, and she had just run away from all her arrangements. She fell into a deep sleep, waking a couple of hours later with a terrifying start, not knowing where she was—from what nightmare came this generic cardboard room with its mint-green carpet and its walls with imprinted tigers above the bed?

And then she remembered that just off the lobby was a glass enclosure with two white tigers, the hotel's signature attraction. On their first trip, Tracy had come up to the edge of the technicolor grid and watched the tigers prowl their picturesque space, looking mutant and improbable.

Slowly she got to her feet, a heavy, unwieldy creature, and walked to the window, staring out at the desert's hazy bloom. She had taken her kindergartners to the zoo in an Oregon town where they had seen a dusty tiger sleeping in the corner of its cage. "Dumb, doo-doo tiger," one little boy had said and Tracy, hurt, had tried to explain to a bunch of kids holding their noses that tigers were all that was left of wildness.

Now she went to her suitcase and pulled out a flowery tent dress. Dolling herself up as best as she could, she then took the elevator down. She traversed the area around the blackjack tables once, twice, with no sign of Octave. Finally she stopped a purple-haired woman who made change. When Tracy asked for Octave, the woman looked back with an awful, empty blankness.

"He's got a ponytail, he wears a sequined jacket, and he's got diamonds on his fingernails."

"There's lots of guys like that."

Tracy's voice rose. "He used to work during the day," she said, "at that table right over there."

"Oh, I know who you mean," the woman said. "He comes on at six. Want any change?"

With a sigh, Tracy got fifty dollars in quarters from her. The senior citizens had settled at the slot machines in a tropical flock and were putzing away at them. After much deliberation, Tracy was just about to sit down at a likely looking Lucky Seven when a large white-haired woman elbowed in front of her and nearly sent her sprawling. The woman wore a hearing aid and a plastic name tag that said, "Hello! My name is Tekla."

"That's my machine," Tracy said, feeling her stomach wrench. She was sure now that luck was here and nowhere else.

But perhaps Tekla couldn't hear her, staring, as she did, straight ahead at the machine. Maybe she had her hearing aid turned off. Full of cold resolve, Tracy moved to an adjoining Joker Is Wild, keeping her eye on Tekla and giving up her own quarters as slowly as she could, angry at Tekla, her pastel shirt, her deaf-as-a-post pose. With satisfaction she watched Tekla swill glass after glass of rum and Coke as she played the progressive jackpot slot. Occasionally Tekla won two or ten quarters, a couple of times she won twenty-five, but it was small stuff. Passing by, the purple-haired cashier slapped Tekla's machine. "She's due, stick with her," she said, and Tracy felt sick, her fingers blackening from her own coins, her lungs searing from the smoke all around. She gulped orange juice, hoping that it would help the baby, who seemed to be spinning around in there, not waxing, as she loved to imagine, in stately phases like the moon.

And then, finally, as Tracy had known it would, the time came when Tekla had to wring out of herself those rum and Cokes. She got up and peered myopically around, throwing her jacket over the seat in front of the Lucky Seven, a jacket that Tracy, without compunction, threw over a neighboring seat as she slid into Tekla's. It didn't take more than twenty tries; Tekla probably hadn't even gotten into the stall. Three red sevens lined up neatly. This started a raucous din. Whistles and bells sounded, along with the clattering of coins spilling into the tray at the bottom of her machine, a clatter that did not stop but came in undulatory waves, each accompanied by further fanfare. Tekla came tearing back, as fast as her short little legs would go.

"That was my machine," she said.

Tracy's plush arms jiggled as she clapped. Twenty-five hundred dollars on the progressive jackpot. "You can't have dibs on a machine," Tracy said.

"She pushed me off my chair!" Tekla shouted to the purple-haired cashier. "I was playing that machine for four hours."

Tracy didn't care. Tekla had been trying to take her luck. A blue-uniformed security guard calmed Tekla down and drew her away. Tracy strode powerfully to the window, where even the cashiers seemed to look at her with admiration. She signed the paper and collected the rest of her money. It was almost by accident that she looked over her shoulder and saw Octave at his table, shining like an apparition. *Octave. Octave.* Vainly she waved, trying to catch his eye.

Even when she came up and looked right at him he stared at her blankly. She let the impression of herself sink in. Probably one of the luckiest people he had ever met in his life. Of course, she had been fifty pounds lighter. Of course, she hadn't been pregnant. And for that matter, Octave himself looked different: He dealt with a sour face. She'd thought he was in his thirties; now it seemed that he might be twice that.

He came to the end of a shoe, and she said, "Octave."

She wasn't sure whether he knew her or not, but felt an image of herself taking shape in the still depths of his pale grayish eyes.

"Hey, baby," he said. "How're you doing? I didn't expect to see you again."

People at the table looked at her impatiently. She remembered: a woman changes the table's luck. Uncomfortable, full of resistance, she sat down. Her fat butt and legs squeezed into the stool.

"Need chips?"

"I've got some." She dug into her bag for the magic fifty-dollar chips, put ten of them in a stack before her.

"Be nice," someone said to Octave, who looked squarely at the green baize. Her chips were gone so fast that she felt it physically, as if somebody had punched her in her big, pregnant gut.

Octave kept winning and, as he kept killing them, four of the five original people at the table got up and left. Now only Tracy and a middle-aged man sat there, a man in a limp, salmon-colored sweater with a plastic button, broken in half, hanging from a thread.

Tracy tried for bravado. She slid toward Octave another two of her chips. "Don't you remember?" she said. "You said I'd always be lucky."

He swiped at his cheek a couple of times with his knuckles, a motion so vigorous that she thought it might hurt. "Maybe this isn't your lucky day, baby," he said. "Maybe you'd better just quit."

Stubbornly, resolutely, she dug into her bag for the rest of her chips, put down two, and watched as Octave dealt himself a twenty-one.

The other player left. The half moon of his broken button had fallen onto the table. This seemed a lucky sign.

"Octave, give me a break," she said. "I've run off from my husband."

She saw the beads of sweat on Octave's forehead. "What'd you come down here for?"

"To see you."

"What'd you do that for?" She kicked the table. "Why?" She kicked the table again. "Baby, I'm going to have to tell you to cut that out." She just kept sitting there, stupidly, as she had ten months before, only this time every time she bet she lost then lost again.

"Look, I hate it when people lose, baby," he said.

"You said I'd be lucky all my life," she said again.

"Wait a second," he said. He looked over his shoulder. She followed his eyes and saw the pit boss watching. "You will be lucky," he said in a low, gritty voice, his lips barely moving at all. "I told you that and it's true. It's your personal fate. But maybe this just isn't the kind of luck you need anymore. Maybe you'll never have this kind of luck at cards again."

Had he signaled for the other dealer to come up and relieve him? Without another glance at Tracy, Octave walked away with spasmodic strides, his shoulders pitching about before he moved recklessly forward.

The new dealer had a large, square powdered face, looked squishy and preserved as a stewed fruit. "Place your bet, honey," she said, and Tracy, shaking her head, pushed away from the table.

Through the dark, smoky, tinkling aisles, she tried to find where Octave had gone. Why was he trying to ditch her when he knew she needed to talk to him? Finally she spotted his distinctive lurching walk and trailed eagerly after. He sat down at the bar, head to head with a woman in green spandex and what looked to be a saran-wrapped conehead. Tracy walked up to him and stood there waiting in horrible mortification, knowing he sensed her with his whole body but was ignoring her.

Finally, unable to keep quiet anymore, she blurted into the conversation, "You tell everybody they're lucky, don't you?" Slowly he turned to look at her. His hand shot out to grab hers. She could feel his long fingernails cutting into the soft pad of her palm.

"Listen, lady, I'm telling you," he said hoarsely. "What you need isn't here. Go back to your husband."

"Are you crazy?" she said. "I can't go back to him."

"Just wait till the baby's born, see? Then you split if you want. Maybe even come back to see Octave." He pulled her to him by her pinioned hand, breathing close to her cheek, almost a kiss. A favor to her in front of his friend. It took all her strength to pull her hand away. When she got into the elevator her palm was sore, weeping with some kind of preblood, sanguineous fluid.

In her room she lay down on the bed, trying to calm herself, but she was furious. Her whole body rippled and heaved. She convulsed in fear of the impending delivery . . . and then, out of the corner of her eye, she saw the print of the snarling tigers. Sitting up groggily, she grabbed the headboard, looking up at them. She had forgotten their rapacious faces . . . and yet she would need that ferocity if she were to birth her baby right here, pull it out of herself all elastic and shining. To take that power unto herself, to be for her baby the keeper of the sacred doorway between life and death—to reign over the moment when both of them hung suspended between those two worlds—Tracy felt herself gasp.

All at once she shuddered. There was nothing to be afraid of. Tigers no longer roamed wild. They were a fragile species, barely hanging on, the finale of an ancient line, their true existence in wall hangings, pleasing patterns in a small frame . . . a series of streaks and colors, flaxen and black with gleaming fangs, the savage expressions redundant and pathetic. Even kindergartners weren't fooled.

Weak, nauseated, she clasped her belly. She had still won a few thousand dollars. It wasn't the fortune she'd hoped for, but it was enough for her to take off, go to Nebraska, stay with Grandma for awhile, decide on her next move.

Then suddenly, as if she had willed it, the phone rang. Who could it be? Only Octave knew she was here. She hadn't even thought he knew her name.

But the voice on the other end came from nowhere but her nightmare, the nightmare she did not remember having. "You don't get to kill the clown, Tracy," it said. "Didn't anybody tell you that? Nobody ever gets to kill the clown. And I would just die if you left."

"You dumb Bozo," she said. "How dare you come after me?"

She slammed down the phone. Immediately, it started ringing again. And yet she didn't move. She lay there, hands clasped over her belly, watching through the blinds as the midsummer sun made its late descent, emblazoning the gilded chamber with its long rays, illuminating the stylized tigers. He was crazed by her, in her thrall. She would kill him before she would let him subdue her like that again. And yet . . .

Lagoon

It was going to be a long sunset. As the plane broke through the black and orange tatters of a stormy dusk, Lydia let the slanting rays stream across her face. On the evening flight back to Honolulu, this was the moment when it seemed the plane would overtake the sun, plunge them again into a brilliant, crimson day. Then, just as they were really gaining on it, the sun would flatten and dissolve, and Lydia would think of the time when she was a child and a butterfly had landed on her hand. Frantic not to lose this sign of grace, she had pinched the iridescent wings with all her might, till her fingers grew sticky with glittery pulp and Bobby had to tell her it was dead.

"Would you mind pulling down that shade?" asked the man across the aisle.

Jesus. She glared over at the sultry-voiced creature who had come slouching into the compartment just before takeoff wearing an expensive sport coat too big for him. Now he made no move to help her as she snagged a nail prying at the stuck shade. With his lustrous blond coiffure and tattooed vine bracelet, he was obviously too evolved to offer outworn courtesies. She knelt on her seat and pulled, finally forcing it down.

"The UVS and radiation pour right in when you're on a plane," he said.

They were the only ones in first class. He was all hers for the next five hours. "Excuse me? Do you really think you can protect yourself from what's out there by pulling down a shade?" she asked, then turned away.

When the attendant came by she got a very nice pillow and laid her head back. In truth, this trip had been an ordeal for her, an unwelcome detour, and for days she had been nagged by the idea that some additional awful thing would happen to her before she could return to her accustomed delightful existence. It was always when life was the sweetest that cruel things came, blasting and withering whatever was in their path.

Her restaurant seemed hopelessly far away, but only a month before, she had been sitting on the lanai after the last guest went home, staring into the inky black of the lagoon, listening to water softly lapping among the tall, dense mangrove trees. The full moon had burned white on the water like scattered petals.

She longed to see that moon now. She could hear tinny music coming from the man's headphones as darkness spread through the cabin. He appeared to be sleeping, although he nodded vigorously from time to time as if to a beat, his hair rippling with a glowing white sheen—except at his pate, where it had thinned to a few tendrils. She waited awhile, then forced open the shade again and found the moon nearly full, just eaten about the edge.

The moonlight was stealthy and quiet as it wrapped the two of them in its graceful coils. Feeling around in the stuffed bag she carried with her, she did not see her purse mirror reflect the disk of her face in several empty windows, a powdered doll face with a pale smattering of freckles like the glaze on a spotted shell. Gradually her face began to shine as the sweat crept up to her forehead and she realized, frantically, that she could not find her keys.

She began tossing items out of her rucksack-sized purse, full of things she had taken from her brother's apartment. His lover, Milo, had surprised her as she rifled through Bobby's rolltop desk, stuffing into that purse all she could lay hands on.

"You ignore him for ten years and now you rob him?"

Milo's incredulous look even now hung on her like a poison cape.

"You delivered a killing blow, but it didn't kill him, did it, Lydia," Milo had said. "He lived on quite well without you."

Her cigarettes, a makeup kit, a restaurant account book, all came out of her purse, but not her keys. Perhaps she had dropped them in front of Bobby's desk. If so, she would consider them lost. She would rather die herself than ever again hear Milo's scoffing, dismissive voice. In truth, she couldn't remember the last time she had seen her keys. During her weeks in Minnesota she hadn't given them a thought.

The man turned toward her as she continued her futile ritual. She had been immaculately groomed when she got on the flight. Now the lap of her peach-colored linen suit was soiled with the marks of blush-encrusted cotton puffs and the streaks of an open mascara wand. Scattered beside her were a dried hibiscus blossom, a postcard of a hermaphrodite, a garnet ring, an embroidered fanny pack, a picture in a tiny crystal frame of the two of them as kids.

"Can I help you?" said the man. She looked over at the luscious-voiced creature, murderously, desperately. "What's the problem?"

"I lost my keys," she said. "I cannot for the life of me figure it out." She crashed her hands to her head. "The mess this is I cannot convey to you."

"Why don't you just lay everything out?" She stared at him. "I mean, just put everything on the seat. That might help." His voice was languorous, friendly, in contrast to his mournful face with its large honker of a nose. Partly to humor him, she started her inventory again, pulling out Bobby's white silk scarf, Bobby's wallet with its pictures of Milo, a pack of playing cards decorated with Liberace modeling costumes. She felt the man's eyes on her, attentive to everything she did. Past the exquisite tailoring of his raw silk jacket, she noticed how spindly his chest was, how looming his shoulders.

"They're hard to miss, they're so heavy," she said. "There must be fifty keys on them, plus a silver dollar from Las Vegas that I got on my honeymoon, and a rabbit's foot some little kid gave me on the street in Oahu. He just walked up and gave it to me."

Everything but the sand and spare change at the bottom of her purse was on the seat. She glanced out the window, looking down at the moonlight reflected on the water far below. She was trapped and would never be able to find her keys.

"This is terrible," she said, thinking of a dozen locked restaurant doors, the secret safety deposit box. The chill moonlight gave a dull luster to the metal of the plane's wing. Wing parts shuddered and flapped in an invisible draft. It was insane to trade safe solid ground for the whine of jets and this thin travesty of comfort.

"It's not worth it to get so upset, is it?" he said. The wispy hairs of his eyebrows were so long that they drooped over his lids. Something was wrong with him, but it was subtle; she couldn't tell what it was. "Name's Win," he said, reaching across the aisle to clasp her hand, and she said her name. He kept holding her hand until she squeezed his in greeting, then cast it back.

"So what's so bad?" he asked.

She shook her head. "It's pretty bad."

"No hope left?" he inquired with an encouraging grin.

She laughed a little, and this time when the attendant came by, she ordered a scotch. "So where are you from?" she asked.

He raised his eyebrows very high and shook his head. "Silicon Valley. I'm in software. You?"

"I own a restaurant on Kauai. The Sleepy Lagoon." He laughed. "It's quite a nice place." And all at once she wished she could express to him what it was like, to be looking out at the inky lagoon in the deepest part of the tropical night. How quiet it was, with the onyx water and the moonlight and the emptiness. "It's rather out of the way." She looked out the window, pressed a palm to the cold glass. "I don't leave there very often." She turned back to him, her head expanding with the scotch. Perhaps she should give him her card. "People rush about so much. Why do they have to get anywhere that fast? What can they really change?"

"My, you're a grim soul," he said.

"Not at all," Lydia said. "There's not even a bit of restraint. Every generation replaces the next as fast and furiously as it can. Don't you feel yourself becoming obsolete already?"

He smiled as if she spoke to charm. "I don't think people need to feel so helpless," he said, then went on like a debater, a fan of discourse, trying to lure her into discussion so he could stick her with his opinions, keep pouring on the lazy honey of his voice. "Every time we turn on the TV we see people just like us who need help. Networks already exist that are going to change the course of human history—for the better, I think." Something was odd about his big hands. "See, we know so much about each other now. There are no more secrets. We can't allow each other to suffer."

His big, sullen, heavy-lidded eyes made her think of bumblebees in pollen—thick blond lashes, a face still succulent with youth. Perhaps she could pluck at the web around him, make her way into his dream. As he began helping her repack her purse, she inhaled the sharp clean soap scent that still clung to his shirt.

He held up a snapshot that had fallen loose. "You and your husband?" he said. "Who's the young woman?"

She hesitated. "My daughter," she said finally. "In college on Oahu."

"Almost as pretty as her mother." He grabbed her hand, peering at it closely. "You're older than you look, aren't you?"

She pulled her hand away. "I don't know, how old do I look?" She tried for a charming pout. Inwardly she was a crone, her ancient features horn and bone, desolate as moonscape. But he looked at her sweetly, she thought, with guileless eyes that wanted to drink and wanted to drown.

All at once she pulled his hand over as he had pulled hers and looked hard at it. "What about this?" She poked a knobby bump between his thumb and index finger, a fat stub and a fleshy pink keloid scar.

"Ah, you noticed," he said with a fond gaze, scanning her face avidly. "Born with two thumbs on my left hand. Born with improperly fused rib and shoulder bones. I'm a mutant, in a way." He looked earnestly at her with his amber eyes. "Honest to God, I'm telling you the truth. People never believe me. My father was in the army working at a Nevada bomb-testing facility in the fifties. He was contaminated during an accident just before I was conceived."

She barked a shocked little laugh. "What?"

"My poor old man and the three other guys who were with him all died of lymphoma within a year of each other, when they were in their early forties." She felt herself turn away. "And I wake up every morning wondering when it's going to happen to me."

The low, mellow tones of his voice filled her with a terrible, piercing sadness. "I'm sorry," she said, sunk for a moment in the finality and hopelessness of everything he had said. But then an idea came to her and she looked over at him slyly. "I'll bet you got some money out of it."

Harshly, he laughed. "Haven't you heard? You can't sue the government unless it wants to be sued. They've denied anything ever happened."

Her eyes roamed the spacious cabin, lighted on the smooth, expensive material of his jacket. "You haven't done all that badly," she murmured.

"Well, if you must know . . ." he began.

"It's always good to know, don't you think?"

He shrugged as if it were all the same to him. "Whatever. Some friends got behind a deal of mine that worked out great." He gave her a quizzical little smile. "I don't know why I'm telling you all this. You must be doing all right yourself, at the restaurant."

She smiled with pleasure. "It's such a lovely place," she told him with a sigh. "It was all my concept. The food, the decor, the ambiance. As soon as I saw the lagoon, I knew it would be perfect for a restaurant. People would want to sit there for hours, looking out over the water, listening to music. I greet everyone; they all know me by name. Whenever I leave for awhile, everyone asks, 'Where's Lydia?'"

Her smile felt sodden, like papier-mâché, her hands like crepe in her lap. Her husband had financed the restaurant, made the initial investment, hadn't he? Without his money it never would have happened. She had begged him, implored him, promised to cross him in nothing. And then a time had come when she mentioned

Bobby's name and he said, incredulously, "Bobby?" From then on he would wrest the wildest, most insidious nuances out of Bobby's name whenever it came up. Only as the years went by had she realized, fully, the deal she had made. Still, she would do it over again in a second. It was not everyone who had a restaurant like hers.

When they ordered a second scotch, her cigarettes fell out of her purse and into the aisle. He scooped them up eagerly and then moved over to sit beside her. "Do you mind?" His linen jacket brushed her bare arm with a rough friction that filled her nerve endings with a vague excitement.

"Are you sure you want these back?" he said, still holding on to the cigarettes. His eyebrow arched up high, and quivered there. "I don't want to be presumptuous," he went on, "but what about this smoking thing of yours?"

"Bobby . . ." she said, slipping, for he, too, was an anointed, singular one.

"Win," he said.

"Listen, Win," she said. "I eat the fat on the steak, I eat the sour cream. I drink vodka and scotch and I smoke what I want. This is the way I want to live, and when the time comes for me to die, I'll say fine, I made the deal."

"But the smoking . . ."

"Do you really think," she interrupted, "that you can tell me anything I haven't been told already?"

The pupils of his eyes were huge as corn kernels; she could scarcely avert her gaze. After awhile she no longer tried, and he did not begrudge her this fascination, as Bobby never had, either, when she had loved him, could not bear to be without him. "Now tell me," she said, "a little about this software thing of yours."

He sat back in his seat, made a square with his big-knuckled fingers, marred only by the bump of whatever had been reaching out of his hand once—a tentacle, a magic wand. "Now, for example, where have you just been?"

"In Minnesota. My brother . . ." she began.

"OK, a family thing. In the future, you see, you won't have to leave Kauai to visit your brother. You'll use the computer to set up a virtual meeting place. You'll put on your goggles, your gloves, and meet—actually hug and walk around—and not even have to leave home."

Lydia looked on wanly. She sat closer to him, pressed herself into his side. "It was a funeral," she said.

They stared at each other. At that moment there was a change in cabin pressure. She felt her ears pop, and then a breeze began to stir, hissing out of invisible airholes. "I'm sorry to hear that," Win said, bending his head for awhile to study his odd hands in his lap, pieces of pottery that didn't match. His bony elbow poked her as he thrust his hands into his pockets. "What about your husband?" he asked, peering at her. "Why isn't he with you?"

She was feeling something else in the sweet weight of his gaze. This indeed was a game she had not played for quite some time.

"He hated Bobby," she said. "You see, Bobby was gay. Because of my husband . . ." Milo hadn't been impressed when she'd tried to explain. All he remembered was how easily she had fallen into the habit of keeping away.

Now she put before Win her prize, a picture she had smuggled out in a book so Milo wouldn't wrest it away: Bobby, nine or ten years earlier, sitting in a Chinese restaurant. It must have been a hot summer day, for he was wearing a tank top, and she could see, behind him, white curtains billowing inward at an open window. A lock of hair fell onto his broad forehead. Milo sat opposite him, looking dotingly on, both of them full of a conspicuous and immodest pleasure in each other's company. Bobby's teeth clenched the crisp edges of a bitten-into fortune cookie; his hand offered the blurred tag of the message up to the camera.

She had asked Bobby once, "Are all gay men beautiful?"

"He could get anything from anybody," she said to Win. "He could have been a scoundrel, a rascal, but he was a good guy." Bobby who could never think ill of his big sister.

"Hey, Robo-sister is down," he had told Milo. "She needs our support."

"I'm not into power queens," Milo had replied.

Bobby had laid his head back on the pillow. "Lydia's about having control. I'm into giving up control. I'm into healing."

Not all of Bobby's friends had hated her. Outside the hospital room, one of his buddies had come up close and run his hand over her cheek, saying Bobby had told him so much about her. "Do you like gay boys?" Au Paul had asked. "Do you like gay boys, cause we love you. We love pretty little ladies with big hair and false eyelashes who put 'Miss' in front of their names. Can I call you 'Miss Lydi?'"

"Say, do you like blackjack?" she said to Win all at once. "You want to play some cards?"

She found again the pack of Liberace cards snitched from Bobby's drawer. "Would you rather play poker?" she said, flailing her hand absently in her purse for a few moments on the impossible off chance that her keys might miraculously appear. "It doesn't matter, I like all the games. Don't you love to play cards? It's always a fresh hand. What's that they say? Cards have no memory."

Playing blackjack, Lydia found herself in the midst of one of those uncanny streaks of luck. She won every single hand. When they switched to hearts, it turned out to be a fairer game.

Win's gold-green eyes and his thick blond lashes reminded her of the summer days when she and Bobby had wandered through goldenrod and clover and swum in their favorite murky warm pond, diving into their reflections. She could fall into her own reflection in Win's eyes right now, for he was as fair as Bobby, and as lanky, and as winsome and young—trying to pretend he was like any ordinary earthling.

"Tell me about the future," she said. "Tell me about a world created by the human mind. I can't wait to live in that future."

He stared at her, his gaze humid and electrifying. They had barely touched, but they were lovers already. Something was wrong with one of her eyes, a childhood injury that caused her lid to droop when she was tired. It infuriated her. Thinking of it, she pried her lid open wide now and thought of how her fingers would crawl up his hot face.

Setting foot on the ground in the Honolulu airport the next morning, she felt for a weary moment that she had been nowhere, that she was stepping onto the same linoleum that covered the floors of the hospital, the funeral home, the Minneapolis hotel.

She never did make up her mind to miss her connecting flight, just stood in an alcove near some vending machines, pressing herself up against Win, trying to feel through his shirt his radioactive bones.

"Just what exactly is the deal with your marriage?" he said.

She buried her face into his shoulder and shook her head. She said a few lying words to him—not that they weren't the truth, but everything she said to him sounded like a lie. Staring down, she counted off the blossoms on her lei, holding its cool soothing petals to her cheek. She and her husband had made the deal long ago. Parting would be too expensive, in every way. Her life was at the restaurant. The night was hers, his the day.

She caught a glimpse of them as they walked past the vending machines, him with his knobby wrists poking out of his jacket, deep seams around his mouth, not aware or interested enough to alter the vacant expression on his face, hustling her along. The blue dents under her own eyes were merciless.

A cab took them to a motel with walls that trembled from the thundering of jets. Disposable walls, a disposable bed. He closed the door after them, and she pressed him into a corner until the roaring in her own ears was all she could hear. They stood by the front closet for so long that they started to joke about it: "We've got the room. We can go in, you know."

As they sat on the bed, she reached for a handful of his white hair, pulled him by it just a little bit so she could gaze at him, turn his head this way and that. "You're really very handsome." She kept her grip on his hair. "No, you are. But your hair is silky, not as thick as mine. Can you feel?" He grasped the hair at her nape and pulled till she could feel the blood pound. After their mother died, Bobby used to help her brush the snarls out of her long, coarse hair every morning till she cried.

They lay down still fully dressed, baking, sunlight on the old blinds casting a tintype glow. She pressed the base of her skull into the long, spongy bones of his arm and rolled her head back and forth. Then she inspected her lei, pinching at a waxy white flower and scoring it with her thumbnail. It sweated its gummy sweetness out into the heat.

Finally she turned sideways and began massaging his crumpled shoulders through his jacket, then opened his shirt to look at his gold skin, his fragile chest. "What else did the radiation do?" she asked.

"What have you heard about? Cabbages that grow and grow and grow, cucumbers like salami? In your dreams, Lydia." She laughed. She made a grab toward his belt, but he held her wrists till they smarted.

And then all she was aware of were his arms around her, his sharp musky scent, and planes thundering like tornadoes that never touched down. She strained into him, burying her head, bathing in the aura that surrounded him, the radiant air.

After many caresses and sighs, when their clothes were mostly off, she put her hand to his chest and pushed him away. She reached her arm over the side of the bed, feeling for her large purse, which she hauled up and heaved onto the bed beside them. "Do you have protection?"

"Of course." He felt in the pocket of his half-off shirt.

"Hold on a second."

He put his knuckles to his forehead. "Now what?"

She pressed her face roughly against his hand as if to dissolve herself into it, rubbing it, turning and twisting it, licking the place where the little thumb had been.

"Listen," she said desperately. "You've got to imagine something."

"I can imagine."

She pressed his vine tattoo to her cheek, trying to hold it there as she lit her cigarette. "Imagine him, imagine Bobby, taking a night off from Milo and relaxing one evening in a bar. A magnificent man comes up to him, smiling, wearing a metallic cape, striding like god. A man nearly seven feet tall." She made a few stabs at the ashtray with the cigarette, but it smoldered there as she sat up on the bed and straddled Win, sweat streaming down her face, her pantyhose clinging to one ankle.

"So the two of them had a beer. Then ten beers, or twenty, and the man says, 'I could have anyone here tonight, but I want you.' And Bobby thought, 'Why not?

He probably has something to teach me, or why did I meet him tonight?' Hah!"

Her gaze wavered over Win's face. "They'd both had a lot to drink and Bobby just had to give it a try. Just this once." She reached into the zippered pocket of her purse, where she had stashed poppers from Bobby's drawer. "So he took Bobby to his hotel room—not one like this, but luxurious, a jacuzzi and shining fixtures and a soft bed with downy covers and languorous jazz in the background—blissful."

She held the popper to Win's upper lip. "Breathe in, breathe in." He hesitated at first. She jolted the fumes into his nose and his head jerked back.

He inhaled and gasped. She gasped herself, then nestled into him for awhile, shivering as pleasure rocked their splayed bodies. "He was all over Bobby, and Bobby was in ecstasy, floating into nirvana, begging for more." She flexed the muscles of her thighs, her hair undone and hanging in sopping braids around her shoulders. "And Bobby asked if he was wearing a condom."

She stopped, looking at him ravenously, letting him know that anything he could give her she would drink, devour. She slid down beside him in the orange gloom of the room and tasted the salt of his sweat, running her arms along his long body, feeling him press his fingers over the curve of her torso, the arch of her shoulder. How sweet it was to be lying there with him, breathing when he breathed. She pressed his face to her chest and held it there, her fingertips on the bones of his frail shoulders and back, that felt porous as an egg carton.

She kissed him, and at first his mouth was raspy, dry, for, she knew, she had frightened him. She tried to go back to the beginning, to the early days when she and Bobby had read *Peyton Place* and practiced kissing with each other, rolling together on the bed in the storeroom one afternoon not too long after their mother died. They had never gone much beyond this, but she still remembered the tenderness of that time and tried to find it in herself so she could give it to Win. Finally his kiss grew softer, and he reached for her with a hand that was gentler than her own. He moved over her, to slam her hard with his downy blond belly. And Lydia had an afternoon such as she had not experienced for a long time, an afternoon that led her to recall how it had been once, in those days so long ago, when she had allowed herself to believe that her life might yet be happy.

Dusk was settling in when she began her tale again. The sweat streaming down their faces had begun to dry. He no longer complained about the cigarettes she smoked incessantly. He fidgeted a little when she began to speak, but she was not to be turned; she had to go on.

"Imagine it. He's starting to fuck Bobby, and he says he's wearing a condom, so Bobby lets it happen." Their sides were stuck together; they panted in the fading light. She lifted herself up on her elbow. "When it's over, Bobby asks to see the rubber. The guy says he's already thrown it away. But when Bobby stands up he sees blood isn't the only thing dripping. A son-of-a-bitch, huh?"

"For Christ's sake." Win lay flat on his back.

She put back her head and closed her eyes. "You know what he says, after it's all over?" She chuckled. "'I want to drink the rivers of love.' That's what he said to Bobby. 'Fuck it to safe-sex Nazi bullshit dry lovers.'"

Lydia couldn't stop her own bitter laugh. The story having dripped out of her, she, too, lay spent.

Win stroked her shoulder with his shimmery mutant hand. "He was lucky to have a sister like you to talk to."

"I only came because he was dying. And yes, he told me the story. A story I didn't feel at all." She stared at Win. "I'm not sorry for him, not in the least. I'm sorry he had to die. But that is a totally different thing." She opened her eyes wide as a jet thundered over, and the bed shuddered again on the creaky old floor.

Win sat up, startling her. "Can you feel it?" he said. "Look at the sun." The angle of light coming into the room had grown more intense, seemingly all at once, but in fact much time had passed since they first arrived. "The solar wind is leaping out at us all the time," he said. He held his hand up to the light, as if he could see the radiant energy pouring through it. "Who knows what's in it? I feel magnetic rays surrounding me all the time. Every time I pass a power line I can feel them, those deadly, jittery rays."

She pulled away from him sharply, an emphatic lurch. Did he have to say such weird, lame things? With all her might she pinched him on his crumpled, papier-mâché shoulder.

"What in the hell is wrong with you?" he said, grabbing her hand.

She was sure she had felt the muscles beneath his skin give way, tearing. "I'm sorry," she said. "I only meant it as a joke." She was ashamed. She stroked him till she sensed he had forgiven her—almost. "I just wish so much, Win. I wish I hadn't gone." As she lit up again, he waved her smoke away. She shook her head. "When we were kids, we were close. We took care of each other. My father nearly blinded me one day. He would have if Bobby hadn't stopped him." She blinked her smarting eye. "My father caught us in bed. But it was nothing, really. He misunderstood." Again, she pressed the strange hand to her brow.

She thought of seeing Bobby in the hospital that first day, his room very quiet, except for the hum of the oxygen, and cluttered and disassembled as a schoolboy's. Bobby had always been a slob, and it followed him to the very end. His face had been small and shrunken and deeply tan, with several days' growth of beard spiking out. He had known she was there, he said, because he could smell the smoke on her.

One morning as she sat with him, he had wanted her to fix his hair. When she pulled the brush through, a handful of dried, feeble strands came out in a wispy clump. Without even thinking, she had cast them down. "Don't you like my hair?" he had said. "You threw away my hair."

Lydia poured scotch into the plastic motel cup, offering Win a shot, too, which he bolted down.

"I couldn't believe he was dying," Lydia said. "I still don't quite believe it. He didn't know it was really over either—isn't that weird? That's what they say. The two things you can't look at for long before turning away: the sun and death." At the end, Bobby had wanted to hold only her hand. "You want to know the last words he ever said to me? 'If they try to make you go away, Lyddie, just act nervous. You're good at that.'"

They were silent then, watching the room darken with the twilight. Lydia thought again of the coldness that had been inside her, the stoniness with which she had watched all this happen. In some way, Bobby had hardened and solidified in her mind long before. Nothing could reanimate him.

"It was great of you to be there," Win said. "You did a good thing."

Her head lashed around. "Will you stop trying to make it nicer than it was? You don't have to protect me. I've accepted it." Bobby had turned into a strange, sad man who'd had something terrible happen to him. It had all taken place long ago. She chewed her lower lip.

Her gaze went right past him now. "Can you imagine what it was like for him to say to himself, 'If only I hadn't gone into that bar; if only I hadn't met that man.' And to relive it hour by hour, year by year? It would drive you insane, wouldn't it?" She sighed. "'Heroes die, cowards survive,' he told me. But it was too late for him."

Her chest rattled when she breathed. "The man in the cape—I guess he hadn't heard that humanity was supposed to be improving." She pressed her fingers to his forehead. "I'll bet there's no fate in the virtual world." She sat there naked on the bed, rocking back and forth, peering at him. "I used to be a nice person," she said. "Do you believe me? I don't know why you would."

"You are a good person," he said, roping a strand of her hair around his wrist. "You're just hurt."

Why did she think of him as a boy? Why did she think of him as young? He was thirty-five, hardly a child, a few brief years younger than she. His eyes, as hers, were glazed from seeing suffering and looking past it. He was just as corrupt as she. So why did she see him, through that long day and night to come, as her child, her baby, her tender young thing?

Still, it was she who got up the next morning knowing it had passed. When he came out of the bathroom, she was dressed and on the phone to her husband, saying, "I told you, I got sick. I haven't been able to call. So of course I'm not there yet. But the thing I wanted to ask you was—I've lost my keys. Yes, my whole set. I want you to look everywhere I was before you took me to the airport." She bucked when Win came up beside her to nuzzle her neck. He laughed so loud that she was afraid he could be heard through the muffled receiver.

When she hung up, he had his hand over his heart. Near it, where she had pinched him and dug in her nails, was a seeping purple bruise. "You're wounding me," he said. "You told your husband you'd be home tonight."

"Well, of course I'm going to leave."

"What do you mean, 'of course.' I didn't hear 'of course' yesterday or the day before."

She watched him walking nude with his penis flopping lazily around, as he continued to speculate in his soothing, gentle voice. "From what you've told me, you've got nothing with your husband. Why would you want to live that way?"

"Ah, such aggressive questioning," she said. She stretched her feet until they reached her lovely clear acrylic shoes with the toy tropical fish and ferns bubbling in the high heels. "How clever, Lydia," her customers would say. "How *you.*"

"Just like that? Back to your homophobe husband, who led you to turn your back on your only brother?"

"Will you shut up?" No trouble getting the volume up now. She put her hand over her eye, which was twitching madly.

Whatever had she seen in Win? She stared at his body, his big kid's body. She winced to think of some of the things she had done to him, the way she had lowered herself, and tended to him, licking him, grooming him, lovingly, lovingly, begging him to let her serve. It made her turn her head in shame. He was marginal, an embarrassing person. He was a decoy, a lost soul from Silicon Valley with no life to keep him from dropping everything and whiling away a day, two days with her, as long as she wanted.

"Ah, I see," he said. "Before you can turn your back you have to turn it into shit." Where had he gotten such churning, mournful eyes? Mutant eyes, green as algae from ancient seabeds.

"My god, you put up a front," he began again, but before she could hear more she walked out, heaving her bags before her, slamming the door.

He was as twisted as her husband, as twisted as she. She shouldn't have wasted her time.

Lydia's husband found her keys under the hibiscus bushes next to the garage. She had never taken them anywhere.

One night a few weeks later, she was sitting on the lanai after the restaurant had closed, listening to the quiet lap of the water, but she could not enjoy the loveliness, thinking of Bobby and of how all the dearest memories had come back to her, but only when there was nothing left to change. The sound system piped out eerie, mournful ballads through the closed restaurant doors. She had forgotten to turn it off, as had happened many times before. This music played tinnily to nobody through the deep tropical night, as if all the ears to listen to it were dead. She sat staring at that place where the moon touched down on the black water and dissolved into a wavering candle, a rich pure paving of shining gold. Her lei was a ruin, with a few discolored flowers still clinging. She tried to snap the string, but it held. She kept it in the closet, where a stale floral stench remained long after the lei had rotted off the hook.

Queen

ADRIAN HAD BEEN HIDING in a corner of the church basement for about fifteen minutes when the bandleader, guiding his blind vocalist to the men's room, backed her into her father's huge birthday cake. "Excuse me," he said insincerely.

Fortunately, Adrian's raw silk dress was sleeveless. Though she'd made a huge dent in the cake, she hadn't soiled the exquisite material of her clothes. She did, however, have a thick curd of frosting along one arm. Dabbing at it with a napkin, she peeked fitfully back at the party.

Under a birthday banner, amid bobbing balloons and his hovering sisters, her father Jeb held court on a couch. Nearest him, shoving the aunts aside, fluttered her younger sister, Luna, thirty-five, long a member of the worker caste. She'd undoubtedly dragged the couch, folding chairs, and cake into the basement.

She had also undoubtedly decorated the cake with ingenious sugary bumblebees, dragonflies, thrips, treehoppers, and a couple of ants crawling over honey-colored frosting. "Don't bug Jeb on his 70th Happy Birthday," it had read, but most of "Happy" was now on Adrian's arm.

Adrian absently brought a gob of frosting to her lips. Sweetness rushed into her and she shuddered, remembering how, all those years ago, she had first started overeating. Involuntarily she gobbled dab after dab of the icing. It had begun so, at her mother's funeral, this shoving of her to the sidelines. She was thirteen; it should have been she who moved into the void to tend to Jeb. But he had looked at her burgeoning bosom as if it were a crippling deformity, then reached out a palp and drew Luna to him.

There Luna bent over him, pouring cream in his coffee, shoving aside the pleats of the dress she wore like a feminine uniform. "Daddy, are you all right?" Luna asked. She swirled, casting tart, formidable glances at Aunt Drew, Aunt Julia, Aunt Jolene. They were supposed to ask, too.

"Yes, Jeb," they buzzed, "is there anything we can get you?" They sent out feelers, petting him, seeming to know everything they needed to know from the brush of a tentacle, the hiss of a feathery leg going by. Luna automatically touched his temple, making sure his hairpiece stayed securely attached. He'd finally made the transition to powdery gray. Fifteen years ago, he'd kept the wig a bold tar black.

A swishing cane flicked Adrian's ankles. The bandleader repeated his accusatory, "Excuse me," and shoved the relieved vocalist past her, back into the celebration.

His sharp tone activated Luna's antennae. She looked up briskly, then gasped. Quickly, she strode through the tables. Jaw slack with disbelief, she stopped within three feet of Adrian. "Adie?" she asked.

Years, years since anyone called her "Adie." Luna came closer, grabbed her with shiny, segmented fingers. Adie, her lips pursed on a morsel of gooey sweetness, felt an intoxicating recrudescence of sleepy, intimate sisterly love.

"What are you doing here?" Luna asked.

"Well, it is his seventieth," Adrian said.

"But you weren't here for the sixtieth, or the sixty-fifth," Luna said unanswerably. "Oh, my God," she cried. "What have you done to the cake?"

"I'm truly sorry about the cake," Adrian began. "The bandleader—" But the music had already started up, and to be heard she had to raise her voice or come in close. "I'm here because I've got a fabulous present in mind for you," Adrian said, drawing near, wanting Luna to notice her costly dress, its rare material. Oh, what Adrian could do for Luna if Luna would give her the chance.

"I want to take you around the world," Adrian continued. Luna was grabbing napkins from around the cake, frantic to repair the damage. "I want you to see that the world doesn't begin and end here. It could be an entomological safari, if you want. Africa, South America, India. But what I'd like you to see are the places in the world where people live like ants, like bees—where they've actually built hives for themselves."

Luna looked up with compressed lips. She'd always been pretty with her pointed nose and her thin eyebrows, jagged as lightning bolts. She was not pretty, however, as she said, "Daddy's had a stroke, didn't you know? He's not going anywhere, and I'd never go without him."

The aunts were beginning to head over.

"How could I know?" asked Adrian.

"Besides," Luna snapped, "given the way you made your money, what makes you think we'd want any of it, Adie? Everyone knows you're a hooker."

The aunts swarmed to them, whispering, flitting, staring with their compound eyes, smelling, feeling, tasting the air with their tongues, sensory organs everywhere.

"Adrian? How nice to see you," said Aunt Drew.

"Are you here for long?" asked Aunt Julia.

"Whatever have you been up to? Luna said you were in—was it Chicago?" asked Aunt Jolene.

Far across the humming room she felt her dad's eye alight on her for the first time, then swiftly move away. Furiously, she drew a finger along her arm and sucked frosting from it, absorbing its sweetness into herself. He always could pretend to be blind and deaf. Or maybe it was the stroke. He looked at her again. She waved and saw his hand rise woodenly. Luna followed the transaction, then flew protectively back to their father. The aunts bumbled uncertainly.

The band played ever louder. "Full moon and empty arms," began the vocalist in a vibrating tenor. What kind of song was that for an elderly widower's birthday party?

Through a series of smells, Adrian gradually drifted into consciousness. First was the dry, dissolving dust on the frames and trays full of insects that filled her old room. She'd pawed them off of her bed the night before, adding them to the precarious arrangements that tottered all around, connected here and there by fragile cobwebs. She opened her own eyes to face minute collections of sightless, petrified eyes from every corner. A dead room, a storeroom, a minimausoleum in a far corner of the hive. There was none of her own smell left in the bed. For long years the sunlight had filtered through the yellow parchment blinds and into her room, the sun lapping up, the sun lapping back, curing, curling.

She lay in a room of preserved oak treehoppers, locust treehoppers, and thorn mimic treehoppers, the strange-looking jumping insects on which her dad had built his academic career, an ill-fated career for that matter . . . he was supposed to get an appointment at the University of Minnesota, then didn't get it, then his own father had died, leaving him nothing. All the collections, all the killings. When he was a young entomologist, he would take Adrian out to observe and draw, collecting notes and victims. She remembered sitting with him on lovely mornings in the woods, Mother and Luna far away, just her and her father out in the forest near the St. Croix, the two of them arrayed on a blanket in front of a milkweed plant, recording all the insect activity they saw for a whole morning—mites, bees, ants, spiders, leafhoppers. She drew pictures for him as he wrote, the two of them baking in the sun, freckles on their arms, caps on their black hair.

Adrian had barely known he wore a wig because she rarely saw him without it. To her he was handsome as a god. In fact, she had thought he was god, the god of bugs.

Mother would tease him about it sometimes, the dreaded encroachment of baldness, and he would soak his feet in solutions while she massaged his head, trying to coax the hair back.

Now, as she opened the dusty bedroom door, Adrian smelled the tang of glue that always told her she was home, vapor from the adhesive that her father used to stick on the toupee.

One shocking day on the school playground, Adrian had overheard Luna laughing with some kids: "My daddy's got a squirrel and he keeps it in a box in the bathroom."

Weeks later, Adrian sat tending their ailing mother in the back bedroom when they heard Luna marching three of her little girlfriends into the bathroom to show them. "This is where my daddy keeps his squirrel!"

Adrian was frantic, with Mother so sick and all her rules for protecting Daddy being broken. Then they heard Daddy's footsteps pass through the living room. He was headed for the bathroom. Surely he would punish Luna severely, murdering her, perhaps, as he murdered bugs in his new business, spraying her with poison, drenching her with liquid nitrogen.

But he didn't. He merely laughed at the squealing

nine-year-olds and with his booming voice chased them from the bathroom, bellowing in that ringing baritone that tamed even Adrian, made her feel connected and grounded.

Why had he suddenly tolerated Luna? Why was Luna now channeling the dead Mother, not Adrian? Why was Luna doing what Mother had always done, defending Jeb and sacrificing herself for others? The pungent glue scent held Adrian at the top of the stairs, filling her with awe rather than comforting her, announcing as it did the presence of royalty, the king of the hive. How strange. Shouldn't it be a queen?

She found her father in the living room, passed out on the love seat. He'd put a napkin over his bare pate but it had slipped off. For the first time she saw his shiny bald head, a blunt, wide, earnest head like the head of her stout, bearish grandfather—briefly, vividly remembered now—Grandfather who had once accidentally burned Adrian with a cigar ash when she was a little girl sitting in his lap. Looking aghast and tender, he had apologized profusely, hugged and kissed her. He'd nearly started to cry. How had such a kind father given rise to such a cruel son?

But he had not always been cruel: those mornings in the meadows, the impassioned lectures he prepared for his students and practiced on Mother and Adrian. He had changed when Mother died, no, just after, when Adrian's huge breasts swelled forth and the junior high school boys soaped on the house windows, even on Dad's car windshield, "Big Boobs," the swarms of buzzing boys. Adrian had been mortified, but when she turned to Jeb for solace, he stared at her breasts in revulsion: "No woman in my family ever had a chest like that—or in your mother's either. It's freakish."

She tiptoed away lest she awaken him. Unthinkable

that he should know she'd seen his naked head. An intrusion into the holy of holies.

A final odor overwhelmed her as she walked down the hall to the back entrance of the shop, the toxic, stomach-turning reek of Pegasus Pest Control. Hardening herself against the awful soaking stench, she opened the door and let the shop's smell hit her, an all-body assault. At the far end of the counter, even Luna, talking on the phone, seemed stiff and pickled, with low affect, as if afraid to breathe too much, as if to keep as many chemicals from getting into her as she could.

Luna's shoulders were hunched, her head bent, as she gave out information. "Well, it could be mice. Where are you from, the South? No we don't have any termites up here, what we've got is carpenter ants." Luna paused, her head tilted attentively. Was she still pleased with herself? When Luna was a little girl, it had seemed to Adrian that she had been born pleased with herself.

Standing in the doorway, tapping her foot, Adrian felt infused by pesticide fumes, not a teasing vapor like the wig glue but an aggressive, odoriferous stench that let you know your neurons were being bombarded, and particles bouncing into nose, throat, lungs. She suspected that inhaling these poisons had contributed to her mother's death, knew this was what had caused her father's stroke, and yet they kept working here.

"Well, the way you can tell carpenter ants," Luna was saying, "is that you can hear them in the walls at night."

But you don't always pay attention, do you, Adrian was thinking to herself, you don't always know when to pay attention because the buzzing and the chipping are going on all the time, aren't they, and you can hear them but you don't want to know what it all means.

"It's kind of a weird sawing sound or a feathery hum. Have you seen winged ants in the house?" Luna checked her log. "Well, we could probably come over this afternoon. About three? No, it's an unmarked van."

When Luna hung up the phone, Adrian walked over to her. Luna's eyes scanned her warily. She knew how to keep Adrian at a distance. "So you're here to amaze us," Luna said. "Well, I told Dad, and you know what he said? She's amazed us enough already."

Adrian felt a pain so dangerous she thought it was going to swallow her up. I am not this evil person, she murmured to herself, but her lips were not moving. Why is she trying to banish me from their lives?

"I've seen amazing things," Adrian murmured. "Things that have changed me and that could change you, too, if you'd just get beyond—" her hand moved in an awkward arc—"this dreary place."

"I just can't forget all the times Daddy and I cried after you left," Luna said, her head bent. "Are you still working?"

"No, I've retired."

"Well, then. Maybe now Mother can rest in peace."

In the plate glass of the storefront, Adrian saw the painted-on picture of Pegasus—a winged horse, creature of power and triumphant sexuality. Adrian couldn't stop staring. Blinding afternoon light etched her reflection into the plate glass, a firm, fit mate for the flying horse.

Luna stood up. "What are you doing?" Adrian asked.

"Didn't you hear me? I'm heading out to Prospect Park to see about some guy's carpenter ants."

"You're going?"

Luna put her hands on her hips. "Dad isn't doing too many housecalls anymore."

"Well, I'll go along with you."

Back in the house, Dad was still asleep. When Adrian came down in a blouse and slacks, Luna frowned. "If you wear those clothes, you'll get stung and bitten to death." In Luna's room, they had trouble finding a long-sleeved shirt and heavy pants big enough for Adrian. Even Adrian's gloves were too fancy to be of use and she had to slip into some old ones of her dad's that were in the shed out back.

"I've got to go wake Daddy up," Luna said. "I have to tell him I'm leaving so he can sit in the store and answer the phone."

"You're sending him into the store in his state?" Adrian said. "Those pesticides probably caused his stroke."

"He's doing very well for seventy," Luna said. "The doctor said it was his strong constitution that helped him survive."

"But all those warnings on the bottles and cans. . . . If you can smell the stuff, you know it's not going to do you any good."

Grimly, Luna crossed her arms. "You'd better go wait in the car. If he sees you here, it will just upset him." Apparently the look on Adrian's face caused her to soften her tone a little bit. "He's got to get used to it gradually. It's just upset him that you've come back so fast, without any warning."

"Let me just say good afternoon to him," Adrian said.

In the living room, Luna put the napkin back on Jeb's head and held it there as she gently tugged on his arm. "Dad? Dad? Adrian's here."

Adrian saw his eyes flutter open. When they lighted on her, it felt like a javelin throw.

"Dad," said Adrian. Her lips stuck to her teeth as she tried to smile.

"Hello, Adrian." He looked away, the father with more powers than Spider Man. Well, somebody had to try to do it. Somebody had to try and halt the circle of pain. She put out her hand to shake his and he stared at it as if it were some vile thing, a hand that caressed strange men's most secret parts, a wanton hand. But finally his eyes rested not on her face but on her breasts, the breasts of the lush, plush sexual woman, flowing with milk and honey.

"I'll wait outside," Adrian said.

Inside the van, Adrian turned on the ignition for the air. Even in here the smell lingered. Anybody who'd ever set off a bug bomb and gotten sick sensed the truth about those chemicals. She had no doubt that she had allergies, dizzy spells, depression, because she'd grown up inhaling the sprays. Luna herself seemed sexless, and there was no convincing Adrian that this wasn't the effect of those toxins slamming into her.

When she joined Adrian in the van, Luna said she was hungry. "I could eat," Adrian said. At the diner, Luna ordered bacon and eggs with hash browns and Adrian ordered turkey on dry toast.

Luna was looking at Adrian thoughtfully. "You're looking fine," She said.

Adrian petted her own clunky arms self-consciously. "You, too," Adrian lied, seeing before her a haunted visage, skin slick over the skull.

"I didn't think you'd look that good," Luna said. "I thought the life you'd been living—that it was hard."

"Hard?" Adrian said, stalling. She had known that she and Luna were going to have to have this conversation. Fifteen years ago, Adrian had left Minneapolis for Chicago and taken a job in a cocktail lounge. As usual, her breasts had drawn looks, and offers. Before too long, she was working in a place that was raided. Someone had obligingly sent the newspaper clips home to Jeb and Luna. She'd written every Christmas, sent cards and money on birthdays, and occasionally received a note from Luna at her post office box. "As a matter of a fact," Adrian said now, "in some ways, it's an easy way to make your living."

"But did you sleep with anybody? Just anybody?" Luna was letting her food get cold, staring at her open-mouthed.

Images flicked through Adrian's mind. She tried a few offhand remarks, but despite her plan, they sounded depraved. Joey, with only stubs of his fingers left, swollen sausagey stubs reaching out to her . . . his patronage alone would have made her rich. Charlie, his penis a pencil stub. Sometimes she felt more like a therapist or a public health worker, only better-paid. "Well, of course I did. I was a professional. I trained myself to be above revulsion."

"But did you get to keep all your money?"

"What kind of question is that? Of course I kept my money."

"You mean, you didn't have to give it to a pimp?"

Adrian laughed. "Why would I do something so dumb? I kept it and I invested it." Adrian looked at Luna dead on. She'd made a lot of money and earned every cent of it. Why should she be ashamed? It was the American way.

Adrian was finished with her food, but Luna had barely begun.

"Don't you want something more?" Luna said.

"No, I licked all that frosting off my arm at Dad's party. You know how easily I gain weight."

"If you ate something once in awhile, you wouldn't always be starving and so interested in other people's food, watching them eat."

"I'm not watching you," said Adrian. She made a deliberate effort to look away now, and her eyes rested, of course, on the busboy she'd noticed when she came in, with his dark brown skin and light green eyes and the faint hint of a mustache. Sexy males had always gotten her into trouble.

The busboy moved majestically about his tasks, his eyes full of defiant resolve. She was used to spending her time around people who lived on the barest fringes of ordinary life, struggling to create a sense of order.

"Have some of my food. I know you want it," Luna said. She made a small plate with bacon, eggs and toast. "Go ahead, eat it," Luna said.

Slowly, Adrian forked up some eggs, chewed on a piece of bacon. "And the sounds you make when you eat!" Luna exclaimed, catching Adrian in midbite. "Little moaning noises. Food is such a big deal for you."

"I told you, I'm not hungry," Adrian said irritably, pushing the food away. Now she felt self-conscious eating in front of the secure Luna, so sure of herself. Luna had her own home. There was no doubt in Luna's mind that she belonged in this world.

"Dad never made you ashamed of your body the way he made me ashamed," Adrian said. "From the time that Mother died he was after me all the time, making cracks about my breasts, expressing his disgust, saying he'd never take out a woman who looked like me . . . and I was thirteen years old!"

"Oh, that again," Luna said, rolling her eyes. "It's Daddy's fault. Everything's Daddy's fault. Why don't you just leave him out of it?"

"He's not a very nice man. I think he felt guilty about Mother, just ignoring her after she got sick and all. Letting her die in the back room. I was the only one who paid any attention to her."

Luna stiffened. "Will you just stop it about Daddy?" Luna said, staring at Adrian with her sickened, burning eyes. "All the money you sent—I gave it away. I gave it to Children of the Night. I knew you did that—job—just to humiliate Daddy."

"No I didn't," Adrian said. "I did it to make money. As unskilled labor, what options did I have?" All she'd had were her love of bugs and her sexual drive, her brains and her bosom—and her bosom seemed a much surer thing.

"Give me a break," Luna said.

"I didn't say everything was Daddy's fault," Adrian continued, looking down. "But don't you ever think of what your life could be like without him? If you could just travel, get away from all the limits he places on you. Luna, listen to me. I'm your sister, I care about you." She spoke firmly, trying to show how she'd reconstituted herself into a robust, whole person.

This was what she had come so far to say. She'd met so many men in the past few years who barely kept themselves together, who lived empty joyless lives they could hardly stand, trapped in dead jobs or marriages, going out of their minds with boredom and despair, men whose visits to her, or her friends, were what made their lives bearable . . . men who, like Jeb, seemed terrifying and all-powerful but who gave all that up in the refuge of a secret place. Yes, people hid a lot of pain, and as her dad had been wrong to condemn her totally, so she, too, had been wrong to condemn. But it was wrong of him to keep Luna from going anywhere, seeing anything. "You used to be such a spunky kid. He's got you enslaved now, too, the way he had Mother enslaved," Adrian said. "He's got you doing everything for him."

"Just because you were so cold," Luna said. "And distant. We all knew how smart you were." Her brain had been a hazard to her throughout her working life, whenever ideas tried to struggle up through her deadened emotions. "You never felt anything for any of us."

"I felt something for you."

"But he caught you with Derek! You were making love with Derek on Dad's bed!"

"Derek," Adrian said, licking a pointed tongue over her sharp front teeth. "What an absurd choice—God, Derek! I was an idiot."

Adrian had been sixteen years old, convinced by Derek to make love in Jeb's bed. Jeb had walked in on them. In the vicious days and months that followed, any claim that Adrian might have had in that family to human dignity was permanently effaced.

She remembered the bulging veins of her father's fist, his furious hand smiting her. This was the first time in years that he'd really noticed her, when she was breaking all the rules.

Luna had been a helpless eleven, but Jolene, Julia, and Drew did nothing to intervene, made no move to protect Adrian against her father's malice, the screaming and beatings. "He just wasn't meant to be a parent," Jolene once said, but beyond that had offered little information. The loss of pride in herself that made her drop out of school, her choice of Derek, the birth of their sick little baby, the death of that baby that had triggered her descent into the worst kind of despair . . . her father knew where it came from, and Adrian knew it, too.

But it was worse to be alone, wasn't it, Adrian thought now, feeling a twinge of envy for Luna. People went to great lengths to avoid belonging nowhere, to no one. They made sacrifices to be around familiar sights and sounds, to grab a piece of bacon with a shiny pincer, as Luna did now, saying, "Let me get this straight. *You* want to save *me?*"

Adrian ignored her. "I wonder what made Dad so mean and bitter," Adrian said musingly, staring off into the middle distance. "Mother's death? Not getting the university job and having to change from bug lover to bug killer? Grandpa leaving all his money to the church? Or maybe it was the way he lost his beauty, losing his hair—the squirrel."

Luna looked at her furiously. Adrian hugged her plush arms. She understood so much more about it now, the hive's ruthless discipline, the necessity of someone to enforce it.

ADRIAN saw a large, outlandish-looking stucco on a cheerful street of splendid and eccentric dwellings built along stiff inclines of hills not far from the Mississippi headlands. Set on a winding street beneath the Witch's Tower, a looming old water tower shaped like a witch's hat, the house they were seeking was fronted by a steep slope of wild flowerbeds and a decaying deck.

"Can you see it?" As they sat out in front, Luna gave Adrian a conspiratorial look. "Can you see the ways those carpenter ants could be getting in?" Luna had picked up her father's competent, professional tone. "The branches extending over the house—they could walk right in on those, perfect tree-branch highways. Or they could trip right in through the wires over there, not to mention walk up that deck and squeeze in the windows." Adrian followed Luna to the back of the van. Clucking, shaking her head, Luna took out a clipboard and a briefcase.

Over her shoulder, Adrian stared at the wooded overgrown hill that led to the witch's hat, where on a happy summer day many years before she and her mother and father had hiked to the top and climbed up the fantastic old tower, pungent with moss and ringing with the rich trickling of water that had fallen through the same sloughs for a hundred years. Luna hadn't even been born. It had just been the three of them, believing unquestioningly that Daddy would get the university job and they'd all live in Prospect Park.

No, Luna didn't remember *that* father, kind, easygoing and benevolent, in the times long before their mother had died. The father Luna had known had been forsaken and in need of saving, while the father Adrian grew up with already had a wife.

In plaid workshirts, gloves, and long pants, neutered workers Adrian and Luna walked up a cobbled path of broken stones. Whitish lace curtains seemed to be mildewing from the inside. They stood on the broken boards of the porch listening to the reverberation of a bell.

"Did you used to make housecalls?" Luna asked with a lift of her brow.

Adrian tried to straighten herself.

"No, of course not," she said, striving to keep her composure. "If you go to their place, you never know what to expect. It was safer just to stay at Candy's duplex."

"The whorehouse was somebody's duplex?"

"That's where we worked, yes."

As the door swung suddenly open, Adrian's face went crimson. A florid-faced man in his fifties stood there. Had he heard? A medium-sized white guy with pale blue sun-faded eyes and a friendly smile.

"Come on in, Pegasus," he said, a little apologetically. "Odean Odegard." Scandinavian, of course—Norwegian, probably, with that rusty, curly hair swelling into a pompadour, a proud vestige of his youth. His hands were shiny with callouses. "Go by Odie," he said, but Odie didn't go with this house. He seemed more like the working men, the plumbers and electricians, who came by droves to Candy's in Chicago.

"Glad you could come over so soon." He pointed up the stairs. "My mother's old cousin just died and willed us the house. So I come up from South Carolina to clean it out. Cousin Viola was married to a professor and they got a ton of books."

They walked into a scene of traumatic disarray, lives moved half in, half out. "I was supposed to get it ready to sell, but wait till you see the attic. " A sagging couch was covered with pristine floral print upholstery. Florid wallpaper of what looked like expiring hydrangeas persisted fitfully, sagging and torn off in places, as they started up the stairs.

"I got here yesterday," Odie said. "When I tried to sleep, I kept hearing these rasping sounds." As they reached the second floor landing, Luna stopped them at the windowsill.

"Aha," Luna said, and, reaching into her pocket, she pulled out a baggy, then swept a rapidly-moving ant into it with her gloved hand. "Dad will want to see this. Look at the size of her." The winged black ant was nearly half an inch long. "Did you see the way she tried to bite me?"

"She?" Odie said.

"Absolutely," Adrian said, moving in, taking over. "It's a mature female. Once they have wings, they don't grow anymore." Luna seemed startled as Adrian took the baggy from her hand and held it up to the light. All three stared at the ant. "Carpenter ants have one node. Can you see it there? That makes them different from other ants. And they have small hairs on their undersides." Adrian squinted hard, trying to detect hairs as the ant squirmed frantically in the baggy. "Could be a queen searching for a new place to start a nest. Then the others will follow. It's amazing how they know how to find her, how to nurture her. When you've got winged forms in the house, colonies are already established." Adrian handed the ant back to Luna.

Luna put her ear to the wall beside the window, then tapped on it. They heard a hollow sound. "Probably in there."

"Look at that, will you?" Everyone followed Adrian's pointing finger. From a corner of the window, a trail of large brownish-black ants marched up the wall and onto some trim about seven feet from the floor, heading up the stairs. "Probably going from the main nest to the satellite colonies."

"Satellites?" asked Odie, crestfallen.

Luna smiled grimly. "I'm afraid you've got a real infestation here." They followed the line of ants, climbing up a narrow passageway where Odie opened a door to a windowless room with books massed up to the ceiling. Hundreds, maybe thousands of books were piled wherever Adrian turned, and all along the walls were little heaps of finely shredded wood shavings and dead ants. Some of the stacks of books, shuddering indistinctly against the eaves, were thick with fungus. Luna began to cough. "Sorry. I guess I've got a touch of asthma." On the floor, in all directions, trails of ants marched silently.

"Luna, how could you have let your health get this bad?" Adrian said.

"I don't think Cousin Viola ever went out of the house," Odie said, squinting at the scene in horror. "When they found her in that back bedroom, she'd been dead a week." He turned away. Yes, it was amazing how the hive took over, how the colony saw its chances, sensing them in its teeming collective brain. Odie shifted from foot to foot, following along as Luna tapped the wall voids, the floors, the hollow place behind a trap door, and began probing with a sharp prong like an ice pick. All through the room, she pounded with her pick. "They're everywhere the wood is moist enough," she said to Odie. "In those shade trees out back, in the stump, and I'll bet they're in your deck—I told you that as soon as we drove up here, didn't I, Adie."

"God, it's awful. How did they all get up here?" he said. "I mean, I heard those rustling sounds at night, and I thought, maybe there are mice up in the attic, hell, I can handle that, and then . . ."

Odie had a crooked nose, an open gaze. Adrian watched him, standing as near to him as she could get, drawn to his confusion. Yes, she had spent too much time at Candy's. She couldn't meet a man without thinking of what it would be like to see him with his clothes off, to imagine the feel of his rubbery penis . . . and then he caught her looking at him.

With a mighty heave of her ice pick, Luna broke open a fungus-covered cabinet near the top of the wall and hordes of ants came streaming out rhythmically, hesitating and then swarming out again. It was like the beating of a heart.

"For heaven's sake," Odie said in despair. "There must be a million of them. How in the hell did they all get in here?"

"Ants are amazing," Adrian said breathlessly. "They find their way by light patterns and gravity." She touched her leg, unfortunately hidden by her thick pants." They can follow a trail of molecules left in the air . . ."

"Adie, chill, will you?" Luna said, but Odie seemed struck by her talk.

"Our father was an entomologist," Adrian said, "and when I was a little girl he taught me about all this stuff. He used to read me articles, take me out with him and . . ."

Luna made a mighty jab with her pick into another hollow place in the wall and bits of soil, wood flakes and ant corpses floated after them in a suffocating shower.

They all fled the attic, Luna coughing uncontrollably.

"We have to go back down to the van, Adie," Luna said, trembling on the landing. Adrian winced with every one of her wracked, resonating coughs. "I've got an electrogun there and some liquid nitrogen and some chemicals that, unfortunately, we're going to have to leave around because the infestation is so bad. If we start an all-out assault on them right now, we may be able to save the house."

"It's an issue of saving the house?" Odie asked desperately.

"I'm afraid so," Luna said, in her most consoling bedside manner. "I'll head downstairs and get the chemicals and equipment we need. Coming, Adrian?"

Adrian looked expectantly at Odie. "I think we've got to get a better idea of where the colonies are," Adrian said. "I'm going to take Odie around and we'll look . . . all right, Odie?" She could feel the late afternoon sun baking down on the top of the house. A miasma of moist, yeasty air shifted around them. "And you, Luna, go down there immediately and put on your protective gear."

To her surprise, Adrian found she still had the authority of an older sister. Obeying her, Luna turned and walked alone down the stairs to the van.

"There are so many different kinds of remarkable species . . . but the carpenter ant is the most incredible," Adrian said, pointing out to Odie another trail of ants, the two chordates walking gingerly, respectfully around the arthropods, Odie listening in what seemed like fascination, drinking in her words, and she couldn't stop talking to him. "Carpenters can eat away large parts of the architecture."

"They eat wood?"

"They don't eat it, no." They sat in the stairwell, watching the ants stream in the cracked windowsill, clearly using the branches of a resplendent oak as their thoroughfare. "They excavate these mazes, these elaborate tunnels, galleries really, and then they live in them. They polish up the galleries. They carry away the woody debris and push it out through slits they cut to the outside. You know that rain of sawdust we were just in upstairs, bits of ant bodies and wood flakes flying out into the room?"

"Christ," Odie said.

"But they're not all bad," Adrian said, smiling at his horror. "I'll bet your old cousin doesn't have any bedbugs. Carpenter ants suck the juices of other insects. They suck them dry."

"Aunt Viola was in pretty rough shape when they found her," Odie said. "Maybe . . ." His voice trailed off. He ran his hands over his body, cringing. "There's a jar in the cupboard with honey oozed out at the top and all along the base. Around there was the first place I saw them."

"Yeah, they'll eat sweets, too, they love sweets." Adrian tapped on the wall, all the forgotten lore coming back to her in an exquisite rush. "My father used to tell me all these things. I thought I was going to be an entomologist, too, when I grew up, and then . . ." She smiled into Odie's eyes. "What do you do?"

"I work for the railway in Charleston. But I live in an apartment building." The two of them kneeled and followed with their eyes a scurrying trail of ants.

"There could be a few thousand in each colony," Adrian said. "The little tunnels they drill for themselves, you can't imagine. They're so beautiful, galleries in the wood . . . the most mysterious works of art." On her hands and knees, she crawled toward the dishwasher. "Here's another colony, anyway, right here in the wall void. See the slits where they've thrown the dead out? This is molted ant skin, right here. When an insect is young, it's covered by skin that's like a shell, only it stretches. Then when there's too much flesh beneath the skin, the shell just splits wide open and a new skin begins to harden."

They heard the thump of Luna's footsteps on the lower back deck as she made her preparations to eradicate the neurons, the ganglia of a huge community brain. Luna, like her father before her, was a warrior against bugs that chomp and bite, trespass on human space, damage houses and antique tables, destroy papers, suck blood, spread bacteria, ruin flour and sugar.

"They bounce back from anything!" Adrian said. "I'm fascinated by the whole concept. They're so . . . streamlined." *Not hulking creatures, bursting and redundant, and sick with it, all that memory . . .*

Luna rose into their sight, appearing gradually, her face in a blue plastic mask with a tube nose and goggles, her body in what looked like a space suit.

Odie opened the door for her. "Shouldn't we go upstairs with you?" he asked weakly.

"No," Luna said, pausing beside them on the landing. Her voice bounced hollowly within the mask. "I'm going to be using chemicals all over the attic. No one should come up here for awhile unless they're masked."

In the kitchen it was hot, but when Odie opened the window he let in the dreamy afternoon outside. Adrian and Odie lingered in the puddle of shimmering, wavering green. He got her a glass of lemonade from a pitcher in the refrigerator.

"I'll bet this is going to cost me a fortune," Odie said drearily. "I told Mother, just hire somebody to take care of it. This is something I know nothing about. But she was sure we'd get cheated if I didn't come up myself."

Adrian looked at him closely. Yes, even he was connected, everyone was connected, to long lines of sisters, brothers, aunts, cousins, and others to whom people pretended to be enslaved but gratefully embraced, thankful to be kept from floating off—but to where?

Adrian took the lemonade from the kitchen table, saw more ants marching across the kitchen floor from the back door toward the dishwasher.

"I know what Luna's going to tell you," Adrian said. "She'll say you're going to have to prune those tree branches and keep them from touching the house. You're going to have to plug the electrical line and pipe entryways with caulk and put pretreated woods all around your window frames. Come down here," she said, leading him over to the dishwasher where they knelt on the floor. "They've excavated all through here, can you see it? They've been attracted by the moist wood near the water. They're in the joists. You're going to have to repair the leaks, correct the drainage system . . ."

Adrian smiled at Odie's quivering lip. "It's really quite wonderful, in a way. It's too bad we have to destroy them." She thought of their silent presence, all the ants in their shadowy galleries, sleeping in the afternoon sun. "Lovely galleries like the Anazazi used to build in the rocks, or the halls the Nabataeans built in Petra. Have you ever been to Petra?" He looked at her inquiringly. "All pink sand and huge pillars carved into the cliffs. Funeral chambers." She looked into his eyes. "I want to take my sister there. Just to look, you understand."

Upstairs they could hear the wheeze of an engine, Luna's heavy footsteps. "I've been all over the world. But it's hard sometimes . . . being alone."

She was older, she knew. She was no longer what she had been in the days when she had been making so much money so fast that the other women hated her and refused to work on the same shift with her.

Yes, interest in her large breasts and in Adrian herself had been declining, definitely dwindling in the last few years. But she wasn't ugly, either.

What would Odie be like beneath his clothes? Pink and shrimplike and shiny, like an arthropod that's just cracked off its old skin? Would he want her to kiss him or would he turn his face away?

She had thought these things about the young man in the restaurant. She'd thought it about the farmers she had talked to in the smalltown bars on her way from Chicago. And she thought it now about Odie, bashful, humiliated Odie, righteous railway worker doing a family task, doing a favor for his mother and finding a house inhabited by a swarming mass of form and feeling that

Luna might, just might, be able to eradicate. . . . Odie looked at her shrewdly now, in a sizing-up kind of way, while upstairs Luna tramped, trailing long arcs through the galleries with her silvery wand.

Sex had been so much a part of Adrian's life—now it had been months since she'd been near anyone at all. She yearned to touch Odie, and that reminded her of how starving she was inside, starving—but it was Jeb and Luna she hungered for. She saw out of the corner of her eye a bumbly, feathery ant feeling its way toward the closed-up jar of honey.

She held her arms stiff, not allowing herself to move toward Odie.

"Adie!"

Luna, electrogun in hand, stood in the doorway.

"I wasn't doing anything."

It was late that night when they came back to the house. Near the shed in the backyard, Luna and Adrian washed their boots, their goggles. They rinsed off their rubber shoes before entering the house.

"I'm going to take a shower," Luna said.

Adrian walked into the house alone and found Jeb in the kitchen. He was sitting at the table having a plate of birthday cake. He'd taken off his squirrel and was wearing a fisherman's hat. The house reeked of glue remover.

Repulsive, vain, Adrian had thought about him when she was a teenage girl, yet she never dreamed of razzing him as Luna had. Now she didn't think anything.

When she sat down with him at the kitchen table, he barely looked up.

"So are you here for awhile?" he asked, staring into the cake. Adrian clutched her arms around herself, watching him eat what was left of Luna's creation, the caved-in assaulted cake with its thick buttercream and egg-rich layers. Sweet, sweet. Although he masked it well, she knew his whole body rose and swelled toward the sweetness.

For awhile she sat there. Then, all at once, she had to resist a powerful urge to put her head down on the table. She was tired, so very, very tired.

"Luna can't really wash all the poison off of her," Adrian said. "The fumes are ruining her brain. And yours, too."

"Our brains are already ruined," Jeb said. "That's obvious. It's been happening for years."

Who knew what had made him what he was? Adrian's eyes drifted to the smiling young man in the wedding picture she could still see hanging in the dining room, the personable young scholar with soft black hair. Even then he had known how engaging he was, and how to throw his booming voice, to use the male charm that would get him through the twistings and turnings of his life wherever it might lead him.

And Mother—would she be ashamed of Adrian, as Luna said? Maybe she would if she had simply heard the word, whore. But if she'd been able to get past the freeze, the deadbolt that the structure of the brain itself put on the potentialities for awareness, for being able to grasp the world around, she was sure Mother would have evolved and moved into a new future, as she, Adrian, had done.

"So you came back to Pegasus, back to the bug house," her father said and Adrian stared at him. He'd always been terrified of her, of all she'd been able to offer up . . . the verdant swelling sexual queen.

"I didn't come back to stay. I came back to give Luna a chance," Adrian said, and just then Luna appeared at the door.

"If she's going to hurt you, Daddy, I say she should leave," Luna said.

"She's not doing anything of the sort. Luna, sit down," Jeb said.

Luna sat.

"It's not that I want to stay," Adrian said, but she felt her voice quavering, felt hit by that terrible tiredness. "What I wanted was to take Luna on a trip, a sort of entomological tour of the world," Adrian said, but he made no response. "It's so interesting, the way ancient people built homes in the rocks. They lived in colonies, and hives."

"Like high-rises," Jeb said.

"Like high-rises," Adrian repeated.

"You should have heard her talking to the client about ants, Dad," Luna said.

"He taught me a lot," Adrian said. "You don't forget those things, do you, Dad. About the tenacity of the arthropods."

Adrian thought of herself, winged form to be tended, extruding out her knowledge through touch, through smell, through powers she herself was just becoming aware that she had.

"Why are you here?" Luna asked.

Adrian narrowed her eyes. "I'm a wealthy woman. I can do a lot for you. Both of you."

No one responded. She felt herself pulse, swell with outrage. "You've got to take me back!" Adrian cried. "It was all your fault, Daddy. I'm so lonely, and I don't know how to love anybody."

Jeb's hands sprang out, flailing at bug mists and the mists of time, flicking at everything she had to say.

"Adrian," he said, but she was grasping his wrists, drawing him near, and he did not resist the stroke of her quivering tarsus, tibia, antenna, that could not be, to him, completely alien.

Geology

How many times she had dreamed him before he finally appeared, she would never know. In fact, at first she didn't recognize him because he was so different from what she had sought, this dissipated-looking professor with his great dark eyes, his face sallow against the white shirts he always wore. He had a huge lion's head, a wild, if receding, corona of black hair. He looked sorrowful as he walked up to the podium, jittery and startled, but left that behind as soon as he began to speak.

"Lava plains," Virgie wrote down, "lakes of molten sulphur, shield volcanoes." Reviewing her notes later, she found that Jeremy Dietrich's words, on the page, were flat and expressionless. Geological time, that's what he had been talking about. "Consider the immensity of it! And our only keys to it are written in codes. We search for them in ancient rocks, we try to interpret their sign language."

He told of funerals in ancient civilizations. When a ruler died, they buried the whole court, too, alive. Layers of such courts had been excavated, bodies adorned with gems and precious stones, beside them gilded plates and goblets and finely woven cloth. Draughts of henbane were found scattered about, drunk to ease the pain of being buried alive. "They knew how lightly our physical bodies lie on us. It is the stones they clutch, metals and minerals that outlast us all." Sometimes Virgie looked around the class, wondering which hapless creatures she would take with her. Certainly Heather, her know-it-all lab mate, sitting there in an insolent slouch.

More than once Virgie had had the experience of seeing Jeremy in a crowd when he wasn't there—his noble face and form would superimpose themselves on some anonymous person just far enough away and then fade out. She'd had to approach within a few feet or so, and stare, and blink for a moment, to confirm that it was not he, Dr. Jeremy Dietrich, her geology professor, but an elderly woman in a hair net or a boy with freckles.

And now she stood in his geology lab, crushing her clipboard to her chest, squinting at the samples on the table, trying to memorize the names of the rocks. "Rhyolite, serpentine, sialic," she said to herself. It was like pushing in a cassette that kept ejecting. She could make no connection between the thrilling theories propounded by Jeremy and the dusty, unspectacular rock that she saw before her, sort of brownish and rough, a little crumbly. She poked at it with her hardness stylus.

Coming toward her was Heather, a formation herself, like a stalactite, a cone-shaped mass of dripstone with a tiny head and a large bottom.

"You've been staring at that rock for fifteen minutes," said Heather sociably; she was chatty, everybody's friend. Her notebook was stuffed with rock identifications. Why couldn't Virgie learn this stuff when Heather had no problem?

Virgie laughed. "I don't have the slightest idea what it is. Do you?"

Heather leaned down, peering closely at the rock. "It's

gneiss, isn't it?" Virgie couldn't remember if she'd even heard of gneiss. Heather's nose was within an inch of the porous, spongy-looking sample. "Sure it is, gneiss," she said. "Look at the coarse grain, look at the streaks." She confirmed her guess, turning over the little identification card. "You'd better know it. Isn't it awful that summer school exams come so fast?"

Virgie pursed her lips. She had thought it would be easier than this, to learn rock names. She hesitated to reveal to Heather that her brain felt bald as an iceberg, identifications melting and sliding away into the open sea.

"I can't remember the last time I had an exam," Virgie said, and Heather began peering at her.

"Why're you in this class?"

"Everyone needs a science to graduate."

Years ago her husband, Lou, had discouraged her from continuing school. Artists didn't need an academic background, he had assured her, but at a party one night he'd expressed it differently: "With all Virgie's got going for her, she doesn't need to be intelligent." Virgie narrowed her eyes.

She caught sight of Jeremy Dietrich now, on the other side of the room, talking to a group of young women. How delightful he was. In the old days she would have taken one look and said, "I'm going to get you."

Heather was nodding enthusiastically. "I admire you, I really do," she said. "I think it's so cool when older ladies come back to school."

Virgie drew back indignantly. She was supposed to be starting anew and already people were categorizing her. Thirty-seven was nothing, an infinitesimal age, wasn't it, in the geological scheme of things—a mere fingernail paring of time. Heather was simply too ignorant to comprehend this, although it was a major theme of Jeremy's lectures.

"That's it, Virgie, that's it. Use that fingernail, take it out of your mouth," said Jeremy, who was moving past tables toward them. "That fingernail can help you with your identification. Now what's a fingernail on Moh's hardness scale? Come on, come on, you know that. Try your fingernail on that rock in front of you. Try to scratch it. What does that mean?"

"Hi, Jeremy." Virgie stood there smiling at him. Of course, she smiled whenever she saw him, couldn't help herself. She thought she detected a pink flush in his cheeks.

"I know, Jeremy, let me try," said Heather, pushing past Virgie exuberantly and scratching the stone with a tinted nail. "It's talc, isn't it, Jeremy?" Over her head, Jeremy caught Virgie's eye.

"You're right, Heather, that's what it is," Jeremy said. "You should know that, too, Virgie. Talc is one on the hardness scale, a fingernail is two-and-a-half. What's next?"

"A copper penny," Heather chimed, in a trance of delight, her mouth open. Virgie watched tenderly as Jeremy bent over the table. He was losing his hair. The top of his head looked as smooth and fragile as an egg.

"Pay attention, Virgie," Jeremy said, raising his finger. "You should know that this is pyrite, this is magnetite, this is obsidian—how can you tell?" He took the stylus out of Virgie's hand, scratched the pyrite, pulled one pebble across the table with a magnet. Then he looked squarely at Virgie, feeling for the crumpled pack of cigarettes in his shirt pocket. His hand dropped.

"Jeremy, I need a conference," Heather said, moving closer yet again. Virgie saw him wince at this boldness. When students tried to talk to him after class, Virgie had seen him stammering and shy. It was as if he used his marvelous voice and words to draw people to him and then, when they actually came, changed his mind.

"Just give me a call," he said. "You, too, Virgie," he added.

They both watched him walk away. "That guy could teach me anything," Heather said.

Virgie looked Heather up and down, surveyed her smart, chatty, dripstone self. "Isn't he a little old for you?" Virgie asked. If she were back at her old studio in front of her easel, she would take a piece of yellow paper and paste it right over Heather. That way, when Jeremy came to talk she could have him all to herself.

Turning aside, Virgie began counting her breaths, a relaxation technique she had learned in group. She must take her time as she started this new life that opened up possibilities previously unimagined. Her past had been flood and earthquake, tornado and eruption—her fault. She was now aware of more profound processes that brought change about slowly but on a much grander scale. All around her she felt the silence of the dead seas trapped in the rocks on the tables, the sediment of ancient tides.

On her way out she passed him as he was talking to another group. She hesitated. He was cordial and polite to everyone, remembering names, concentrating with that mild, inquiring gaze. Although his back was to her, she felt in it a curious attentiveness, as if he knew she were leaving.

SHE had been gorgeous, a scoundrel, a rascal, a heart-breaker in her time, and an artist: galleries here and there still held her collages of handmade paper, with their ravishing colors and serene geometric shapes demurely juxtaposed. But she had gotten cancer and her husband had left her and she had gone to live with her daughter, thirteen now, in a big gray slab of a building, not too far from the Mississippi, not too far from the freeway. It was what she had been able to get with the settlement; it was paid for, but sometimes she thought it was the last place she would ever see—she, still so pretty, so much life left in her.

She had never worked away from home, but now she took a night job filing in an insurance company. She abandoned acrylics, torn shapes, and jamming her arms up to the elbows in hot solutions. At the support group they told her that the only way she could respect herself was to start paying her own way. She decided she would go back to school.

There was a long period of time when she had no eyebrows, no eyelashes, no hair. She learned several techniques for wearing a headwrap—side twist, contrasting side twist, and wrap with beret. She also learned to use a pink undertoner to camouflage the sallow gray pall of her skin. She waited for inner strength to engulf her, but sometimes it was depressing; no flames sprang from her quenched bald head.

One day, long before she took the class with Jeremy, she had stood at the bathroom mirror after a shower, rubbing the steaming glass with her hand, trying to conjure up the genie who had once faced her there. It hadn't been that long ago. She'd had luminous blond tresses and a heart-shaped face, clear eyes as dark as dates. "You're a bride doll, Virgie," her husband had said. "You look like you've just been unpacked from a carton full of tinsel and silver dust." Yes, that was what he had said. She had thought it would always work for her.

"What's wrong, Mom?" her daughter had said, coming up next to her at the mirror. Her name was Leilani, but she preferred, recently, to be called Lani. She was a sweet, chubby daughter, with lips shiny as candied fruit and smoky ringed eyes. Virgie sometimes felt tortured by the wounded, yearning way in which Lani followed her around, as if expecting her to come up with some kind of profound answer.

"Hi, honey," Virgie said, still inspecting her face. She winced at the sight of her hands under the bright light, fingernails ugly and bumpy from the radiation.

"You don't remember at all, do you?" Virgie asked.

"Remember what?"

"Remember what I used to look like," Virgie said. "I was pretty."

"You're still pretty, Mom," said Lani. Lani hugged her close, a passionate little hug. "Don't feel bad." She didn't know how frail her mother was, her heart violent and exposed, an outboard motor of a heart.

Lani smelled like a ripe peach. Soft and gentle, she outweighed Virgie by thirty pounds. "You know," said Virgie into her fragrant hair, "sometimes Mom feels like she'll never be pretty again . . . that she'll never have another boyfriend." At these words Virgie felt her daughter stiffen and push away, turn to look at her with sorrowful eyes.

"Mom?" she said.

"Yes?"

"Mom," she said again, "they told you in group you're not supposed to do that. I mean, you're the mom, I'm the kid. You're not supposed to make me the mom."

"Oh, for heaven's sake," Virgie said, bending down toward the sink to splash her face. In her support group Lani had been made to think there was some preordained right way to do everything. Virgie didn't like the mother role anymore. Lani kept trying to draw her into a drama she didn't want to play.

THREE months later, after the chemotherapy, Virgie's hair had started growing back. It grew and grew until it began jutting out from beneath the wig.

"What should I do?" she had asked Lani.

"Cut it," Lani had said, but Virgie was fascinated by the new growth, it was different from her old hair, it was bushy and streaked with gray. "You've got to do it, Mom," Lani had said. "Cut away all the bad stuff of the last year."

So she had. She cut it short and dyed it and threw away the wig and saw that she might be beautiful again. She thought maybe her body might be giving her its last miracle.

HUNGRY she was, ravenous, and she woke up that way. She was on a beach, sweating, basting, as if on a spit—in the hot sun she dripped, gleaming. The other bodies were gorgeous, too, glistening and scantily clad, but of them all she was the nugget. She would rise and strut, glide along the beach and take her pick. Nobody could stop her—they never could. The sun was ferocious, it beat down on her.

"Mom," said Lani, pulling on her arm. "You're having a dream." It was late morning. The curtain had fallen loose and the sun was directly on her. She felt cooked, scalded on her cut, seamed body. Sweat streamed down her forehead. "Don't you have a test this afternoon?"

"I do," said Virgie. She struggled, blind, to her feet. "Aren't you supposed to be at camp?"

"I said I'd stay home to help you study, remember?" But she'd spent the morning watching the TV, which was blaring out a program with a loud laugh track: "Love Connection." Virgie walked past the mound of clothes, covers, CDs, and books that rose over Lani's bed. What did the kid do under there? Virgie threw water on her face, steeped herself some tea.

"All right, come on, if you're going to help me." Virgie pulled the rock specimens from behind the saltshaker and the napkin holder. Limestone, microcline, mica, pyrite all were there, but which was which? "Time to put on our goggles. Here." She handed Lani a pair of white plastic spectacles, practically a headset, and then they both started hammering. *Crash! Bang!* It wasn't long before they had hit every piece of rock on the table. "Okay, now smash them into little tiny bits," Virgie instructed.

It was funny seeing Lani in her goggles, hammering away. With her round arms bulging out of her shortie pajama top, she looked like a baby hardhat. If something happened to Virgie, who would love Lani?

"Ouch," Virgie screamed as she hit her thumb, then sucked on it, shaking her head at Lani. "Now get out the magnifying glass. You know what we're looking for. Crystals and cleavage." Virgie pushed the goggles back on her forehead, examined the silverish gray stone. "It's mica schist," she said. "I can tell by the way it's separating into thin sheets." She rubbed her fingers together. "Say, all right! I figured it out.

"Did you know," she went on, "that if they made a movie called 'The Complete Story of Earth,' that lasted a month, a human life, even a long one, would last only one-sixteenth of a second?" Lani knew. "I can't understand how you can be so *blase* about it."

"How is hammering rock going to help you to pass?" Lani said.

"Oh, I'll pass," Virgie said, hunching over the rocks and grinning at her. "I think the professor likes me."

"Oh, right. Have you got a crush on him or something?" Lani's look annoyed her. Since the divorce Lani had adopted a sneering attitude toward men.

Lani resembled her father, who was part Hawaiian and had at one time considered being an all-star wrestler before opting for dentistry. Since babyhood Lani had had the round tan face so enchanting on the Poi Boy, and pretty, hefty, little arms.

Virgie continued peering at the rock samples, some of which she had collected herself along the riverbank. To think that she had been living here her whole life and had never been aware of breccia, terraces, and limestone formations. She repeated her resolve to be courageous when she talked to Jeremy about this and other more urgent matters.

Though she didn't look up, she could tell that Lani was giving her that daunting stare. "Can we go out and see how the little turkey chicks are doing, Mom? And then go out for dinner later?" On the river flats near their home, a small flock of wild turkeys had been introduced to see if they could be made once again to thrive.

"Tonight would be bad," Virgie said, eyes on rocks.

"As usual," Lani said, pressing her thumb into the schist. "We used to go out all the time. You were always taking me places. You used to be the nicest mom." She tugged at Virgie's arm. "How come you changed?"

Virgie didn't have an answer for her. It was true. Her daughter was no longer first in her mind. Sometimes it perplexed her that her heart had grown so hard. How had she gotten this way?

Besides, she shouldn't be so sure of Jeremy. Things were different now from how they had been in the old days, when her looks had been the one thing she could count on, the cream that rose to the top of her. Jeremy was ignorant about her. He did not know that she was sewn together. He could not tell that she was scarred, that her flesh rose up in ugly, curving ridges—she'd turned geological. Every part of her body oozed with sticky gum, out of all of her incisions she wept.

After the test she located his office on the sixth floor of an old building near the defunct stadium—no elevator access, no air-conditioning. She came to a stuffy room, crowded floor to ceiling with books and papers. He didn't see her come in. Terror gripped her as she saw him sitting there, head in his hands. When he looked up, she started.

"Oh, hello," he said, poised as if for flight. "It's you, Virgie Wahine. I remember your beautiful name."

"And one of the people who flunked the identification test."

He laughed aloud, as if this were nothing. "Sit down. Come on, sit down."

Trembling, she sat at the chair next to his desk. "As soon as I saw those rocks, I forgot all the classification criteria. I can't tell you how hard I studied." He was friendly, solicitous, waiting for her to go on, but her confidence was crushed. "This is my first course after many years. I can't afford to get a bad grade. If I drop the course now it won't go on my record."

She had meant to be pleasant and firm, but now she stared wanly at him, trying to read his expression.

"You must be patient. Maybe you just studied too hard. A lot of people are intimidated by identifications at first. It's like learning a different language." He opened a lower drawer of his desk, taking out a weathered box of cards. On one side of each card was a bright picture of a rock, and on the other side a name and list of characteristics. "You get someone to give you these once a day," he said. "I personally guarantee that by the final you'll pass."

Virgie took the box, fingers clammy as she looked through the cards, inhaling his smoky smell, hearing his hoarse breathing, so different from her own. "Besides, you don't really want to drop the course, do you?" he said, gazing at her. "What fun would it be for me to look out at all those bored faces?"

She glanced up from the cards. "But you're never boring," she exclaimed.

"That's why it's your face I always look at," he said. He

rose suddenly to his feet. "God, it's hot in here. I've got to go. Which way are you headed?"

"I live back there, over across the river."

"Excellent," he said. "There's a famous limestone formation that outcrops just by the bridge on the other side—did you know that? It doesn't exist anywhere else in the world. I'm giving a talk on it tomorrow. Want to go have a look at it with me?" Already she was following him, his swift strides. She rushed down the stairs. People, buildings, shadows of bridge railings like harp strings, flashed before her eyes as she panted, matching his steps. He lit a cigarette, puffing as he walked.

She noticed, looking at the side of his mouth, that he was missing a couple of teeth. Didn't this show that he really wasn't a superficial person, overly concerned with appearances? His true interest was the abyss of geological time, not paltry human time, in which a missing tooth, be it that of a reptile or human, was of no consequence unless it could be used for carbon dating.

As they walked down the steep slope to the river, he held on to her arm, keeping her from stumbling among the twigs and moss, toppling into the rich, fragrant earth. Rough and calloused his hands were, rasping to the touch, a workman's hands. She watched them as he pointed out the features of the formation then took notes on a little pad. No, he didn't live here, didn't she know? He was a visitor, just here for the summer to study this particular limestone formation and to teach.

"I've lived here all my life," she said, "but I've never even looked at this." There was much she longed to tell him, but the fear bubbled up in her again. "Come, let me show you something," she said all at once. "I've got something for *you* to see."

Farther down the riverbank, deep in the undergrowth, she looked for them. "We must be careful," Virgie said.

"Otherwise, we'll flush them out before we have a chance to approach them slowly. The turkeys," she said to his quizzical look.

"Turkeys?" he laughed.

"Hush," she said. "I know we'll find them if we just look for awhile." Her eye roamed the weeds and flowers of the flats, scanning for them, the flock that had been introduced in an attempt to start a population in the wild, but they didn't know they were wild. On Virgie's many walks with Lani, she'd become acquainted with them. They'd come up to her and she'd fed them—cracked corn and bread and the fortune cookies from Leanne Chin that were their favorite. Yes, they'd been the only thing to come close to her leathery, mottled fingers, so ruined from the radiation—but Virgie didn't tell him that, it was too soon.

As they turned down a curving path they heard a panicked rustle in the brush.

"Here they are," Jeremy said. "Are these your friends?"

Virgie knelt and held out her arms as three turkeys approached. "Aren't they ridiculous?" she said joyfully to him, so happy was she to see them. "That's what people say. But, you see, they're really not. They're magnificent." The turkeys came close, imperious and stately, with glossy brown feathers and arrogant displays, tails like quilted round fans. They were bobbing their crone heads, pastel pink with purple mottling, little skulls. "Do you like them?" Virgie asked, but the turkeys, seeing Jeremy, were already veering away. "Come here," Virgie said, but they had already rustled past, cooing—such a plaintive, sweet sound they made. Only for Virgie were they tame.

"They're disappearing," Virgie said. "There used to be six."

"Maybe they're somewhere else on the riverbank."

Virgie shook her head. "They stay close. They always

know where the others are. Can't you tell by the way they call to each other?" The turkeys hung clustered together, making little clucking sounds, picking caterpillars off of trees, making quick motions with their grotesque little heads. "Little sweethearts," Virgie whispered after them, "where are your sisters?"

"It looks like somebody's shooting them," Jeremy said, scanning the length of the bank. "That one that's bumping into things? It looks like its eye's been put out with a beebee or something."

They sat down to rest on a stone bench. "Who would do such a thing?"

"Hey, guilty as charged," Jeremy said. He looked away. "I used to shoot birds when I was a kid. Hate to say it, but it's true." Virgie stared at him till he regarded her again with his great dark eyes. "Not very nice, was it?" he said. "What can I say? I don't do it anymore." He pinched at his lower lip. "I question the wisdom, though."

"Of what?"

"Of releasing them around here. It's too close to congested areas. They'd do better away from the city." Virgie thought about this for awhile. "You take all of this very seriously, don't you," Jeremy said.

"Yes, I do," Virgie replied. "I've been watching them since they were small. I love them."

The sun was growing low in the sky, highlighting, at an odd angle, the trees and buildings across the river, giving them an eerie, peachy cast. She could see that he was as hot and sweaty as she was from their hike. Her heartbeat was still wild. She watched him feel in his pocket for his cigarettes.

"You mind a smoker?"

"No, I like it." She hated smoke, actually, it was dangerous, if not lethal, for her to breathe it, yet she leaned toward his smoky plumes, feeling them circulate pleasurably in her lungs again and again, as if she loved smoking and hadn't given it up. She wanted to bring up a deep subject, to show him that she was profound . . . perhaps talk of the thousands of generations of humans that had been born and died without a trace, hordes and hordes of them, an endless phalanx into the earth. She wanted to discuss with him the nameless dead, how you didn't have to go back more than a generation or two before you felt the huge vast pit of them, their lost faces, their lost stories. It would be a start. Instead, she listened to him wheeze.

"Must be getting old," he said.

"You're not old." He said he was forty-four. Virgie was silent. She didn't have the slightest idea anymore whether forty-four were old. "When you think of that limestone formation," she said, "or that shale." Jeremy laughed.

Virgie felt her face grow hot. "You see, I'm an artist," she said. "I mean, I don't do art anymore, but that's my training." She turned to look directly at him. "When you laughed just now, it was because I was stupid, wasn't it?" She shook her head. "That's the worst kind of laugh."

"Oh, come on, now, I don't think that at all," he said. "I think you're very charming." He paused. "I think you're all charm." He reached over, slowly, carefully, touching her necklace with a broad, thick finger. "What do you call that?" he said.

"A choker."

He laughed. "You should always wear chokers."

She touched her throat, felt shame at her worn clothes.

Much later, he dropped her at her door in his car. "Forget about the test," he said. "You'll pass. You'll get an A. You'll see I have some pull around here." She made a move to touch his hand, then drew back. "Go ahead, it's not that hard," he said. He was gazing at her passionately. She leaned over to kiss him, but they both stopped before it could happen.

A couple of weeks later Virgie sat at an old hippie cafeteria near the university studying her flashcards. She had just been to the mall and was wearing a new silk dress. In the past she had gone there to spend joyfully. She was supported, she'd had unlimited credit. Today, the purchase of the dress had dazed her. On her income, it seemed an insane thing to do, to spend to the maximum on her credit card. And now she couldn't take off the dress. She couldn't bear the thought that anyone would see her not wearing it.

She sat for a long time, her flashcards before her, meditating on these things, staring out the window, watching young women with baggy pants, their scarves flying in the breeze. If you created buildings, people could feel your imagination and fantasies long after you were dead, as she responded now to the droll scrolling on a tall, skinny, compressed building, and admired the weathered, cherry-colored brick, the iron grillwork. An old man with black bell-bottoms walked by, taking careful, stately steps, his hand at his beard. His jaw moved up and down for awhile in jerky rumination. He was so skinny, this old man, that his pants slid down around his pelvis; he kept hitching them up with a rope. Sparrows pecked around him, vestigial dinosaurs . . . Jeremy had told her this.

"How little we know of what has come before," she had said to him as they sat in a downtown bar last week, and he had squeezed her hand. He was listening to her as no one ever had before, seeming to understand, and she had longed to say more: that even in our brief time, the people who see us into the world are not the people who see us out. We start our children on a journey that we hope never to see them finish. We live parallel to each other, but in such ignorance: the women walking by, dressed in yellow and signing to each other, the bell-bottomed old man, they didn't know about Virgie, or care, they didn't know about mica schist or about Lani, but more than anything they didn't know how happy she was at this very moment, and this seemed to her quite strange.

Someone slid into the stool beside her. "Mind if I sit with you? I promise not to talk about uniformitarianism."

"Oh, hi, Heather," said Virgie, rubbing her forehead. "How's it going."

"What are those?" Heather asked.

Virgie stretched her hand over the box. "Dietrich loaned me his flashcards."

Heather looked astonished. "He gave those cards to you? Why to you?" Virgie shrugged. "Giving them to one person and not another—that's not very nice. I wonder if it's even ethical."

Heather was glaring at her. "I was pretty desperate," Virgie said.

Heather rolled her coffee cup back and forth between her palms. "Is it true that he just got a divorce?"

Virgie looked up from beneath her brows. "Where did you hear that?"

"You know Jennifer, that soil science major who's always wearing shorts? She says he's practically hitting on her."

Virgie's chin swerved the slightest bit. "Well, he's the kind of guy who's friendly to everyone."

"Friendly. I'll say," Heather said with a tight little grin. "Come on, tell me, you're not trying to go out with him, are you? He'll be gone soon anyway, isn't that right?"

"I guess," Virgie said, standing up.

"I guess it gets pretty lonely for a horny, lonely single dude out on his own."

Outside, classes were changing; she passed the frantic people all in the midst of their purposes. She cast glances at the men, trying to gauge their reactions to her, but faces told her little. People hid their secret thoughts.

How good at that they were, and she was, too. She had her own secret. She thought of the cancer, like silt at the bottom of a river, gradually building up. It had started as a single simple layer, a primary sediment, and then, imperceptibly, began to grow. She might not be able to name rocks, but she had a feel for the eternities it took for strata to be built up, undersea, over time. She looked around her. She would be in it again, joyous in this hot tide. People go on like this forever, the group said it every week—they live with it, they learn how. The cancer layer had been sandblasted out, leaving her dry as a desert.

VIRGIE and Jeremy sat by the river, sipping wine out of a bottle in a paper bag.

"Seriously, though, who was your ex?" he said. "You've never told me."

Virgie drank deeply. "Well, he was a dentist," she said. "I swear to God, a dentist, Dr. Wahine. He was an emergency dentist, actually. I met him when I had to have a root canal on Christmas Day." Jeremy chuckled. She put her palms flat in the grass. "He was Hawaiian, a big guy. When I lay with my head back against his broad belly as it rose and fell and he drilled—well, I saw the future right before my eyes. I'd never felt so secure in my life."

Jeremy put his arm around her. "So what happened to all that bliss?"

She tried to answer his expectant look with lightness, but it wasn't there—her voice grew quavering, thin. "It's hard to explain," she said.

"I'll bet I know," he said. "You fell in love with somebody else, didn't you?" She moved away in aversion to this tone, but he didn't understand. "You're still in love with this other guy, isn't it true? Are you going to be honest with me now or are you going to wait until I'm madly in love with you and then devastate me?"

"I'm not in love with anybody else," she said.

They walked farther along the river and sat on a stone bench. There they listened to the black lapping water. High above them a crushed full moon dripped gold and silver on the cloud tips. Jeremy moved closer. Virgie lay her head back against his outstretched arm, feeling her hair bunch up, thick and glossy, on his white sleeve.

"Do you think we should stay buddies?" he asked. She turned her head to look at him. "How about if I asked you to make love?"

"How about your other lovers?" she said. "How about the other people in the class? Like the soil scientist in the shorts?"

Jeremy groaned. He pressed his forehead. "What have people been saying about me?" He looked at her for a moment, then turned with a sigh. His face looked careworn and drawn in the moonlight. "It happens every time. Don't you trust me, Virgie? All right, all right, don't bother."

"Have you been honest with me?"

His body was coiled, he seemed furious. "You want honesty? I'll give you honesty. I told you about my divorce? It's my third divorce. Yes it is, Virgie, that's the truth. And I haven't been able to get it up for the past year. How's that for honesty?"

She felt the bench, cold and hard, beneath her bony thighs. "Neither have I," she said.

"What?" he said.

"I haven't had sex for awhile."

For a long time they just sat there, close in the moonlight, listening to the water. Virgie moved her hand to his arm. "That's all right, you don't have to pity me," he said.

"I don't pity you." She hesitated before him, a hummingbird hovering before the bright splash of a feeder. "But if you really like me, then why get involved when you're just going to be leaving?"

He sucked in on a cigarette, still looking at the ground.

"Ever hear of phones? Ever hear of plane trips? I'll be on sabbatical next winter in Italy. Think you could get away?" Her face was burning.

"Do you think I would say this to you if I didn't care for you?" he asked. "Can you really think that I'm casual or promiscuous?"

"No," she said, realizing that she had never thought that.

"Tell me," he said. "Tell me what you want from me."

She dropped her eyes, gave him her most winsome smile. She was in a flutter of feathers at his feet. "I want to know if you think I'm beautiful."

He looked amazed.

"Please, just tell me once. Am I beautiful in your eyes?"

Later, riding the elevator to her apartment, she watched herself in the metal grid of the car; she extended forever in the trim, a long plum stripe with a silver crimson flush on top, a creamy silver crest. She felt the damp curls that framed her face, she pursed her swollen lips.

She was sick that she had asked him that, that she had humiliated herself so. And yet he had been so kind, breathing against her cheek. She'd almost told him then, at that moment, when he was so tender. But no. She'd drawn away instead. Even he had said it. When classes were over at the end of the next week, it would be better.

She ran her palms along the jagged terrain of her body and went cold with terror.

AFTER exams were over, on the afternoon of the class party, Virgie came home from work early. As she walked up the path to her building, she grabbed the railing with her right hand, a twinge going through her whole body. She stood there, waiting for the waves of pain to subside, then started up the stairs again, took the elevator to the empty apartment.

As she turned to go into her room, she felt something tip, heard the rolling and banging of a hundred bottles clattering their way into the far corners of the living room. Lani had left it out for her, the ugly bag of bottles that she was supposed to take to the recycling center. The support group was giving Lani all kinds of ideas about responsible behavior. She was becoming uncannily sophisticated. The jargon of support was marbled into her speech: victim psychology and acting out. Once Virgie had come in and found her watching a program on teenage prostitution. It was hard to tell what she knew.

She wondered if Jeremy would be surprised that she had a thirteen-year-old daughter. She hadn't told him that, either. One part of her story had seemed to lead to another; she'd been afraid to begin. If he knew of her cancer, of her plight, perhaps he'd start feeling sorry for her. He would be like the people who said, "Virgie, you are so brave," but who treated her as if she were the fatted calf, prepared for some great tragic destiny so that they could be spared.

How cramped their apartment was, a cubicle in a maze of cubicles overlooking the freeway, not big enough to contain their many possessions from the old house. Lani, in particular, lived in chaos; Virgie had to swim through her junk. Sometimes Lani's mess made her the angriest of all.

Now, as she arranged the comforter over Lani's things, Virgie saw hidden a lost phone bill. She snatched it up, hands trembling, then ripped it open and flung it away. Lani had run up a bill on that 900 number again, seventy dollars, mostly at home but also using the credit card. She looked at the statement: National Nu Age Teen Action Rap Line. A few months ago there had been a couple of calls. She had hit the ceiling and Lani had promised never again.

In her bedroom, her quiet bedroom, Virgie leaned her head against the maple bedstead, her old bedstead, one of the few possessions she'd salvaged, and tried to balance herself, but she couldn't stop it, this wanting to know. Gingerly, she dialed the number, then hung up before it connected. This happened once, twice. Then, wild with adrenaline, she let it ring till a cheery-voiced girl came on and told her to press one if she wanted to hear messages from across the country and maybe hers from last week. She pressed one. She listened to Alison from L.A. tell how she'd been dumped by a sailor seven years older, and to Theresa from New Jersey who said take personality in a guy, not hot looks—she'd gone for hot looks and gotten burned, man—and Virgie was not really at all surprised when the next person was Lani from Minneapolis who said that her mom had just gotten a divorce and was fighting cancer and there was nothing but cancer books and cancer tapes all over the house and cancer support groups two or three nights a week with other people who were related to people with cancer and who were mostly a bunch of dweebs. "But the worst is that she's got a crush on this guy. She used to be real pretty, but now she's all skinny and she's met this stupid professor and all she thinks about now is him. Forget me! Really! Totally!" Lani's voice trailed off. "The last thing in the world I want is to be so mad at her when she's so totally clueless."

After Lani's quaking voice stopped, another girl's came on. Virgie slammed the receiver down, unable to listen to yet another spoiled teenager trying to convince the world that life began and ended with her. Virgie felt congested, her side ached. She lay back against the bedstead. And as her hurt subsided, she started to think of how she had failed Lani.

How could Virgie counsel her? How could she be a mother to her, instruct her in the ways of getting along, when she had gotten so much wrong herself? The only way she knew to get along was to get love from men. It had always worked for her. When she, Virgie, had been thirteen—well, she was already a woman. She had had her first man then, a guy in his twenties, and she had clung to him fiercely. Her parents hadn't been able to do a thing. They never had. She'd stepped off into the dream of her own body and had never come back.

It had lasted a long, long time, that dream, and then she had gotten sick. During the bad days Lou had turned away, when she shrank and walked with a halting step, when her wild milkweed hair swirled around her like a drowning woman's.

Now she saw Lani as a bobbing boat on the water, her little sail up, trying to catch the wind. And this was the message Virgie had given her, a message she hadn't intended at all: Don't look to me for help. Watch out for yourself.

Virgie remembered that last meeting at the Wellness Center, the cancer survivors meeting, no children. "Is that your new wig, Virgie?" Moon Calf had asked. Moon Calf was reborn, wore a long gray ponytail, had sagging earlobes weighed down with turquoise.

"It's not a wig, it's my own hair," Virgie had said, shaking out the new growth till it curled around over her shoulders in a hot spill. Luxurious it was, and she, Virgie, was glorious, ravenous—she saw Moon Calf's eyes narrow to little points.

"Your aura is purple, Virgie," Moon Calf had said. "Such display isn't worthy of you. You're on your way out. You'd better start making your peace."

The facilitator had jumped in, saying Moon Calf was inappropriate, didn't everybody hear, but sometimes, still, Virgie could feel that spear in her side.

She rested her head on the cherrywood bedside table, her temple against the honest wood, warmed with the late afternoon light, and she told it that she was a good girl, she just needed a little time. She squeezed her eyes shut again and again until she saw it: a field of yellow tulips, shimmering in the sun; a fragrant riverbank lush with blossoming trees, the wind in their branches, and she walking through it in flowing robes, her attendants scampering behind.

She sighed. She had it. She was there. She felt her shoulders, her back, flex and relax. If she defied the ache it stopped, it changed into the faintest buzz, as if she tamed it by not acknowledging it.

She was still bent that way when Lani came in from camp.

"Mom, are you all right?" Lani said.

"I thought your dad was taking you to his place."

"He's coming at five," Lani said.

Virgie looked up at her brown-eyed Hawaiian child. It was as if she'd gotten everything from her dad and nothing from her mother. Virgie gestured at the crumpled phone bill.

"Tell me about the Nu Action Rap Line," she said. Lani looked around frantically. "Look on that garbage heap you call your bed."

"It's you that's wrong," Lani screeched at her. "Where do you get off, snooping through my stuff? You're supposed to respect my boundaries."

"Oh!" For a moment this was all Virgie could say. She wiped her moist lip, closed her eyes. Finally she said, "Boundaries! You talk to me about boundaries! You who call up strangers—strangers!—and use my illness as a way to make yourself queen for a day."

Lani looked stricken. She moved toward her clothes heap.

"I can't get over it," Virgie said, rising. "That you could be so self-serving. That you could use my sickness to make up a good story about yourself." She wanted to stare Lani down, but Lani had turned from her, humiliated, a long-legged bird in her summer camp shorts, bursting with wronged virtue.

Virgie paced. "I don't know where the money's going to come from to pay for this bill, but I'm not paying for it, you can be sure."

"Dad'll pay for it," said Lani in a voice so low Virgie barely heard her.

Virgie swallowed hard. "If you want to ask him for extra, after all he's done to us, you just go ahead," Virgie said.

"Oh, you're so noble it makes me sick," Lani said, starting to cry.

Virgie watched her. Well, she wasn't going to let Lani ruin her evening.

"Where are you going?" asked Lani, still huddled on her clothes. "On a date?"

"Yes, if you must know," said Virgie. "Why don't you call your 900 number and tell them all about it. 'Cancer Mom Goes on Date.'"

She walked toward the bathroom. "I don't feel sorry for you," Lani called after her. "You didn't take care of yourself. For three years you were having symptoms, for three years you ignored them. It's hard to have sympathy for a victim who brings all her problems on herself."

Virgie hummed to herself. Not one bit sorry. "I know who you heard that from." Virgie spun, stood in the bathroom door. "Well, if you're so crazy about your dad, why don't you just go stay with him and his perfect new bride? I'm not going to be home tonight anyway. Go hang out there and tell them you want to stay."

"Mom, Mom," Lani called to the shut door. She was

apologizing desperately, but Virgie, furious and proud, did not answer. Ah, how glad she was to be so absorbed in getting herself ready. The acrylic fingernails she'd attached made it so difficult for her to hold the pencils and the brushes that by the time she came out, Lou had already been by to pick Lani up. "I'm not one bit sorry," Virgie said to her reflection, but her reflection wouldn't tolerate it. What terrible things was she doing to her daughter? What ill omens hung over Lani's head because of her? She put off the thought yet again.

GORGEOUS in purple, Virgie found her way over to the house Jeremy was subletting on Lake Harriet, following the precise map he had handed out in class. It was a stuffy old place in elegant disrepair. When Virgie walked in, late, she came upon a scene of eerie quiet: her classmates sat still, their faces illuminated by the white glare of Jeremy's slides. Instinctively she reached inside her purse for her notepad: "Coquina, bioclastic formation, carbonate mud." Then she sat on the edge of a couch, awkward and nervous, holding a heavy silver lighter in her hands, running her palms over the smooth, icy surface as her classmates eddied around her. Jeremy turned off the projector. Heather, next to her, winked and looked away.

"Congratulations," Heather said.

"On what?"

"Haven't you seen the grades posted? Haven't you been over at school? You got an A."

Virgie stood numb. There was food and chat, but she remained aloof, unable to talk to the friends she'd made. Jeremy, too, was less social than usual, taking glasses to the kitchen even before they were empty. As people began to mill out, Virgie still stood there, dazed, savoring it, that all her tireless, hopeless work could come to this.

But by the time the last person walked out and Jeremy stood, his back against the door, smiling in pleasure and relief, she felt as flat as an antimacassar on one of the old chintz chairs.

Gently, he took her arm. "Come sit with me," he said; he must feel her trembling. She kept her hands on the lighter, fondling it. Jeremy, too, seemed nervous. His words came just a second too late. They laughed a bit at the furnishings of the absent professor, particularly his cactus collection. They watched passing car lights make cones and trapezoids on the walls. Jeremy poured her a drink from the bottle on the table. Virgie didn't take it. She felt the cold, reassuring weight of the silver lighter, snapping its catch back again and again.

"It doesn't work," Jeremy said. "It's beautiful, but it doesn't work," and the sound of his voice so startled her that she pulled one of her glossy fake nails on the catch and the lighter dropped through her fingers, leaving on the coffee table a star of shattered glass.

"Oh my God, I'm sorry," Virgie said. The table, the carpet, were spattered with the blood red liquid he'd poured.

"It's all right," he said, coming closer to her, kissing her fingers, her neck. "I'll get it fixed."

"I've spoiled everything," she said. "Look at the mess I've made." She got down on her hands and knees, trying to scrub the carpet with a napkin, turning to wipe the table, but Jeremy caught her wrists.

"Virgie, what's wrong with you?" he said. "Calm down a little." Virgie tried to turn from him, but his grip was strong. "It's an old carpet, I'll get the table replaced," he said, his voice rising. "Come on, look at me."

"I heard about the A," she said.

"What about it?"

"I know it's not a real A. You patronize me."

He looked at her intently. "But Virgie, it is real. Your classifications were impeccable. Your essay was one of the best I've ever seen."

She sighed, almost convinced. No one had worked as hard as she had. "You mean I'm really smart?"

Jeremy laughed. "Of course you're smart," he said, drawing her up to him on the couch, putting his lips against her ear. "Now tell me honestly. You've always, deep down, known you were smart, haven't you?"

She heard the words in her dark, secret heart. "Yes," she whispered.

He stroked her shoulder, her arms, easing her head down on a pillow. They lay side by side in a shimmery heap, drenched from time to time by the strobe of a car's headlights. After awhile he said to her, "You're desperately smart and I desperately want you. You must know it now." He took her hand and pulled it to the front of his slacks. "See, I'm allergic to you." His voice was light. He pulled her in even closer. "I've got a swelling." She felt the hairs rise all along her arms and pulled away her hand.

"What is it?" he said sharply.

"I've got something to tell you."

He waited a moment to see if her words would go away. When they didn't, he groaned. "Christ," he said. He sat up, propping his back against her stomach as she lay on the couch, and reached for his cigarettes. "OK, I'm ready."

"I had an operation," she said.

"Whatever," he said wearily, inhaling his smoke. "What was it?" He looked sideways at her. She touched her breast. "Are you kidding me?"

She shook her head. "Gone."

"It's all right." He raised his eyebrows. "Well, then . . . let's see it."

"You mean, you just want me to show it to you?"

"What else did you have in mind?"

For a moment she was too shocked to move. "Why not," she said at last, and the words came out on a wonderful wisp of breath, burning, burning. Of course he was right. Why hadn't she seen before how simple it was. She got up from where he had her pinned and moved to the center of the room. She pulled at the purple silk dress, that slid down her long limbs like water, pouring onto the carpet. Her bra was satiny, eggshell-colored, another extravagance. She could smell her own musky hot scent. Then she stood there like a maiden, crossing her arms.

Jeremy rocked back and forth; he gazed. "No, it's not bad for me," he said. "It's not bad at all."

"You see how it is?" she said in a low, intimate voice, running her hands over the scars and ridges that merged with the perfect, velvet flesh. "It's geological," she whispered.

"Ah," Jeremy said, nodding. How fond of him she felt. She wanted to press herself against his chest, stroke his wide, stooping shoulders, look into his face that was so tender and forlorn. "For heavens sake, you could have told me," he said. "I knew there was a secret. How could I figure out what it was?"

"But you can deal with it now, can't you?" she said. "You *are* dealing with it."

"Of course I am. Of course."

She moved next to him on the couch. She caressed his stomach, his legs. "I see you're not allergic to me anymore."

"Ah, it's nothing," he said, taking her hand and clasping it. "Maybe I'll come back."

Much later, he pulled her to him tenderly. He kissed her face and her neck. He kissed the breast that was there and he kissed the scar. He kissed her face and her hair and made love to her body with his tongue. He tried again and again, with gentleness and passion, and she loved him back, in all the ways she had learned how to love a man.

He did not move to get a blanket. She did not move to cover herself. But when she tried to leave, he pulled her back down beside him and would not let her go until the room began to come into raw, scratchy focus with the dawn.

ON HER way home, in her great happiness, her great magnanimity, she stopped the car on the river road near the place where the turkeys roosted. Sitting there, watching the sky begin to brighten, she thought how wonderful it would be when she met him the next year, in Italy. Would he invite her for a brief visit or ask her to spend the whole term with him? She should have mentioned it before she left. It was all at once impossible to imagine.

With a sigh, she got out of the car. She went first to her favorite oak where she often found the turkeys spending the night, perched at the ends of the long branches. Then she looked through the tangled undergrowth nearby. They were nowhere. She made the cooing sound, calling for them, for they always slept in the trees around here. Could they all be gone?

She heard a rustling in the scrub near the bank of the river and she tracked it. There, beside a bush, she found a single turkey, shivering, and she knelt down next to it. "Hello, darling. Hello, beautiful. Why aren't you in the tree? Where are the others?" she said. It looked at her once, reproachfully, it seemed, and bobbed its little skull head as if trying to tell. But it couldn't tell. It had a small hole beside its eye. Moisture oozed from it, making the matted feathers look sticky.

Virgie hovered near. "Poor sweetheart." She leaned

closer. The turkey's head swung to the ground. As she tried to pet it, it stiffened, but she was determined to hold it in her arms, to take it away from the brush and into deliverance. She was pulling it towards herself, feeling the awkward thrashing mass of it, when suddenly, more quickly than she could have imagined, its quick beak gouged her arm, drawing blood. The turkey tore itself from her and she dropped it, watching as it pitched itself toward another bush, where it huddled, head bent.

By the time she got back to the apartment, there was blood on the front of her dress. She pulled it over the top of her head as soon as she walked in and was contemplating what to do about the fragile, stained silk when she felt herself observed. Lani was there watching her, not in her own bed but in her mother's.

"What are you doing here?" Virgie asked. "I thought you were going to stay with your dad."

Lani rose to greet her, her face full, fleshy, with broad, high cheekbones. Virgie could smell the sleep on her as she walked up close, looked deep into her mother's eyes. The rawness, the sharp, ripe tang of her, made Virgie shiver.

"I like you best, Mom. I like you."

Virgie felt breathless at the power, the force of this daughter. "I like you, too, Lani," she said. "I like you, too." She grasped Lani by her shoulders. "And you know what? He loves me, honey," she said. "He loves me and I'm going to be his girlfriend, just like in the old days."

Lani's pinched, weary look made Virgie remember. How could she ever go away for any length of time? What would Lani do? And all at once she felt with overwhelming sureness that she would never go to Italy.

Pushing this terrible thought from her mind, she pressed a finger to Lani's smooth cheek. "Come on," she said, sitting down on the bed and pulling Lani with her, holding her head against her chest. Lani nestled in.

Virgie ran her fingers over the nasty gouge on her arm. "You know, the turkeys?" she said. "I was just down there. Only one is left. Someone shot it in the head with a beebee. I tried to bring it back home with me, but it got away. We could nurse it back, don't you think? The two of us. We could save it."

She could feel Lani's head shaking against her chest. "I don't think it's a good idea, Mom. I don't think we could save it. We had somebody from the wildlife rehabiliation center come to class . . ."

"We could take care of it," Virgie said again. "We could bring it back here for awhile. We could catch it with a pillowcase."

Virgie pulled deep inside herself for the breath. Finally it came, flooding her arms, her shoulders, with keen waves of warmth that sank into her like a salve.

"And when it's well, we can take it out to the country," Virgie said. She would find some safe and lovely spot. It would rustle up into the branches of an oak and roost there, dreaming of the others.

"It's so early. Do we have to go now, Mom?" Why was Lani crying?

"We can't just leave it out there," Virgie said, wiping, with her silk dress, her oozing cut, Lani's streaming eyes. There was no time to lose.

Hatshepsut

JUST DOWN THE STREET from Luxor temple, a few miles away from the Avenue of the Divine Rams at Karnak, Louise woke in the dark. In her dream she had been on the barge of the god Amun, trailing her fingers through the waters of the sacred lake, drifting with the lily pads. Perfumed sails billowed in the breeze—and yet all was not well.

Tentatively, Louise traced down her pelvis with her fingers. She was no lily. But she was very wet. Stiffly awake now, she lay in a strange hotel bed in a strange city in the middle of the night.

"Ah, hah, hah." From the bed next to hers, Uncle Tony was yawning. "Hah, huh, hih." She'd grown used to his vocalizing yawn, like someone pretending to laugh.

Scrunching her eyes shut, curling her body around her pillow, she held herself rigid.

Please don't wake up, she silently begged him. She must concentrate fully. It was crucial that she glide, like a barge on the waters of the sacred lake. Without the slightest abrupt movement, she must float to the bathroom.

Slowly she slid her feet to the floor.

"Hah, heh, hih."

Steadying herself, she took a step, then panicked. With a wild leap, she ran across the carpet and quietly shut the door. Flipping the switch, she found herself immersed in fluorescent light, looking down to see—nothing. She was not bleeding. Her thighs were white and bare. Only her nails were red, a deep carnelian, though beginning to chip after this week on the road.

At least they were still long. She drummed them on the counter next to the sink, next to the plastic Kotex bag decorated with Arabic printing and the demure line drawing of a maiden. She'd been sure her period was going to start, and it hadn't. After years of taking care of Mother's wasting body and adjusting herself to its routines, Louise now seemed to have lost the rhythms of her own.

Thank god the water blasted out of the showerhead pelting and hot. She stood beneath it for a long time, the cramps pounded out of her by the healing spray.

A LARGE, untidy woman of forty on her first trip out of the United States, Louise was perpetually scared. She was scared of being away from Minneapolis, she was scared of being without her mother. She was scared of Islamic militants, she was scared of tourist buses. She had gruesome fantasies about dead bodies and the consequences of exposure to toxic substances.

When she came out of the bathroom, the air was thick with Uncle Tony's smoke, but the cigarette had vanished. She couldn't complain, either, because Tony was talking long distance to Mordecai, his spouse, who was supposed to have come on this trip with him. But Mordecai, also in his eighties, was frailer than Tony and suddenly going blind.

"Fine, fine," Tony was saying. "Cairo was unbearable, but Karnak last night was superb. The columns are so immense it's like being at the bottom of one of those crevasses in Kashmir or Nepal, darling, and looking up at the sky. Remember?" Swigging from a Coke can, he was downing pills one by one: multivitamin, E, blood pressure drug—and Prozac, for sure. She could see already on his face that fuzzy, guileless smile. He stroked the froth of white curls at the opening of his lilac silk pajama top, the latest to appear in a series of perfectly pressed garments meticulously folded into his suitcase by Mordecai.

Louise couldn't look at Tony without thinking of her mother—the broken keyboard of her chest, and, where her breast had been, the sealed lips of a scar. But Tony also had Mother's attentive, listening manner. Even if you didn't like her, you liked her, someone had said about Mother once, and Louise thought Tony had that same quality.

"She's far more impressed by everything than I am—far more impressed." It was Mordecai, not Tony, who had planned the trip. But when Mordecai became too ill to travel, the money being spent, he'd urged Tony to go through with it, taking Louise.

"Find her a boyfriend," Mordecai had said.

"My impression is that Egyptian men aren't that attractive—and she's such a soft little thing." Uncle Tony had pinched her on the cheek.

"Tony!"

"I didn't mean it cruelly. Louise knew I didn't, didn't you, sweetheart?"

She should have declined to come, but how could she turn down Uncle Tony? In the year since Mother's death, she'd called this stranger crying every weekend, sometimes every day. Her three-hundred-dollar phone bills showed how dependent on him she'd become.

"No, she still doesn't brush her hair in back and she's wearing three earrings, but she's being nice to her old uncle."

Louise walked over to where Tony sat on the bed and called "hi" into the receiver. Mordecai was reporting to Tony about their orchids, those most evolved and solitary of plants, which hung from every trellis and fence in their tiny yard overlooking the Pacific. "Tell me about the youngster in the front yard. Is it coming back?" How kind Tony's voice grew when he talked to Mordecai. They protected the tenderness in each other.

Six A.M. in Luxor, so it must be early evening in San Francisco, later in Minneapolis, where she lived, wasn't that right? For someone who, at home, tore each week as it ended out of her planner and crumpled it into the wastebasket, Louise certainly had a poor sense of time. No one waited for her in Minneapolis. She had no one to call. So why should knowing the time concern her in the least?

ON HER way to the dining room for breakfast, Louise stopped in the gift shop, where she found a book with graphic close-ups of warehoused mummies, generations of them, named and dated. So this was how they showed you they loved you: stuck you on a board, turned your body into a plank, and let your dead flesh tatter, shrivel off in papier-mâché rags. She studied the array of faces in all their perky individuality—like class pictures, only everybody's dead.

Leaving the shop, she ran into Uncle Tony in the lobby. "Have you seen Safa?" he asked. "She's been calling up to the room. Did she say she was going to pick us up early? I don't remember that." He smiled. "See how pretty you look today. You got a little sun. It's just as I told Mordecai. You've got Rose's looks, but you let her bully all the spirit out of you. I wish I'd been around. I'd have been able to keep that from happening."

Louise had no regrets about the time she'd devoted to Mother. But it was impossible to talk to Tony about this.

An hour later, Louise and Uncle Tony stood in a barren wilderness, staring at a white temple that had been carved directly into a vast corrugated cliff. In a succession of terraces, the temple rose against the sheer rock, imitating the rippling of its alluvial pleats.

So steep are the chasms, so boundlessly blue the sky . . . Louise blinked in the daylight, trying to summon an intensity of concentration that would allow her to take in the age of the precipice, a frozen waterfall one hundred million years old, and the human ancientness of the temple's collonades, like something the cliff had dreamed.

"Louise." A scent drifted over to her, but not the scent of the desert—no, nothing so dry as that. Safa, who had been their guide in Cairo for five days, was now in her hometown of Luxor. She was cold today, more distant, and something else about her had changed: wherever she walked, there followed a waxy honeycomb fragrance.

"This is my favorite person to talk about," Safa said. "Imagine her standing here thirty-five hundred years ago, Queen Hatshepsut."

"Say again?"

"Hot-CHEP-soot," said Safa. "Like 'hot chicken soup.' No, that's not quite it. Maybe more like a sneeze. Anyway, this queen has decided to herself become a pharaoh. A woman, they say, cannot be divine, and thus cannot be pharaoh, but she *will* be divine. As she walks up this ramp, on either side are pools and flowers and trees, where now is desert."

Louise gripped Uncle Tony under the elbow, trying to keep pace with Safa, who leaped ahead, the golden bangles on her arms clinking.

Both of Uncle Tony's knees had been replaced the previous year. Other than that, as far as Louise could see, he had the stamina and appetite of a draft horse, if not the strength, for every step had to be deliberate. Tony felt the ground tentatively with his cane, then took a step. Feel and step—that was the rhythm of his careful travel. Louise helped him along as she had helped Mother along.

"See that tree stump? A poor wrinkled thing, you say, but it's thousands of years old, from Hatshepsut's expedition to Punt—what we call Somalia today. To the Egyptians, Punt was like the Garden of Eden. That's what Hatshepsut said about the god that made her: all his odors came from Punt."

Louise tried to smell Hatshepsut and the lush perfumes of the god, but around her the sands were parched and baked. It was only Safa's sticky fragrance that lingered.

"Safa, could you slow down?" Louise called out. Safa turned her head and stared at them from behind a column. In Cairo, Louise had been crazy about Safa—a woman alone, yet boisterous and loud, a smart and confident tour guide, in contrast to Louise, who for ten years had been a nurse for Mother and still hadn't gotten back to teaching full-time. Louise was hooked on substituting, hooked on kindergartners and first graders she only had to know for a few days. "Roll around on the floor," she could tell them, and they'd roll around on the floor. "Let's curl up and be snails," she could tell them, and they'd all turn into snails.

Yes, Safa was fearless and Louise was a coward, still taking Mother's pain medication even when she didn't have cramps. But she'd left the codeine back in Minneapolis, afraid of customs, afraid Uncle Tony would notice, and the pangs she had today made her long for it.

Safa tossed her mahogany-dyed hair, which flowed down her back, bare to the sun. It was a woman's choice whether to take the veil or not, Safa had explained; wearing traditional garb certainly saved you money on fashion expenses, but she didn't wish to do it. Louise should forget the publicity about Islamic oppression of women.

It was phony, just like the propaganda about terrorists in Egypt going after the tourists. She should come again and bring her friends. There were a few nuts, of course. Didn't they have nuts in America?

Safa waited, arms crossed. "Your uncle—I don't think he can take this temple. We have to walk a long way up." She spoke as if Tony couldn't hear—Tony, with Mother's innocent, trusting eyes.

"Then what's he supposed to do?"

Squinting at the temple, lighting a Marlboro, Tony began quoting something from memory, his voice resounding even in this vastness. "Hundred-gated Thebes—wasn't that Homer? I believe the Greek boys came over here to complete their educations. Have you heard anything about that?"

"I don't know nothing about any Greek boys," said Safa.

Guilelessly, he lifted his chin, turning his face up to the sky like a sunflower. His eyelids fluttered and he smiled. "Now, you said this was the Valley of the Queens?"

"No, no, no," Safa shrieked, poking at him. "You're leaning against a pillar. Those are sacred writings, they're crumbling away. No leaning is allowed."

Ashen, Uncle Tony straightened himself, brushed off his jacket. "This is the Valley of the Kings," Safa went on. "We'll go to the Valley of the Queens this afternoon. Yes, there are some men buried there. Even in ancient days they had a few of those kind."

Louise felt the hairs on her back rise. Tony's locks were silver in the morning light, his ARTS over AIDS T-shirt a fluorescent, stubborn pink.

Safa stalked on ahead.

Up the incline, they made their way: Poke the cane, step. Poke the cane, step. Louise held on to the elbow of his cotton jacket.

Everywhere they'd gone, Egyptians had been glad to see Uncle Tony. In the Cairo Museum a group of smiling youths had greeted him as if he were a dignitary. "Take good care of him," a curly-headed boy in a burnoose had said earnestly to Louise, as if the elegant old man were a blessing. Today, however, the boon seemed to be getting on Safa's nerves. Louise suspected it had started the night before, when Tony first met Waleed, their Luxor driver. Helped in and out of the car by the handsome Waleed, Tony, despite his infirmity, had begun to prance. At the end of the evening, he gave Waleed, and not Safa, a tip—a large one, too, of twenty dollars. But Safa was a professional, and well paid up front.

"Stiff little bitch," Uncle Tony muttered now. "Sounds like she's got everything memorized. Say something that's not in the guidebook, and she wouldn't know what you were talking about." He stopped abruptly in his tracks. Louise pitched forward, halting herself just in time. He had only paused to say, "That's the thing about the people here. They either fawn all over you or they're rude to you."

Only last night he'd been praising the Egyptians, so gentle, yet dignified.

"She wasn't rude yesterday," Louise said.

"That's what I'm saying."

When they joined her in the forest of columns, Safa began her speech, indicating a pillar topped by a carved head. "Perhaps Hatshepsut's face. 'How beautiful is she.' That's what she wishes us to say about her. Or when we see the splendor of her obelisk: 'How like her it is, who always honors her father, Amun.'"

Louise squinted up at the sculpted woman, her chipped lips cracked open and parted by the sunrises that had crossed her face every day for 3,500 years. *How beautiful is she.*

"They believed their lives were bound up in their

names. You could help the dead by saying their names aloud: Hatshepsut, Hatshepsut."

"Hatshepsut," Louise murmured. To think that Hatshepsut's pillars had been standing like this, tranquil and composed, while she went about her life in Minneapolis, driving on the freeway, doing errands for herself and Mother. But of course, Mother, too, was dead now. "Rose," Louise whispered.

"She created a story of divine conception for herself—sound familiar?" Safa lifted her brows high. "If her father was a god, she was divine, right? But it had never happened before. So, she tried to have it both ways. In this drawing, here"—Safa pointed to a curved nail—"she is portrayed as a man. 'Hatshepsut, he.' She wears male clothing and a false beard."

"I can't believe anybody bought that," Tony said. "Is her mummy a man?"

Safa shrugged. "It's disappeared."

"Gone?" said Louise. What a tragedy for someone who wanted her body preserved—unlike Mother. Louise had been thankful for Tony and Mordecai's helping her through Mother's cremation, for spreading her ashes in the garden.

"And over here, more of the things the old ones said." Safa pointed at a column. 'Your members shall continue to be. You do not decay, you do not rot. You are not turned to dust. You do not stink, you are not corrupt. You shall not become worms.'"

Tony guffawed. "Hah, what a joke. I should put that up beside my bed." Louise wished Tony would back off. What was Safa supposed to say?

"'Awake from the swoon in which you sleep,'" Safa said. "That's how the god calls the mummy. 'You will triumph over everything done against you. Ptah has overcome your enemies. They no longer exist.'"

"What a bunch of garbage," Uncle Tony said.

Safa's face was impassive. "Of course, before they could meet with the god, they had to face judges and go through The Negative Confession: 'I have not committed evil against men, I have not mistreated cattle, I have not copulated with men.'"

Uncle Tony tripped.

"Are you all right?" Louise kneeled beside him. His reflexes had been sharp. He'd sat down fast, flat on his butt, and hadn't injured himself. But it took Safa and Louise both to get him back on his feet.

"We're done here anyway," Safa stood between them. "Tell Waleed to drive your uncle over to the tombs. We'll meet them there. I see my girlfriend, Liala. You and I, Louise, will ride with her. It's not far."

Walking away, Uncle Tony said to Louise, "Whoever married that girl married her for her looks, not her personality."

"She told us she's divorced," Louise said.

"That's what I meant. She just lectures. I was a teacher for fifty years. I know the tone. She's arrogant."

Before they got to the cab, Waleed came loping toward them, a brown-skinned man with eyes a waxy yellow color, the hue of lima beans. "I've got Daddy," he told Louise. "Don't worry." Tony clamped onto Waleed's arm.

Atop the second ramp of Hatshepsut's temple, Louise found Safa smoking a cigarette.

"I didn't know you smoked."

"At home, in Luxor, I smoke. And I drink, too. That's why I look so old."

"How old are you?"

"I was born in 1959."

"You don't look old," Louise said. "I was born in 1955."

"I know. I saw your passport. You seem young." It was not a compliment. Safa tapped her toe. "It's hard to tour—with someone like that."

But she was their employee! They were paying her hundreds of dollars, and she should defer to them. Safa looked narrowly at Louise. "The two of you are very close?"

"Well, actually, for a long time we didn't know each other." Her mother had never spoken of her older brother, till just before the end. By the time Tony and Mordecai arrived, it was too late. All at once, Uncle Tony had become her only living relative, quick to add his distinct perspective: Why didn't she have a love life? Why didn't she have a full-time job? Yesterday it would have been possible to tell such things to Safa.

A cramp, the throb of a headache, gripped her, then disappeared. Louise looked around her. Once the temple had shimmered with radiant color. Now its life was stamped out by the weight of the years, the heaviness of all the feet that had trod here.

At the bottom of the ramp, they met a tan woman with dyed-blonde hair standing among a dozen Asian tourists. She wore a jaunty beret, a silk scarf around her neck. Forty, fifty, she had a few broken teeth, a game smile.

"Liala, hi. This is Louise. Can we go over to the tombs with your group?"

"Of course," Liala said.

"But what about Hatshepsut?" Louise said.

"They're ready to go now. Come on." While Safa spoke Arabic with Liala, Louise fell into step with some of the tourists. Listening to the Japanese talk among themselves, Louise wondered if they felt as stranded as she did, as trapped in an identity brought along from the native country. Here she was, in one of the most fabulous places on earth. Asked about Luxor on her return, what would she say? *I had PMS.*

If Mother were here, she would understand. That Mother was dead and only Louise really remembered her didn't seem so bad: Mother's being, her personality, permeated Louise's life. But that wouldn't have been enough for her—for Hatshepsut. It was her wish to conquer this land, to command its attention. In these surroundings you must make statements gross and bold if you want to keep your name alive. Without monumental statues and architecture, bombast endlessly repeated, a single human being might just seem . . . pathetic.

Atop another pillar, another Hatshepsut stared out. Cracks and weathering had almost eroded away her nose, but Louise admired the plaited hair, the full, swollen lips, the expression both wistful and determined: *How beautiful is she.* To live in this desert, to live for eternity, you had to be . . . hard.

A Japanese woman joined her, mouthing quick syllables. Hastily, Louise made sure her pad felt snug, in place, then turned puzzled to her new companion, who spoke again insistently: "Tina Turner."

Louise peered up at the ancient carving. "Hungh?"

"Nah, nah." The Japanese woman adamantly shook her head. "Tina Turner."

When Louise climbed out of the van at the tombs, Safa was waiting. Louise mimicked her style, never looking at men, the *fellaheen,* straight on, but casting down her eyes, and thinking of Hatshepsut, so loved by her subjects: *When Hatshepsut's accession was announced, the people leaped and danced. The god said: It is she who will sit upon my wonderful seat!* All over her temple she had spelled it out for them, the children of the future: Louise, Safa, Tony, Waleed. How she had craved their attention, her dreamy gaze fixed on them with an unquenchable yearning: *I will shine forever in your faces.*

A cramp pinched her gut, stopping her abruptly. "Where's Uncle Tony?" Louise said. "I thought he was going to meet us here."

"Waleed will take care of him."

"But . . ."

"Let me show you where they buried the pharaohs."

A scattering of tourists milled at a ticket booth, the gateway to the tombs. "The funeral procession would move along through here." Safa was pulling her down a wide dirt road. "The family, the priests, the mummy, all of them came up to this entrance. Here in the tomb was his true and everlasting place. Imagine them, where we are now."

They stopped before a cave, a simple hole gouged out of the rock that ended with a crude downward plunge into darkness. Safa wiped her eyes. "Right here, at the entrance, they stood the mummy upright on the ground. Now came the Opening of the Mouth. The priest touched the mummy's face with adze and chisel, then rubbed its face with milk: this renewed its bodily functions. The priest embraced it to bring back its departed soul."

"What bullshit! It's crazy that they believed all that stuff."

Safa turned.

"Uncle Tony!"

With Waleed, he had ascended the hill. He spoke directly to Safa. "This religion. It just doesn't turn me on."

In the noonday sun, a sweet waxy scent emanated from Safa's hair and wafted over to Louise, as if it had melted in the heat.

"You can never get in here, never," Safa said to Tony. "It's too much climbing."

"I'll just sit here awhile and have a smoke," Uncle Tony said, pulling Waleed to a stop. He halted in all the dignity of his years. "Leave me alone, I'm fine."

"Are you sure?" Louise asked.

"Go on. Get going. I'll just sit here with my friend for awhile, and he'll tell me what's really been going on in these mountains. Right, Waleed?"

Along with some other tourists, Safa and Louise entered the cave and climbed underground, took a long walk through a rocky corridor, and then arrived at the burial chamber. Beneath ceilings of heavenly blue and shiny gold stars like xs were paintings as fine and clear as porcelain. The protecting goddess Nut spread her graceful arms over the vaulted ceilings, her attenuated body supporting the stars that shimmered as they swam from her womb. Night after heavenly night, the revived mummy would enjoy all the pleasures of life within these gilded caves, so enclosed, so safe.

"The tomb paintings are here to let the sun shine in and drive out darkness and death," Safa said. "Each night, down here, the mummy is cast aside, the detached parts of the body come together again. The pharaoh enjoys what he enjoyed in life, but with something more—peace of soul."

So enclosed, so secure it felt in here, but the tombs had been thoroughly ransacked in ancient times, as everyone knew, the dream violated almost at the moment of its conception.

They returned to the dirt road and stood silently for awhile, side by side. Finally Safa said, "Go in there." She pointed to a bare doorway in the rock. "Go see King Tut." She reached in her purse for her cigarettes. "It's almost pristine. A small extra fee. But I cannot go in with you. The place must be approached, how do you say, with piety. His mummy has been returned to rest there."

"Not another mummy." Would she ever be able to get those carnival grimaces out of her mind? Even at home she woke in the night, her mind full of stalkers, dead bodies, slit throats, partial cremations. She recalled Safa's description of the removal of the blood, the siphoning of the brain through the nose, the canopic jars stuffed with viscera. But Safa had already started her cigarette; Louise could see her eyes flutter as the smoke flooded into her lungs. She shooed Louise, pushing her elbow.

No other tourist descended with her down the shaft. For a moment, in this cool seclusion, Louise felt calm for the first time since arriving in Egypt. Yes, that was what she needed, a few moments to herself. To her relief she saw no exposed mummy as she reached the back of the cave—just the dirt burial chamber and, set within it, the famous Tut sarcophagus: 2,500 pounds of solid gold molded to depict a changeless being, two, three times larger than life. She felt faint just looking at it: A dreaming face, sheltered in this secret house and left to gaze with tranquil certitude into eternity. *You breathe when you hear my voice.*

No, they didn't want to be found shrunken and decrepit, as Tut was beneath this massive coffin—that was the last thing they would have desired. They wanted to be endlessly poised in perfect golden youth, not consumed by people who greedily drank in images of decay . . . chipmunk teeth, penis a tiny stub. She leaned on a wooden railing, trying to concentrate on the profundity of it all, but the headache stung again behind her eyes, and she felt for her pad: *King Tut, riding on a donkey, King Tut—was my favorite honky.*

Suddenly the lights went out.

In icy fear, Louise began to slink her way out of the cave, bumping into the cold dirt walls, inhaling mouthfuls of dust. When she finally clambered up to the entrance of the tomb, Safa was nowhere in sight. A man in a turban and gelaba came up to her and thrust into her hands an alabaster necklace. "Good luck," he said in English, "good luck," and Louise, hands still shaking, began taking dollars out of her purse, one, two, three, and he kept accepting them. She probably would have started to give twenties if Safa hadn't appeared with words that sent him scurrying.

"They're like robots," she said. "They see me all the time, yet they approach me, too, and say the same thing. It's like somebody put a chip in their brain."

"The lights went out," Louise said. "I was alone with King Tut." She clutched her necklace.

"The generator probably blew. Sometimes it happens."

"Isn't there a curse? And all those mummy movies—I don't know if they show them over here—these angry mummies coming to life and lurching around, seeking revenge?"

Scrunching her shoulders, Safa said, "You know, it's funny. My girlfriends and I, we're all tour guides, and we all have bad luck. We lose all our money, we never have any boyfriends, we're all divorced. Hah!"

Safa's pretty face was baking in the sun. But it was she, Louise, who was sweating. "What about the curse?" Surely it would find her. Now she'd really done it. Arcane chemical compounds she had heard about, sprinkled on the mummy, essences so potent that they could affect the life rhythms of others even after thousands of years.

Safa wrinkled her nose. "Sure, there are spirits. They have their world and I have mine. There's no curse."

Louise started to laugh. "I've got the curse. The curse, you know? I mean, I keep thinking I'm going to get it."

"I told you, there is no curse," said Safa.

"It's an idiom." Louise said. "You know those funny idioms we were talking about the other day? It's what we call menstruation. The curse?"

Safa frowned with distaste. "Who wants to hear about it. Are you bragging or something?"

Louise felt the blood rush to her face, hot and prickly.

"No tombs, not one more tomb," she said, turning away.

Safa shrugged. "You're not getting your money's worth."

Safa's bracelets clanked as she led Louise down the hill. Either she was no longer fragrant, or Louise couldn't smell her anymore.

They found Waleed and Uncle Tony beneath an overhanging rock, smoking Tony's Marlboros and laughing like old friends.

"Oh, you'll never believe what Waleed showed me," Tony said. "We went to a cave, back over there?" He giggled in delight, dabbing his eyes with a napkin and tilting his face upward as he spoke. "Well, there's some graffiti inside, from the time of Queen Gesundheit—whatever her name is. And there's a drawing, a perfect cartoon drawing, of her getting buggered. So you know what the common people thought of a woman who had herself declared a man, even if she was a queen." His shimmering eyes were full of wicked fun. "If she *was* a man, really, you know, it was the only way she could get fucked." Uncle Tony turned to Safa. "Do you think we could show that to Louise?"

Safa hissed in Arabic to Waleed, then said, "There's no reason for anyone to see that." She and Tony glared at each other. "Back to the cab. Back, back." By the time they'd ferried across the Nile and were driving once again, they were all tense.

Waleed was talking to Tony. "Oh, yes, I have children. Eleven," he said. Louise wanted to touch Waleed's strong brown arm, see again his sunny eyes. The pharaohs had hundreds of children. All of them, Safa and Waleed, must be the children of the pharaohs. *His love passed into her limbs, which the fragrance of the god flooded.*

"No more temples. I want to go back to the hotel," Uncle Tony said from the front seat.

"But we've only done half the day," Safa said.

"I'm canceling you. I'm canceling the tour."

"You still have to pay."

"I'll pay for the part of the tour I took. No more."

"We'll see about this."

"We certainly will. To the hotel, Waleed. The hotel," Uncle Tony said.

Louise sat back, mortified but relieved. Beside her, Safa began talking softly, her smile never wavering. "He's, you know?" She flicked her pronged hand. "Someone like him brought AIDS to this country. When I was going to Cairo University, we had an American teacher, just like him." She laughed musically, staring at the back of Tony's head. "He got into it, with all the boys. One guy. One person. And now there is AIDS all over Cairo."

"He's in a monogamous, committed relationship," Louise said, the syllables in her mouth like soft bread. Safa's vacant stare showed not a trace of comprehension.

BACK in the hotel room, Uncle Tony immediately lit a cigarette.

"You promised," Louise said.

"Give me a break," he said indignantly, then stalked into the bathroom. She heard his cigarette fizz in the toilet.

When they ordered drinks and lunch from room service, he was still angry, commanding Louise to bring salt, extra water, and to wipe off his face with a washcloth. Finally she was able to enjoy her pita and tahini, the fresh dates and pomegranates. Not far from here, Hatshepsut had sat in her palace, inhaling the perfumey air, thinking of what she should do next.

Yes, there it was. She would hold on to it, the presence of Hatshepsut, wafting in from the blossoming trees. The hotel bath foam, perhaps, was scented with local flowers, essences Hatshepsut would have known. "Do you mind?" she asked Uncle Tony. He was pleased to let her leave him alone. For an hour Louise soaked in the dark bathroom, easing her sore limbs, inhaling lush perfumes, the intoxicating odors from Punt.

She dabbed at the sweat that was stinging her eyes. They broke into the tombs, those awful robbers. They tore the arms off the mummies to get at the bracelets. They smashed the faces to kill the magic. And yet today we come into what is left of those secret places and find the spell still alive. We ignore the spoilers. Our belief, our love, is with the dreamer.

"Aren't you done in there yet?" Uncle Tony called, and when she opened the door, she found the room closed up and Uncle Tony smoking cigarettes next to a full ashtray. Louise nearly burst into tears.

"I told you I couldn't stand smoke," she wailed. "I told you before we went on this trip that I wouldn't go if you smoked in the room. And you promised you'd stop."

When she'd visited Tony and Mordecai in San Francisco, they had smoked so much she'd had to take breaks in the guest room with the door closed.

"When people care about each other," Tony said reproachfully, "I think they can make allowances for one another's habits."

"But I told you I didn't like smoke." She opened the balcony door. "If I pull a chair outside, will you smoke here?"

He scowled as she scraped the chair as far out onto the balcony as she could get it. She stood for a moment at the railing. From the distance came the call to prayer, a melodious voice, full of longing.

Louise lay on her bed in the smoky room, a towel over her face. Smoke was death, exhaust, a toxic by-product. For years she and her mother had avoided smoke, but her mother had died anyway.

Uncle Tony called from the balcony, his voice melding

with the sweet monotone of the chant. "That Safa—what did she turn out to be? Sleazy."

"It was disappointing, wasn't it." Louise inhaled the towel. "They're everywhere."

"Indeed they are. Your mother was the same way." Uncle Tony coughed. "Forty years ago was the last conversation we ever had. I came out to her, and she never spoke to me again."

"But she died, Tony."

"It was forty years ago."

"If she hadn't died, I'm sure you would have been friends again."

"You have absolutely no basis for making a statement like that," he said. "I never forgave her."

"Then why did you ask me to come along on this trip?" she asked.

THAT night Louise woke again in the dark. In the other bed, she heard Uncle Tony's peaceful breathing. Sleep had finally come to him and she didn't want to wake him, but she was tense with alarm. Smoke hung in the air, and another scent. She'd been dreaming of Mother as a lost soul, searching among the blue tombs for her body. She raised up on her elbow, snapping on the bedside lamp, which cast a brutal cone of illumination: there was the chair onto which she'd dumped her clothes. "Neat, neat," Uncle Tony had hissed earlier, folding her clothes into her suitcase. But the room was quiet except for Unle Tony's gentle snores: truly, no one was there, just her tennis shoe askew next to the bed, the tan carpet like the carpet in any other Hilton, the fragrant desert air wafting in from the balcony, and—Louise lifted up her hands—and the blood. Her hands were tacky with it and the sheets already stiff, the floral bedspread scorched with handprints where she'd pulled it down. She leaped to the floor. Her nightgown and underpants were soaked, and the blood was streaming down her legs, trickling round her ankles even as she stood, speckling the sand-colored carpet.

She pulled off the sheet, the spread. The mattress cover was already wet, too. She left behind her a bloody trail. In the bathroom, she turned on more glaring light. She put her bloody hand to her lips. It was odd. She felt strange, but she looked pretty to herself, so pretty, and her limbs firm in the full-length mirror on the door. Drawing closer, pulling with bloody hands at her hair to arrange a pleasing pose, she saw that her thighs were marked with sticky fingerprints.

It was Waleed's green eyes she had summoned up when she was rubbing herself the night before, afraid that she would awaken Tony but in such a heightened state of excitement that she had lain sleepless for hours and would have continued to do so if she hadn't allowed herself some discreet rubs, in time with his snores, never knowing that the room was full of her menstrual scent.

Trying to muffle her sounds, she wrapped herself in a clean towel, then turned on the bathtub water, sloshing the sheets around. Her stash of pads was in her suitcase. Should she stuff a towel between her legs and make a break for it now, hoping not to wake Uncle Tony, or wait till she'd taken a shower?

Drip, drip, drip. She looked down at her bloody footprints on the white bathroom tiles. Then she caught sight of herself in the mirror once again. Pretty she was with her bloody hands, raw with power. She was still young. She put her hand to the glass: "Louise . . ."

"Are you all right in there? Is something wrong?"

She froze. My God. Now it was really over. The fight about neatness had been bad enough. The fight about smoking she'd thought would end it all. But here, now, really, was the moment after which there could be no recovery.

Uncle Tony stood in the doorway in his pajama bottoms.

Scratching his back with his left hand, he surveyed the tub, the tiles. "Looks like we need some more towels. And a new set of sheets? A spread? I'll call down."

She exhaled, her shoulders slumping. "It's OK, baby," he said. "It's OK."

He walked out of the bathroom. She turned on the shower, gulping down water, flooding away the handprints and footprints that were everywhere. When she went back out, a maid was changing the sheets. Uncle Tony was dabbing with a wet towel at the floor.

Suitably padded and staunched, Louise crawled into her fresh bed. Uncle Tony tapped her comfortingly on the shoulder. "You'll be all right. It's 3:00 A.M. Try to get some sleep." His hair was silvery white, his look fond. Louise could see the ghost of her mother's large eyes in his bright blue ones, hear the cadence of her voice, the song of its upswing.

"I miss her," she said into her pillow.

"I know," said Uncle Tony.

Beyond his pink cheeks, beyond his Prozac, she saw her mother's lovely long neck, her happy smile. "Hatshepsut, Hatshepsut . . . Louise," she murmured, feeling for the smooth, cool alabaster of her necklace on the bedside table, and, for a moment, all was not so completely lost.